Date the Alphabet

Laura Langa

By Laura Langa

LOVE TUCSON
Haley and the Yeti
Date the Alphabet

My Heart Before You

A Guarded Heart

Between Our Hearts

For the teachers—we'd be lost without you

Chapter 1

"I'd rather not," Ann said to her slice of pie. Scrutinizing the dessert she'd made for her father effectively diverted her attention from her sister's gelid gaze. The tart apples and sweet pears had blended perfectly, but next time, toasting the hazelnuts before mincing might provide a nuttier flavor.

"It's my wedding. I can have whatever I want."

Ann struggled to keep her eyes from rolling. It was her younger sister's *third* wedding, all before her twenty-ninth birthday. Ann had already played reluctant henchman to Rene's bridezilla two times over. She didn't mind helping again, but being bullied into bringing a date was where Ann drew the line.

Ann didn't date, and Rene knew that.

"Mom, tell her she's being unreasonable," Rene whined.

Their mother took a deep breath. "Priscilla just wants the tables to be balanced. If you show up without a date, then there will be an empty seat."

Unlike Rene's first two marriages, which their parents had scraped to pay for, her fiancé's wealthy mother was footing the bill for this one. So apparently, what Priscilla says goes—even if that meant scrounging up a nonexistent date.

"Are single people forbidden from attending this wedding?" Ann caught the dramatic uptick of her voice and mentally calmed herself. It wouldn't help to get caught up in her family's chaotic milieu. Poking her fork at the golden pie crust, she said, "There must be a widowed grandparent or lone uncle who needs company. I'm not picky about who Priscilla seats me with."

"You know you could always do one of those long wedding party tables," Dad piped up, mouth full of pie. "The ones where you face the rest of the room. Then Ann wouldn't be sitting by herself."

"I did that for wedding one. I can't repeat myself."

Oh, the irony of her sister's words.

Ann brought her chin up. "I'd prefer to come alone."

Rene's steely gaze bore into her. "Sometimes, you're so selfish."

A heated wave licked at her skin, prickling the hairs of her arms, but Ann didn't react. That would only leave her sister more satisfied than an overstuffed cat after eating too many lizards.

"Why don't you ask that principal of yours? He's a handsome man," Mom said.

Benedict, her boss and the principal of Hillcrest Academy, was an obscenely handsome man. He was also extremely married with three beautiful children—something Mom had been reminded of thirty-seven times.

Two seconds was all Ann let herself pause. She let out a silent breath while staring at the glass-doored buffet behind her sister—barely a centimeter separated the hundreds of Precious Moments figurines crowding the shelves.

"I could bring a friend, if you'd prefer." Ann's coworker and friend, Kennedy, would never say no to a chance to dance the night away. Though they'd only known each other a few months, Kennedy had "loves weddings" energy—along with puppies, babies, and babies holding puppies at weddings. It'd be right up her alley.

Dad's barking cough sliced through the dining room. It was surprising that he'd made it to dessert without coughing with an intensity that made his face change color. Ragged impotence always surged through Ann, watching her father struggle to draw vital oxygen into his body.

Four years ago, he'd been diagnosed with COPD from his years working at a small air filter factory on the outskirts of town. In his first few years at the job, they hadn't known that spun fiberglass was as bad as asbestos. Even though he'd worn a professional mask after that point, the damage had evidently been done.

When Dad excused himself to get his inhaler, Ann's worried eyes followed him out of the room. Had his spine been that curved last Sunday? The hilly line of his vertebrae seemed to protrude through his gray cotton T-shirt more than normal.

Rene's voice brought her back to the room. "How about I make you a bet?"

This time, Ann did roll her eyes. Rene's bets had been the backdrop to their entire childhood.

Bet you can't jump from the roof into the pool.

A broken collarbone proved Ann couldn't.

Bet you can't steal cookies from the kitchen without Mom noticing.

Success—time and time again. But how could Mom keep track of anything when their home was always a disjointed mess?

Bet you can't kiss Ross O'Neal before fourth period.

She could and did, but it wasn't one of Ann's prouder moments. Especially because poor Ross expected a relationship afterward.

Whenever her sister started a sentence with *Bet you can't*, something visceral fired up in Ann. She'd never backed down from a bet—a fact Rene knew.

"No, thanks," Ann said, ignoring her tightening shoulders.

"You haven't heard the terms yet." That Cheshire grin tugged at Rene's lips.

"Don't need to."

Though Rene play-pouted, her eyes sparkled as if she'd already won. "Come on. I'll even make it fun. How about you date twenty-six men between now and the wedding—one for every letter of the alphabet. Bring one of them to the wedding, and you win."

"Alphabet? Oh, because she's a teacher. I get it." Mom snickered as she began stacking the used dishes.

"Win what?" Ann asked, ignoring her mother's inability to see how messed up this whole conversation was.

Rene paused, always one for dramatics. "Two grand."

"What?" Ann choked on her sip of water. "Since when can you throw away two thousand dollars?"

"Pretty soon, I'm going to be well taken care of." Rene waggled her four-carat engagement ring. "I can do whatever I want with my money after that."

As much as people sometimes called Ann a control freak, Rene had manipulation down to an art. Wanting her students' folders color coded by subject was not the same as playing puppet master in another person's life. Her sister had snagged man after gullible man over the years. The alimony she currently received was pennies compared to what she'd have access to when she married her successful dentist fiancé.

"No," Ann said after a controlled exhale. "Thank you."

She never stood up to Rene like this. It felt like wearing clothes that were four sizes too big. The ticking of the grandfather clock, bookended by an eye-level stack of newspapers and five unopened toaster boxes, hovered over the quiet dining room table.

Dad ambled back into the room. "Are we still talking about the wedding?" He took their stilted silence as confirmation. "It wouldn't be the worst thing for you to bring someone," he said, lowering himself into his chair.

Someone.

That word echoed in her mind as *someone* popped before Ann's vision. Someone with curly, blond hair and a playful scattering of freckles banding his nose and cheeks. Someone with the most relaxed and carefree smile she'd ever seen.

Ann forced out the unwanted image, reminding herself that there was no way *that* someone could be anything more than an acquaintance.

There were rules about these things.

"Your sister's only a year younger than you, and she's found love three times over," Dad continued. "It'd be nice to see you settled."

The knife strike to the chest was the way her father's blue eyes softened as he brought his gaze up. Fatherly concern tripped and fell into the creases around his frowning mouth. Ann knew that part of his worry was due to his diagnosis, to the potential eventuality that he couldn't be there for her, but couldn't he see that Ann was fine? It was him she worried about.

"You're almost thirty," Mom said, gathering up errant silverware. "The dating pool only gets smaller as you get older."

Subtle, even breaths kept Ann from showing her irritation at this conversation topic—one that arose way too frequently at her parents' table. There was no way to politely explain that it was after a lifetime of watching her family's disastrous relationships that Ann had concluded that what they were trying to sell you in movies wasn't real.

True love. Soulmates.

Yeah, right.

Real relationships were messy and complex, like the pathologically codependent one between her parents, or Rene's fleeting ones where she was perpetually trying to trade up.

Just . . . no.

Ann was doing fine on her own. It was better to be fiercely independent than bitterly disappointed by the fact that she would never be loved like a rom-com heroine.

Another coughing fit left Ann alone with her sister as Mom shooed Dad from the table.

"Think about how many erasers that would buy." The inflection of Rene's voice curdled Ann's stomach. "So many erasers."

Sharp spurs raced over Ann's collarbone, but she remained quiet.

Since she was paid more than the average third grade teacher working for Hillcrest Academy, Ann already used her extra income to anonymously supplement other schools' classrooms. Her private school was ridiculously well-funded, but that wasn't the case for most of Tucson. Ann also attempted to bridge that inequality gap by offering free tutoring at a public library twice a week.

Rene picked up her phone and lit the screen. "Tomorrow's March 1st. That gives you thirteen weeks to find a willing tribute. All you have to do is sit across from a nice man, twice a week, pick one of them to bring on May 29th, and boom—two grand."

Ann let silence infiltrate the room a third time on account of how ludicrous this conversation was.

But . . .

Finding a man for each letter wouldn't be hard. Some letters might be more difficult than others. Ann had grown up with a Quintin, so there had to be an Xavier or Yuri in Tucson. She could make profiles on a few dating apps, compile a spreadsheet of possible candidates. And if Ann planned coffee dates instead of dinner, she could get through them quicker. Plus, the number of underfunded classrooms she could help with two grand kept ticking at her temple.

"You're being petulant for the sake of being petulant. Your sister is offering you money. You should be grateful and take it." Mom stole Ann's almost-full plate.

Her mother followed the narrow path not cluttered by belongings leading to the kitchen before noisily dumping Ann's pie down the disposal.

Ann's spine sagged, feeling outnumbered yet again. "What if I go on twenty-six dates and they're all terrible people? They could be rude, or allergic to bathing, or object to your union."

Rene could have mutilated a herd of cattle with her death stare. "Then you lose. You have to bring someone suitable."

Ann collapsed with an audible exhale. "What if I meet 'the one' on date two? Then what happens?"

This time, lightning flashed in Rene's identical green eyes.

They were often mistaken for twins growing up. Both sisters had matching eyes, dark-brown hair, and flawless olive skin. The biggest difference between them was that Rene's figure matched their mother's—shapely, feminine—while Ann's only curves were provided by the muscles she worked hard to maintain.

It didn't matter that her father often labeled her "the sporty one" when helping others tell them apart. Ann was approached by men just as often as Rene, but she wasn't interested in whatever doomed relationship came at the end of saying yes to a first date.

"Then you happily date your Prince Charming until the wedding, sister." The S's in sister sounded like a snake was spewing them. "That is, if you can keep him around. Remind me again how long your last relationship was?"

Rene knew her only "relationship" had been the three weeks she dated Ross O'Neil out of guilt in her senior year of high school before gently breaking it off.

"Do I have to go in ABC order?"

"*Gah.* I don't care, rule follower. I just need you to bring a nice man to the wedding." Rene gestured at Mom like her request wasn't completely outlandish.

Mom shrugged with a commiserating *I know, she's an oddball* expression while filling the dishwasher.

Ann's polished nails pressed into her mother's best tablecloth.

"Make it four." If she was going to engage Rene in this ridiculous bet, Ann was going to maximize the amount of good that came from it.

Mom's gasp ripped through the kitchen doorway, but Rene didn't flinch. "Fine. Four grand. Double your erasers for all I care, just don't embarrass me in front of Denis's family."

The corner of Ann's mouth lifted, triumph skipping over her muscles. She could do this. She'd have to schedule the dates around her tutoring schedule, but that shouldn't be too challenging.

The sensation of Dad's cool, papery palm over hers drew her attention away from Rene. "What'd I miss?"

"Ann's agreed to try and find a nice man to bring to the wedding," Rene said sweetly.

With those words, Ann understood that Dad wouldn't be let in on the parameters of the bet. He'd often been left out of the comings and goings of their lives growing up because he'd always worked such long hours, and Mom had instructed them both not to bother him with unnecessary details.

Better for him not to worry.

"Oh, good." He set the tablet he'd brought with him on the table and opened the Wordle app.

Mom returned to the room, slapping Dad on the shoulder. "Are you going to be on that thing all night? Your daughters are here."

Every muscle in Ann's core tightened. "Rene and I are done talking. It's okay if Dad plays his game."

Rene picking at Ann was a direct reflection of how their mother chipped at Dad. But no matter her harsh, nagging words, Dad looked at his wife with this loving disbelief that he was lucky enough to have her.

True love, folks. That's what it does to you.

"I wanted to talk with you anyway." Rene rose and hooked her arm with Mom's, leading her through the piles of debris. Before the door to the back porch closed, Ann could hear the words, "Priscilla wants me to sign a prenup."

Ann barely tamped down the laugh bubbling in her throat before reminding herself that she didn't partake in schadenfreude. It was poisonous to derive pleasure from another's misfortune.

After she finished washing the pots and pans, Ann moved the rest of her pie into the garage fridge where Mom was less likely to see it and throw it away before Dad could finish it.

The garage was one of the only organized places in her parents' home. The rest of it was overrun with her mother's hoarded belongings, but the garage had always been her father's domain. Ann's fingertips brushed the needle-nose pliers on the pegboard, resting in their hand-drawn outline, before moving to touch the adjustable wrench.

She'd already washed his and Mom's cars and used a video tutorial to fix the latch on the side gate, but his pegboard and work shelves could use a quick dusting. Even if her father couldn't come out here and tinker like he used to, she wanted it to be ready if he had a good day. Though, those were becoming fewer and far between.

"I'm going to head home," Ann said with a pat to her father's shoulder after she'd finished in the garage.

He was still in his spot, his breathing more even, and had moved on to Scrabble.

"Drive safe, Annabanana." His smile lit his entire face.

Her grin mirrored his joy, affection flooding her bloodstream.

"I know Rene's methods are unorthodox, but I think she just wants to see you happy," Dad said with a wink. "That's the reason she's pressuring you to find a date for the wedding."

It was hard to keep her smile and nod. Both were a lie, but Dad didn't need to know that. The less she troubled him with, the better.

"And who knows, maybe you will find 'the one.'"

Even though certainty to the opposite ran through every cell in her body, Ann lied again. "I just might."

Chapter 2

Zane eased his white Volvo around the cement curb, following the flow of traffic in the pickup line. Two tweens laughed at something on one of their phones before a staff member ushered them into an awaiting minivan in front of him. The neon-green sign with his daughter, Caroline's, student number was resting on the right side of his dash, fluttering inconsistently as the warm mid-March breeze snuck through the open window.

By this point in the year, Zane could've picked up Caroline without having a school staff member check his number to the smaller one zip-tied to his daughter's backpack. Everyone knew each other.

"Hey, Sal," Zane said to the school security officer, opening his back door for Caroline. "Can you believe we got that inch of rain last night?"

"We needed it. It hardly rained this winter." Sal's white mustache twisted to the side, rueful.

Talking about the weather was one of those easy topics between acquaintances, but Tucsonans would often gab about each quarter inch of rain that fell on their parched desert home like it was revelatory news.

Zane was nodding along when Sal shut the back door with a cheerful, "You two have a good weekend."

"Hey, noodlepoodle," Zane said to his daughter's reflection in his rearview mirror. "How was your day?"

"Not one of your better ones, Dad." Caroline rifled through her backpack, not looking up.

Ever since Caroline's first day at Hillcrest Academy in August, Zane picked her up with a new pet name. It was just one of the small ways he was trying to infuse a little more fun into her day. Now that Caroline's mother, Tessa, had been in remission for a little over a year, and they'd all gotten used to life after the divorce, Zane was trying to shake free the joyful daughter who used to live in Caroline's body. The one that had disappeared once words like "cancer" and "chemo" had entered her young vocabulary.

His knuckles rubbed the seatbelt over his sternum before Zane recalled the word he and Caroline had read on the word-a-day calendar in the kitchen this morning.

"My apologies, crepuscular cutie."

"That's better." When the corner of Caroline's mouth lifted, all the tension mounting in Zane's bones abated.

Zane grinned, filling his lungs with the sweet smell of the spring desert as he followed the minivan toward the exit to the parking lot.

The moment of peace was swiftly decimated when Caroline shoved her backpack on the seat beside her and crossed her arms. "Great. Just great. I forgot my science notebook in my desk."

Forcibly loosening his muscles, Zane laced his lips with an easy smile and signaled to turn left instead of right so he could circle back into the school's parking lot.

"No biggie. Let's head back inside and grab it."

Caroline heaved her small frame with a dramatic sigh, crinkling the starched fabric of her navy skort. Though Hillcrest didn't have a dress code, his daughter often looked like she was vying for prep-school president with her wardrobe choices.

The restlessness in his chest didn't fully settle until they got out of the car and his daughter wove her small hand in his. Most of his life hadn't turned out like he'd expected. Wrenching plot twists had mangled what should have been an orderly progression. So when simple moments like this happened, Zane relished them. Even his largely independent eight-year-old—the one who'd progressed from *Dada* straight to *Dad*—still needed her hand held in a parking lot.

They waved to Sal and a half-dozen other teachers finishing dismissal on the way back into the building. The linoleum floor was colored with various lines that always reminded Zane of Tron. They served a purpose, helping the younger grades follow the right color to their respective wings. Since this school took students from kindergarten to eighth grade, before they graduated to the prep school nearby, it was a spacious campus. The first week of third grade, Caroline had complained about how much walking she had to do each day.

But each extra second it would take them to get to the third grade "hub" was needed for Zane to slow his already accelerating heart rate. It was sickly Pavlovian how the scent of construction paper and glue made his blood thump against his throat. If he got lucky, Ms. Powell would've already left for the day, preventing the arduous task of him trying not to stare.

When they got closer to the woodland-animal-themed classroom, Zane could hear her speaking. There was an almost imperceptible rasp layered under her voice, like the dead space between vinyl-record songs. Most people probably missed it, but Zane was trained to hear the resonance and textures in a voice. That sound ricocheted between Zane's ears like a crystal bell tone.

It was just one of the numerous things he knew about Ms. Powell—many of which Caroline supplied with her daily recountings of school. Since his daughter was enamored with Ms. Powell, little details trickled home. Like how her teacher loved dried mangos, even numbers, and "couldn't sing to save her life."

Others, Zane had learned over his many encounters with Caroline's teacher. Like how Ms. Powell looked with a whistle between her teeth as she organized the three-legged races for the Spring Fair, or how you could tell she genuinely loved working with kids, or that she'd bite the inside of her cheek when trying not to laugh when a student said something funny but she was supposed to maintain her position as the authoritarian figure.

Parents were encouraged to be active in the many after-school clubs and events, and being new to Hillcrest, he and Tessa hadn't wanted to stand out by not doing their part.

Zane's chest rose with a deep inhale as his knuckles rapped at her door jamb. He'd expected her to be conversing with another teacher, but Ms. Powell was facing the courtyard overgrown with lantana and California poppies with a cell phone to her ear.

When she spun, Zane hoped it wouldn't happen again, just to give his twisting stomach some respite.

But no, Ms. Powell's eyes locked on his, and everything else dulled.

Those irises, a deeper green than anything that grew in the Tucson desert, stared.

They didn't bounce. They didn't waver.

It was the same body-seizing, time-altering occurrence that happened every time they were in the same room.

Ever since that first time.

Zane turned the corner to yet another corridor, eyes on his phone. Was this place a school or a labyrinth? Tessa had just texted to inform him that the third-grade classrooms were at the end of the teal line, not the burnt-sienna one. Zane picked up his pace. He was already ten minutes late to their scheduled teacher meet-and-greet after getting caught in traffic.

Just before Zane turned another corner, the scent of orange blossoms swept up and caught him. It was brief, but he was temporarily transplanted to his grandmother's snug home in San Jose, the back of which bordered on an orange grove. A ghost of a smile lifted his lips before his body slammed against the source of the scent.

Green inundated him—bright and mossy from widely stretched eyes. His automatic apology was trapped in his vacant throat. Meanwhile, her jaw worked over her own silent words. Zane should have noticed that her mouth was left parted in this action, that he could hear her hard swallow, but he was free-falling in green.

She was tall, so her eyes were only three inches below his eyeline. Zane was used to women being at least a head beneath him, but her wedge heels helped obliterate that distance.

Confusion was the first emotion that clamored for attention as his heart thumped against his breastbone. Zane didn't understand what was happening. They were strangers, standing centimeters *from each other. Societal norms dictated that, even after an accidental collision, they should have sprung apart by now.*

But they hadn't.

Zane could feel her breath on his neck.

A shaky exhale left his chest, and the motion dragged her eyes to his lips. If Zane thought he'd been frozen before, it was nothing compared to the excruciating seconds he spent watching her focus on his mouth. Every chemical signal in his body felt as if it had been poured into his bloodstream, and the noxious mixture rendered him frustratingly inactive.

Then the beautiful forest was obscured as her eyelids fluttered closed. A small shake tossed her impossibly long hair before she took a sizable step backward.

"Sorry." The word was raspy, uneven.

It didn't matter that she'd moved. Zane remained immobile.

Until the crisp, order-up ding of his text message sounded in his clenched palm.

Right. He was supposed to be meeting his soon-to-be ex-wife (as they were signing papers in a week) and his daughter in her new teacher's classroom.

Zane mirrored her distance with his own. "Yeah. I'm sorry."

Was he?

No, definitely not.

She nodded and continued on her way, the rhythmic click of her wedges piercing his eardrum with every distancing step.

How Zane ended up in the right place after that interaction was a miracle. His mind was replaying the short seconds he'd spent entranced in the hallway. He'd never been so captivated by a woman. It was . . . unsettling.

The second Tessa came into view in the empty classroom, Zane could almost put the unexplainable interchange away. He dropped a kiss onto Caroline's head and gave Tessa a hug, just like he always did whenever they greeted or left each other.

"Hey. How are you feeling?" Even if they no longer made sense, Zane still wanted every one of Tessa's days to be good ones.

"Good." Tessa smiled at him. Her light-brown hair was growing back nicely. It was now long enough to look like an intentional pixie cut instead of growing out after chemo. "Did you—"

"Sorry about the delay. Here are the handouts I wanted to—" The voice cut off, and even though Zane's back was to the door, he didn't need to turn around to know that the woman he'd just had a life-shifting moment with was the one speaking behind him.

Zane tried to mollify the impact Ms. Powell's eyes had on him by glancing down and adjusting his glasses. It was after his hand grazed his temple that he remembered he'd put his contacts in this morning—something he rarely did. Covering the movement by tucking a strand of his curly hair behind his ear probably wasn't fooling anyone, but Zane was already at a loss.

"I forgot my science notebook," Caroline said, bee-lining to her desk.

The only saving grace was that his daughter never seemed to notice the tension in the air whenever he and her teacher were in the same room. Zane made sure to minimize eye contact with Ms. Powell if Tessa was also in attendance.

He'd never been good at hiding his emotions, but he'd never really wanted to. Bottling things up only led to devastating consequences. Zane wasn't about to be the one launching emotional shrapnel into the skin of his loved ones. The last three years, though, had taught him to keep some things inside. The only benefit from that unwanted life skill was that he was able to obscure *this* emotion from Ms. Powell.

The one he didn't want to feel.

Zane didn't want to be mystified by his daughter's teacher.

Not when he had almost gained back everything he'd lost. Tessa was healthy, and though it'd been over a year since their separation, their friendship was still as strong as ever, making co-parenting effortless. Caroline had struggled when Tessa began to date three months after moving out of their home and into her parents' house last January, but now their daughter was used to Isaac being a part of their lives.

Getting involved with Caroline's third grade teacher would annihilate the delicate balance he tried to provide his daughter.

Though Zane had initially been grateful that he'd broken their eye contact, looking down had been a mistake. Because now his gaze was stalled on Ms. Powell's long legs, the feminine ruffle detail on her wedge sandals, and her tangerine-colored toenails. Ms. Powell seemed to favor flowery, frilly, form-fitting things, like the pink blouse with half-sleeves highlighting the slight curve of her toned deltoid.

Pull yourself together.

"Sorry to bother you after hours," Zane said to the whiteboard, forcing cheer into his voice. "We'll just be a minute."

Zane hated not speaking to her directly, but it was like his cellular structure rearranged itself whenever Ms. Powell was near, making him incapable of being his affable self. The person who could walk into a room and walk out with seven new best friends. If Zane looked at her again, his cordial words would dry up, and he'd drift farther into the room than he already had, drawn to her against his will.

"It's not a problem." Her answer was said in that low rasp. It washed over his skin like silky soap bubbles, touching everything. "No. Sorry, Mom." Her tone was instantly stronger, clearer. "Someone's—" she began but was cut off by the small voice on the phone.

Zane smiled to himself. He liked that Ms. Powell called her mom after work. His day wouldn't be complete with at least a short check-in with his.

His fingers drifted to touch the green-painted wooden apple on her desk, rotating it a quarter turn before gently pushing it two inches toward the center. It was a discreet motion, done slowly. Zane tried to ignore the reason why he'd moved it as Caroline bounded over to him.

"Thanks, Ms. Powell." Caroline hugged her green composition notebook to her polo-covered chest, her mood instantly improved.

"Yes, thank you." Zane rotated away, heading toward the door.

Caroline followed close behind, grabbing for his hand as they turned to exit the room. When Zane reached back to catch his daughter's fingers, it was impossible to miss that Ms. Powell was now beside her desk. One hand pressed her phone to her ear as her mother continued speaking, while the other clutched the wooden apple to her chest.

Chapter 3

Ann frowned into the large plate mirror. Just beyond the smudge mark that looked like a sweaty forearm, that same man was talking to the two high school girls again. The girls were taking turns on the assisted pull-up machine when *he* came by a second time.

The first time had been a quick interaction, and both girls had smiled, so Ann assumed the man had been one of their fathers or a family friend. He looked mid-to-late forties with gray peppering his dark hair. Now, however, the two girls in Ocotillo High School T-shirts kept trading uneasy looks. Ann watched each microexpression carefully, pausing in her set.

When the man stepped forward, reaching out to touch the brunette's waist, the girl backed into the handlebars of the machine to keep out of reach. Ann's weights clattered to the gym floor. Ignoring the tiny voice inside her that chided her for breaking the gym rule against dropping weights, she listened to the louder voice beneath her collarbones. Ann disliked conflict, but she would go into battle time and time again if it meant protecting a child.

"Hey, girls," Ann gushed. "So good to see you outside of school."

It was impossible to miss the relief flooding the brunette's irises. The taller blonde softly shouldered her friend, reaching down to twine their fingers together.

Ann's heart wrenched. A feeble part of her had hoped she'd misread the situation.

Keeping her emotions from splashing across her face, Ann shared a secret, reassuring smile with both girls. Then she stepped over to give them each a quick hug, putting her five-foot-eight frame between them and the man.

"Hi!" Her voice was unnaturally high as she turned to face him. "I teach history at Ocotillo High. I love seeing families outside of school. That's so sweet of you to bring your daughters to the gym, Mr. . . ." She left the end of that sentence open for him to supply his name.

It was obvious to anyone with eyeballs that the girls weren't sisters.

"Oh, I . . ." He opened and then closed his mouth as Ann artificially blinked at him, a saccharine smile plastered on her face. "I'm not . . . I'm not their dad."

"Oh?"

Rene would have been proud of the poison that sweetly infiltrated that word. Though Ann had spent a lifetime watching her mother's and sister's subtle manipulations, she had never used them herself. Doing so made her feel as dirty as hot-dog water. But having this sleazeball squirm and trip over his words only filled Ann with righteous indignation.

"Then why are you hitting on teenage girls?" A lifted brow accompanied her loudly asked question, prompting several people in the gym to pull out earbuds or lower headphones.

"I'm not hitting on them." The panicked words rushed out as he took a step back. "I was giving them advice."

"Did they ask you for help?" Ann tilted her head, and the long braid she'd plaited her hair into slid over her shoulder.

"Well, no." The man's gaze was flitting around the room.

An early-twenties man in a singlet, who looked like he could crush a watermelon in the crook of his elbow, stepped closer.

"Did they ask you to *touch* them?" Ann continued.

Another stammering "No" filled the suddenly quiet weight room.

"So you, a nearly fifty-year-old man, were hitting on two teenage girls." Ann let her hand settle gently in the pocket of her loose, gray joggers.

Acid was pouring through her veins, and she wished her words were blinding venom, but Ann kept her outward appearance serene. Eerie calm when one should be screaming in anger was often more effective. Silence was equally powerful—few people are comfortable with attentive silence.

"I—" His mouth slacked open again. "I've got to go." He nearly knocked over a pregnant woman on his way out of the gym.

"Eat glass," Ann muttered beneath her breath, watching the man until she was sure he was gone before turning to the girls. "I'm sorry about that. You two okay?"

"That was incredible!" The blonde's eyes were as wide and bright as her smile.

"For real, for real," her friend said. "Like, wow. I wish you were my mom or, like, my older sister."

The pain attempting to overtake Ann only hit for a split second. She'd gotten better at overriding the memory of that day, dealing with triggers like this, and rationalizing that she wasn't broken—just different. Even still, Ann picked up the collar of her baggy black shirt and wiped sweat off her forehead to give herself a moment.

"Are your parents here?" Ann asked, dropping the fabric.

The blonde shook her head. "My mom is picking up my sister from soccer practice and then coming back to get us."

Ann nodded. "You should let her know what happened. I'll tell the front desk once I rack my weights so they're aware too. Hopefully, he'll keep his distance from now on."

"We'll keep an eye out too," the younger man said before introducing himself to Ann and the girls, telling them that he and his friends usually worked out in the afternoons.

"Thanks." A grateful smile smoothed Ann's face.

Ten minutes later, Ann was finishing up explaining the situation to the kind woman behind the front desk when her phone alarm sounded in her pocket. It was time to get ready for Date "H."

Her mother had called right after dismissal this afternoon to inform her that Ann had even less time to find a date. Priscilla wanted the name of Ann's plus-one within six weeks so that monogrammed crystal placemarkers could be hand engraved. Ann had reassured her mother that she was already hacking through the list of alphabetized suitors she'd complied from several dating apps, seeing someone every night she was free.

Last Monday, Archie had kicked this ridiculous escapade off with a no-show, and so far, those thirty minutes of wine bar solitude had been Ann's best date. Last Wednesday, Braxton had arrived at the coffee shop with his girlfriend, Willow, and Ann had to inform the both of them that, respectfully, she wasn't interested in that type of relationship. Dates "C" through "G" had gone progressively from bad to worse.

Tonight, she was meeting with Holden, followed by lunch with Ian tomorrow. Ann had planned on leaving her Saturday night free, but maybe she could fit in a Jayden, Jacob, or Jonathan.

Though each soul-sucking date moved her down the list of candidates, the worst part was that, eventually, she'd have to find someone suitable enough to bring to Rene's wedding.

Holden seemed like a hopeful candidate. He was a veterinarian who had requested she join him on a picnic dinner to watch the sunset at Gates Pass. Though she'd been intentionally picking busy areas to meet her dates, Gates Pass in the Tucson Mountains was a popular location to watch the last of the day's embers blur into night, so they wouldn't be alone.

Plus, something about Holden's black-framed glasses made him appear familiar, approachable.

It hadn't been until Zane had walked into her classroom this afternoon that Ann realized why she'd agreed to bend her "Date the Alphabet" location rules. Holden's frames were exactly like the ones Zane hadn't been wearing today. Seeing him without them for the first time had been a punch to the stomach. Ann hadn't realized how much she'd needed that thin layer of glass as a barrier.

Ann shook her head and hoisted her gym bag higher on her shoulder, thanking the gym employee before heading home.

◊◊◊

"This spread is impressive." Ann folded her flat boots under her legs and lowered herself onto the thick picnic blanket. Though she almost exclusively preferred her heels, dates at rocky trailheads required more practical footwear.

Holden had initially met her at the edge of the parking lot before leading her just slightly off the trail, still within reach of the thirty other people also watching the sunset tonight.

Despite the drier-than-usual winter, the saturating rainstorms that had peppered the desert over the last week had nurtured the awaiting spring blossoms. The tiny purple flowers of Coulter's lupine and owl's clover now broke into the expansive tan and speckled green around them. The yellow of the brittlebush and cheerful desert mariposa made the evening more alluring.

Ann had to give it to Holden. With the awaiting sunset, this was the most scenic and well-planned date she'd ever been on.

"I'm pleased you like it." Holden opened a bottle of sparkling grape juice and poured it into two plastic flute glasses.

Conversation was light and easy as they made a dent in the elaborate picnic dinner. The points kept stacking in Holden's direction. So far, he'd shown up, hadn't brought another woman, and had made a delicious dinner of various pasta salads, fruit, cheeses, and dark-chocolate truffles.

"Do you have any pets?" Holden asked before biting into a strawberry.

"Unfortunately, no. I've always wanted a cat, but I work long hours and tutor on Tuesday and Thursday nights." Ann twisted her lips, leaving out how much she helped her dad. "It doesn't feel fair when I'm gone all the time."

"You could always get two. Then they'd keep each other company." Holden smiled. He had a sweet smile, slightly uneven at the edges.

Ann relaxed more into the cushion he'd brought to further separate her from the rocky ground. This could work. She knew men generally didn't like being asked to go to weddings on the first date, but maybe if she was clear that it wasn't going to mean anything, that it was casual, it would be okay. She'd never had the chance to bring it up on dates "A" through "G."

"I know this is a weird question, but how do you feel about weddings?"

Holden stared at her with an open mouth, the piercing sunlight reflecting off his glasses and obscuring his eyes, before he shook his head. "I can't believe it."

Words of explanation were rushing forward, getting jumbled behind her tongue, when a wide grin stretched his cheeks.

"I was thinking the same thing." He rose to his knees, fumbling to get into the front pocket of his chinos. "Wait." He stopped. "You should meet Nana first." Holden leaned back on his heels, twisting to reach into the second compartment of the large wicker picnic basket.

"Nana?" Her forehead wrinkled.

When Holden rotated around, Ann scattered to her feet, accidentally backing into a nearby staghorn cholla. She barely kept a yelp from freeing her mouth as cactus spines pierced through the light sweater over her right tricep. A wince and a large step brought Ann forward, the cactus piece hitch-hiking along with her.

"Is that . . . ?" She used the plastic fork in her hand to detach the cactus segment before focusing back on Holden's beaming face. "Is that a possum in a diaper?"

His confused gaze fell on the animal being held like a newborn lion cub being displayed to his awaiting pride.

For a breath, Ann half expected Rene to jump out from behind a saguaro cactus, laughing her head off. This is just the type of prank she would have loved to pull.

But no. It was just her and the man holding a possum aloft. *How is this my life?*

"Oh, Nana." Holden laughed, setting the animal in his lap and then reaching into the basket to gather a pink, frilly scrap of cloth before fastening the "dress" around the surprisingly compliant possum's neck. "She's always wiggling out of her clothes."

Ann held her fork between them like a kind of makeshift weapon. "That's your grandma?"

Holden laughed again. "No. That would be crazy."

It was a struggle to keep her eyes from widening further. *That's* where he drew the line on crazy? Not the dressing and diapering of possums?

"My grandmother's soul lives within Betty. So until Nana decides to move along, Betty kind of has to share." He shrugged like he was explaining something simple, like he doesn't like mayo on sandwiches. "But that will happen now that we're getting married. She always said she couldn't leave me until I settled down."

Though Ann had piled her hair into a high bun because she hadn't had time to style it, she was instantly grateful for the tucked-away style. It kept her vision unobscured. Looking around to make sure the area was clear of cacti, she began baby-stepping away. A middle-aged couple sat at a bench twenty feet down the trail, and many more were resting on the rock half-wall near the parking lot.

"I think there's been a misunderstanding. Thank you for the picnic, but it's time I left."

"Wait." His eyebrows furrowed. "You don't want to see the ring?"

Ann weighed the option of fully straightening him out versus saying whatever she could to get out of there. She eyed the couple again.

"No, Holden. I'm sorry, but we can't get married."

He sank. "But—You—"

"It's not you. I can't marry anyone."

When Holden silently digested this piece of information without a volatile reaction, Ann lowered the fork to her side.

"Why?" he asked. "Why can't you get married?"

"Because I don't believe in love." Ann heard her abrasive tone and softened it. "Well, I don't believe in balanced love. Someone always suffers, loves the other person more than they love them. Gets taken advantage of. I'm not about to spend my life being miserable because I love someone." It was already hard enough to watch her father get pummeled time and time again.

She cleared her throat. "I'd rather be alone."

The reasons sounded so sad out in the world, in the cooling desert air. She'd only ever thought of them in her head, but the veracity etched into each one was undeniable.

Holden slowly began to nod, his hand lightly petting the tranquil possum. "It's better to be alone than be with the wrong person."

"Yes." Ann waited another beat. The sun bent and disappeared around the earth, but she missed it. She still didn't trust this man enough to turn her back on him. "This has been nice." *Mostly.* "But I should get going."

Holden nodded again, resolute. "Yes. It was nice to meet you, but we're obviously not a good fit. I'd still recommend getting the two cats. Especially since you plan on living alone forever."

Ann tried not to show how the word *forever* had slashed at her skin. "Good idea."

When Holden turned to fasten "Nana" into the basket, Ann let the fork fall to the blanket and briskly strode to the parking lot. Fortunately, she'd backed her silver Honda Civic into the parking spot, so she could make a swift exit. Only when Ann was securely within the tidy garage to her condo, forty minutes later, did she allow herself to take stock. She'd been too numb to even notice that four cholla spines remained in her arm.

Her eyes sheened, seeing the six tiny droplets of blood on her favorite sweater. The cream cashmere garment had been a birthday gift from her father, something she'd never buy for herself. Ann had been overwhelmed by gratitude when she'd received it. After giving her father a huge hug, the room had exploded with her mother and sister's wrath. Before the cake could be cut, Mom and Rene had made Dad order each of them the same sweater.

Ann sighed and went inside her condo, looking for a comb to remove the remnants of the cactus.

"The children," she murmured, wincing as each sharp spine came out. "You're doing this for the children."

Because what she'd confessed in the desert air had been true. Ann was better off alone.

Chapter 4

"**G**ood snatch, Zane!" Kevin shouted from the sidelines, jumping out of his camp chair.

"It's called a tackle," Rowan said, adjusting his aviator sunglasses.

Every other Saturday morning, Zane and his friends Kevin, Kyle, and Rowan met at Ground Street Coffee to catch up. It was their way of staying in each other's lives since they no longer lived together. In college, they'd shared a bachelor house just off campus after they'd spent their freshman year smushed into a dorm study room that the university had turned into a temporary living space.

Since today was the championship game of Zane's winter flag football season, his friends—or, as Kevin had coined them, 'dorm bros'—were all here to cheer him on instead. Even though this league ran year-round, and in two weeks Zane would start another season with the team he'd played with for years, his friends were sentimental about supporting each other and celebrating accomplishments—big or small.

"Why? He grabbed a flag. He didn't knock anyone over. It should be called a snatch," Kevin argued. "He *snatched* it."

Zane chuckled as he jogged to set up for the next down, focusing back on the game. Though he was usually a wide receiver, the defensive line was short a man, so today he was also playing safety.

After Zane stopped another play and handed back his opponent's flag, his eyes caught Caroline's. Zane smiled and gave a little wave. She gave a small grin and an even smaller wave from her chair. Someone watching might joke that being embarrassed of your parents started early nowadays, but Zane knew Caroline wasn't the kind to scream and cheer for anything. The fact that she was intently watching instead of sketching was her own kind of love letter.

Tessa caught their interaction, placing her hand over her heart before giving Zane an enthusiastic thumbs up and shouting, "Snatch all the flags, Z!"

"Yes!" Kevin's word was louder than the unorthodox cheers he'd doggedly been trying to get Kyle and Rowan to join in on. "*See*, it's called snatching!"

Rowan shook his head, shifting his weight from foot to foot to dissipate his irritation.

Zane understood Kevin's lack of knowledge. Before becoming a father, Zane had never played organized sports. With both his parents working in film, he'd been more likely to attend a Francis Ford Coppola movie marathon at an indie theater than participate in a Little League game. It surprised his high school friends when Zane hadn't made a run of working in the industry and instead left LA to get a degree in writing at the University of Arizona, attempting to follow in his late-father's footsteps.

This flag football club had been a lifesaver once he'd unexpectedly become a stay-at-home dad at twenty-two. When Tessa had become pregnant their senior year, Zane had asked her to marry him, moved them into a small apartment, and did the minimal coursework to graduate, spending his free time working any job he could get to save up for the baby. After receiving a chemical burn pouring concrete, Kevin and Kyle had gotten him a barista position at Ground Street Coffee where they'd both worked.

Zane's mom also helped him pick up some voice-acting work. The community he'd been so entrenched in before moving helped him find used but quality supplies that he'd need to record from home—microphone, preamp, pop filter— and donated the funds for him to buy a dedicated computer to receive audio. After four years of arm-wrestling words together against their will, following his mother into recording was effortless. Upon graduation, Zane accepted his Bachelor of Arts in Creative Writing and put his diploma in a drawer.

He'd started with commercials and company policy videos, recording every second Caroline was asleep. Those helped them scrape by while Tessa continued with her Master's Degree in Social Work. The grandparents also chipped in when they could with gifts of diapers or grocery store gift cards. At that time, Zane didn't have a formal home studio like the one built into his current home. A heavy blanket over his head in the closet of their small apartment did the trick most of the time.

With Tessa often at classes, those early days consisted of him, Caroline, and the closet.

Outside of seeing his friends every other weekend and his in-laws when they cared for Caroline, Zane was mostly alone.

In a confined space.

Something that tore at his extroverted soul.

Though Zane had already felt the dragging effects of isolation, he couldn't justify taking time for himself—not when he could record and render another piece of audio that could provide food for his family. Sleep became something Zane trained himself out of needing—not that he'd slept well since his father had died. When Caroline would sleep in her bassinet next to Tessa at night, Zane would steal three or four more hours of work.

It had been Rowan who'd insisted that Zane find some activity, preferably one outside, to break up his reclusive routine. He'd convinced Zane that his mental health was just as important as his family's financial health.

Then right after Caroline turned three, when an old writer friend from college asked Zane to narrate her science-fiction debut, everything changed. The novel, and its audiobook recording, immediately shot to the top of the New York Times Best Seller list. A few years later, that book and the other two books in the trilogy had been made into blockbusters.

Zane became so sought out that he finally had enough income to move his family into a spacious, ranch-style home in the Catalina Foothills, in the neighborhood next to Tessa's parents. He contracted for a proper at-home studio to be installed and counted himself lucky to be one of the higher paid narrators in the business. Now his genres included not only sci-fi, but horror, spy thriller, and even the occasional romance.

Though they were financially secure now, Zane couldn't quite kick the habit of staying up late to record. Plus, it had been a helpful distraction when life skittered off the beaten path yet again with Tessa's diagnosis.

"Nope. Not this time." The player Zane was supposed to be defending faked him out and rushed for a touchdown.

Zane blinked. He hadn't even seen his opponent. He'd been staring at a smaller version of Caroline, crying at the bleating of medical machines as his chest bottomed out, not focused on the AstroTurf beneath his cleats.

"What was that? He was right in front of you," Micah, his team captain, said, coming up beside him.

"Yeah. Sorry. Sweat got in my eyes." Zane picked up the hem of his jersey and swathed his face.

Two more downs and the game was over. His friends and family wore placating smiles as Zane returned to the sidelines.

"It's okay, Dad. You can't win every sportsball game."

"Football. He's been playing—" Rowan abandoned his sentence, turning to fold the chair he'd never sat in. Though Rowan's even-tempered demeanor often edged on stoicism, he always got agitated watching football. Zane had assumed his friend's twitchiness would be resolved by participating, but Rowan declined every invitation to join the team.

Zane's automatic chuckle froze in his throat when Caroline's warm brown eyes, the same ones he shared, caught Zane's. Then the corner of her mouth crept up as she bounced her blonde eyebrows once—subtly, discreetly.

It was incomprehensive, the pressure building against his ribs. Air wanted to vacate in a punched laugh but swirled behind his breastbone instead.

Caroline had intentionally used the phrase "sportsball" to razz Rowan. His daughter knew the name of the game. She'd been watching him play her whole life.

Messing with each other and gentle practical jokes had been an integral part of Zane's relationship with his daughter. Something that got lost over the last few years as they worked through Tessa's Non-Hodgkin's lymphoma diagnosis, treatment, and remission.

When his eyes flushed with tears, Zane grabbed the hem of his jersey again.

"Can we still get eegee's even though Dad lost?" Caroline asked.

"Sure, honey." Tessa rose with a stretch. "Does everyone want to go?"

Tessa had been such an integral part of his friend group for so long that, even with their divorce, they still occasionally did things together. His friends had all accepted the peaceful dissolution of their marriage as easily as he and Tessa had.

"Actually, I have a call with Ethan in twenty minutes," Kyle said, unfolding his legs and standing. "I had to reschedule from Thursday."

Now Zane allowed himself to laugh. "I have one every Monday, like clockwork."

"Wednesday," Rowan said, softening with a smile.

"Tuesday." Kevin beamed.

"Yeah." A grin lifted Kyle's beard as he rubbed his head. "I kind of figured Ethan would have disappeared again when he moved to Maryland part time, but with all the effort he's putting into being in our lives again, it looks like I'm going to have to mail him a wedding invitation."

Ethan had been the fifth member of their friend group from college who'd pushed them away years ago after a personal tragedy. Last month, he re-entered their lives with the help of his joyous girlfriend, Haley. Ethan had moved to Maryland to be with Haley two weeks ago. They'd planned on spending half of the year there, with her family, and half of it here in Tucson, with his. To show them all that he was serious about staying in touch, Ethan had scheduled a weekly video call with each of his friends.

"You haven't invited Ethan yet?" Tessa slung her chair on her shoulder. "Kyle. What are you waiting for?"

Kyle pushed his hands into the pockets of his shorts with a shrug. "The wedding's not until October. *You* haven't gotten an invitation yet."

She tucked a strand of her short bob behind her ear. "But *I* know the date." Tessa set a defiant hand on her hip. "Does Ethan?"

"I don't have to reveal all my secrets at once." Kyle picked up the wool blanket he'd been sitting on. Had the field and sidelines not been AstroTurfed, the fabric would have been covered in dust.

"Can we argue about Uncle Ethan later? I want a Piña Colada." Once an idea was introduced, Caroline often grew irritated with excess conversation and dawdling—something he and his friends *excelled* at.

"Anything for my number one fan." Zane dropped a kiss on his daughter's eye-rolling head before giving his friends hugs goodbye.

◊◊◊

"I think it's good that it ended up being just us," Tessa said after spooning up her half-Strawberry, half-Lemon-flavored eegee.

The popular sandwich and icy drink restaurant was a Tucson mainstay. Eegee's frozen drinks were delightful—a cross between a thick smoothie and a finely shredded snow cone—perfect for Tucson's mostly hot weather. After running around in the mid-seventies sunshine all morning, Zane was gulping down his Lucky Lime flavor of the month.

Caroline slipping down farther on the curved wood bench and becoming mystified by her bright-yellow drink should have been a warning, but Zane missed it. He was too busy scarfing a veggie grinder. Tessa's shoulders lifting with a large breath, Zane noticed.

She always did that, rose up like she needed to increase her short five-foot-three frame as much as possible. The frame that was a full foot shorter than his. When they used to argue, she'd sometimes sit on a counter or pull him down to the couch, just to level the distance between them.

"Isaac and I have decided to move in together." Since they'd been dating for almost a year, it was an expected step, but the words still stung a bit.

"I'm going to the bathroom." Caroline had already used the bathroom before they sat to enjoy their sandwiches and eegees, so their daughter was obviously excusing herself from the situation.

Tessa's slight sigh blew a crumpled straw wrapper closer to Zane as she watched Caroline retreat to the restrooms.

When Tessa had started dating Isaac three months after she'd moved out, twin emotions had corkscrewed through Zane's bones. He'd been genuinely happy that Tessa had found the love she'd been searching for, but it was Zane's doubt over his ability to do the same that left him bereft.

Every relationship he'd ever been in had just sort of . . . happened—including the one with his ex-wife.

"I'm sorry," Tessa whispered.

When Zane looked down and saw he was rubbing his knuckles against his chest, he placed his hand on the table. "You shouldn't be sorry. This is great news."

The squeezing beneath his sternum wasn't caused by Tessa moving on. It was because he couldn't. Even though he'd found someone with whom he might be able to have that all-encompassing, firecracker kind of love that Tessa had found with Isaac, it was his duty to put his family first. Yet again, he'd need to impound what he really wanted. It didn't matter that, for the first time, Zane wanted to explore what was behind the stolen moments of eye contact with a particularly captivating, off-limits woman.

Life had already hamstrung him.

The sympathy on Tessa's face made everything worse as she laid her fingers over his hand. "I wish you'd yell at me sometimes."

"I know." Zane met her gaze. "But you don't deserve it."

Chapter 5

"I don't think I have it in me to go on another date today." Ann slumped onto Kennedy's hand-me-down sectional, rubbing her aching temples. "Why did I agree to two dates in one day? It's Saturday. I should be relaxing."

"Because I've never seen you take on any project and not go three thousand percent?" Her friend's voice came from the kitchen where she was rummaging around, preparing snacks to soften Ann's memories of her failed "I" date.

Newly divorced Ian had spent the entire lunch showing Ann pictures of his ex-wife's OnlyApp account. Her social media page included—much to Ian's dismay—a plethora of photos and videos of his ex-wife with her new boyfriend. Halfway through her salad, Ann had asked the server for extra napkins because Ian's tears had made a sodden, shredded mess of his.

"You're one to talk," Ann quipped.

Like Ann, Kennedy gave three thousand percent of herself to her students. The two of them often walked in with Sal as he opened the building in the morning before making sure their classrooms had everything laid out for a successful day: pencils sharpened, papers distributed, laptops charged, lessons reviewed. They both relished in the challenge of working with advanced students, curating personalized learning experiences for each of them.

When Kennedy had come flying into her life at the beginning of the school year—new to Tucson and the kindergarten faculty—Ann realized how much she'd missed having a close friend. Since her father's diagnosis, she'd been too distracted with how she could help him manage his illness, excel at her new job at Hillcrest, and keep up with her tutoring schedule to do much socially. And even though she had great working relationships with the rest of the third-grade team, none of those friendships had bridged the after-school gap.

The corner of Ann's mouth tugged, recalling how Kennedy had asked if they could spend time together outside work.

"I should warn you," Kennedy said. "I'm allergic to basically all the foods, so I don't make the best dinner guest. And I don't drink caffeine because it makes me crazy." She pressed her lips together. "And I don't drink because my dad finally got sober when I was eighteen, and my family went dry in support." Kennedy clicked her cheek. "That leaves pogo sticking, snake charming, and bungee jumping. Do you have a preference?"

A laugh burst from Ann's chest. "As much as snake charming sounds like a blast—"

"Oh, it is." Kennedy winked.

Ann smiled, remembering how Kennedy had mentioned that she used to play volleyball for her college team. "I have a counteroffer."

Before Ann asked the question, she already knew the answer. Excitement over the prospect of being able to share that part of her life with someone who equally wanted to be there sent tingles down her forearms.

"How do you feel about the gym?"

Kennedy plopping a plate of dried and fresh fruits, gluten-free cookies, and sparkling flavored waters on the table in front of Ann brought her back to the room. The goodies nestled beside Kennedy's woven plate topped with a variety of crystals of different shapes and colors. Ann's fingers traced the edges of the rose quartz before picking up her flavored water.

"I think it's nice that your sister created this fun setup. It's a lot more interesting dating alphabetically than just slogging through online accounts." Kennedy popped a dried fig into her mouth.

Ann winced. She'd been too embarrassed to fully explain the bet with Rene, so she'd painted the concept of *dating the alphabet* in a positive light, saying her sister was simply encouraging her to get out there—something Kennedy had softly suggested over their short friendship.

It wasn't the first time Ann had obscured the reality of her family life. As far as Kennedy knew, Rene was as sweet as the two older sisters Kennedy had in Colorado. One truth Ann *could* share was how this ridiculous bet was upending her ordered life.

Ann scratched at her neck. "I don't think any part of this can be categorized as fun."

Her friend's expression sobered. "No, you're right. So far, each one has been a dud."

Ann set her passionfruit-flavored can on the faux-marble coaster and ticked off her fingers. "Chris spent forty minutes trying to show me how he could beat Mortal Kombat at that bar/arcade place downtown before asking if he could lotion my feet."

A suppressed smile flickered on Kennedy's lips before she took a sip of her own condensating can. "You *do* have very nice feet."

"David showed up to last Saturday's lunch drunk and threw up on the table before we ordered."

Kennedy dry-heaved reflexively, even though she'd known that was coming, having already heard the recounting of that date at their after-school gym session on Monday.

"Ezra met me at an art museum, opened a can of olives from his pocket mid-exhibit, and kept passing gas and then looking around dramatically as if searching for the source." Ann steam-rolled along.

"Ford seemed like a decent guy at first, but then he criticized me for ordering wings at a wing place. The restaurant *he* insisted I meet him at because"—Ann paused for effect—"they had amazing wings." She shook her head. "He said I should have ordered a salad."

"That's so dumb." Kennedy frowned. "Why do men think we don't get to eat? Or that eating should have some morality attached to it? This is good. This is bad. It's fuel. It's meant to nourish your body or for you to enjoy. That's it." To accent her point, Kennedy shoved an entire cookie in her mouth.

"I agree. You know I love food too."

"And you're so cute about it," Kennedy mumbled around smashed crumbs. "Like when you put ketchup on peas and mix them up."

Kennedy was the only soul who thought Ann's food quirks were "cute." Her whole life, Mom and Rene had grumbled each time she deviated from standard food preferences. *"Why do you have to put a lethal amount of parmesan on your pasta?"*

Ann shook off the critical voice, moving on. "Grayson had no concept of personal space. He literally sat on top of me on the couch at the coffee shop. Then he claimed he forgot his wallet and asked me to cover his coffee and buy him four muffins to go."

"Did you?"

Ann bit the corner of her lip. Saying no wasn't one of her strengths. Ann could defend one of her students until she was beaten and bloody, but she could never apply those protective instincts to herself. Overextending herself had become an artform. If asked, Ann could give an articulate TED Talk on how to breathe while underwater.

"Ann," Kennedy admonished. "What are we always telling our kiddos?"

"No is a complete sentence. *No, thank you* is a polite, complete sentence." She sighed, slipping down into the cushions.

Though Kennedy's kindergarten students often needed that lesson more than Ann's third graders, it seemed, at twenty-nine, Ann also required a re-education.

Her friend squeezed her knee. "And tonight is . . ."

"Jerry."

Kennedy sucked a breath through her teeth.

"Yeah, I know." A sour taste punched Ann in the mouth as chilly, dread-filled fingers trailed down her bare arms. "I'm not too hopeful either."

If there wasn't a spectacular reason for her to continue this torture, Ann would have been done with it after the first no-show. Lately, though, she'd been thinking there *had* to be another way out of this.

"We shouldn't be so judgy." Kennedy tugged at the ends of the straight black locks dusting her collarbone. The top half of her hair was pulled away from her face, secured in a stubby ponytail.

"Judgy-wudgy was a bear . . ." Ann began.

"Right, because you never know. It could be perfect. Matt and I met under disastrous circumstances"—she snorted—"and look how that turned out."

During one of their first gym sessions, Kennedy had divulged how she'd met her husband while skiing—something she'd done so often with her family that Kennedy felt like skis were a natural extension of her feet. She'd been enjoying pristine slope conditions with her sisters when first-timer Matt had careened down the mountain, knocking into her and breaking her arm.

But then Matt had stayed with her until she'd been whisked away by ski patrol. Determined to make up for his mistake, Matt had pestered her sisters, asking questions. After Kennedy had been taken to the ER, Matt had driven an hour out of the way to find a nut-free, gluten-free, dairy-free bakery to create a cake in her favorite flavor—strawberry. Kennedy had said that when she'd seen the strawberry icing character with enormous, apologetic eyes above the cursive *I'm berry sorry*, she'd known Matt was a keeper.

"Jerry could be your one true love." The wistful sigh accompanying that sentence left no doubt that her friend was also remembering her meet-cute with Matt.

Ann didn't want to trample Kennedy's misplaced optimism, so she asked, "Where is your adoring husband, anyway?"

"Business trip. I half joked that if he knew this job would take him away so much, we should have stayed in Colorado." Her shoulders bounced. "But then I wouldn't have met you." The end of that sentence held equal quantities goof and genuine sweetness.

Ann let the indirect compliment roll by as she stretched. "Can we go see the horses? I need to settle myself before heading back onto the dating battlefield."

Kennedy and her husband had snagged a small house just outside a twelve-acre property. Their neighbor's estate held a mansion and a barn with six horses. Every time she drove here, Ann liked to count each flicking tail beyond the split-rail fence. Often, she and Kennedy would walk to the property line, rip grass from beyond the fence, and lay their palms flat to be tickled by wet, velvety lips.

"Sure. Just let me grab my sunnies." Kennedy hopped up.

Sunglasses were one of those essential desert items every Tucsonan used, like sunscreen, a good hat, and a reusable water bottle. Looking like you were doing a strenuous trail hike while walking your dog half a mile wasn't uncommon.

"You just need to shake up your energy for this date," Kennedy said once they were outside. "Wear something different. Go in the out door. Show the universe you're not tolerating these bozos. You want the real deal."

As they picked through the brush, careful not to step on any cacti hiding beneath the preening desert marigolds, a copse of cholla reminded Ann she hadn't shared the events from last night. "At this point, I'll try anything. I didn't even tell you about last night's 'H' date and the possum."

"The possum?" Kennedy spun around, spraying sand in between Ann's exposed toes.

"Prepare yourself," she said, continuing toward the reassuring scent of sun-warmed hay. "You're not going to believe this one."

Chapter 6

Zane grimaced through another set of chest presses, staring at the black-painted ceiling tiles. The baseline to Missy Elliott's "Work It" blasted through the gym's speaker system. Since Zane spent hours wearing headphones, listening to the resonance of his voice, he forwent them while exercising.

After he'd left lunch with Tessa and Caroline earlier, Zane had locked himself in his home studio. It was easy to ignore the world when you were acting out another one, particularly if that world had different rules, species, and technology that was essentially magic. Except, then, he'd been out of material. His next contract was late with delivering his next script, leaving Zane with an empty house.

He'd made a stir-fry and put on a few records but ended up ripping each one off the turntable after thirty seconds. His phone had nestled in his palm for ten minutes before Zane texted his friend Ethan for advice on what to do. After a back and forth where Zane hadn't been honest about what was really bothering him, Ethan had typed, *Go to the gym. Nothing beats natural endorphins when nothing else works.*

That was how Zane ended up in this musty weight room. He only had a membership to this gym because Caroline took swim lessons here in preparation for the pool that was to be built in his backyard. He'd never stepped into this excessively mirrored room until tonight. Zane would happily run up, down, sideways, and complete any body weight exercise his team captain asked for during practice, but he didn't see the point in lifting weights just to lift.

And the mirrors always bothered him. Why would you want to stare at yourself, anyway?

The only good thing about the gym right now was that it was mostly empty. Ten-thirty on a Saturday night was apparently the time to come if you wanted your pick of machines. Zane was two seconds from abandoning the weight bench altogether in favor of the treadmill upstairs when the unmistakable click of heels pierced his ears.

When Ms. Powell stomped into the room, arrowing toward the squat rack, Zane nearly dropped the bar on his chest.

You could smell the testosterone swell the second everyone registered that she was wearing a sleeveless, skin-tight teal dress instead of sweats. Zane wasn't much better than the handful of men left in the room, sitting up to stare as Ms. Powell flung her clutch on the ground, slipped out of her strappy gold heels, and rolled her neck.

While Ms. Powell layered plates onto the bar with an almost terrifying ferocity, Zane watched two thirty-something men in the corner pull their headphones down, muttering to each other. The second she swept her long hair to the side, stepped under the bar, went seamlessly into a squat, and then struggled to push the massive weight back up, every single man in the room lurched forward.

But Zane was faster.

Speed had always been one of Zane's strong suits.

"Ann, be careful." He caught the bar, crowding behind her and helping her return it to the frame's J-hooks.

Zane had never used her first name before. He knew it, of course, but had mentally referred to her as Ms. Powell to assert some feeble distance between them. To protect against the way his body rearranged itself whenever he was near her.

Now "Ann" was out in the air, hovering like smoke.

Her eyes shot to Zane's in the mirror before darting to the red-headed, Viking-looking man approaching them from the left.

"Hey." The Viking sent a loaded smile Ann's way before gratuitously flashing his abs by wiping invisible sweat off his brow with the hem of his shirt. "Need me to help lighten that bar for you?"

Whatever irritation she'd carried through the door, it doubled with his words. Ann's fingers gripped the bar tighter, and Zane felt an upward tug. He hadn't let go of the steel rod, his hands two inches outside of hers.

"Ann." This time, he let her name be a whisper only she could hear.

When her gaze dragged to his again, her eyes confirmed what Zane had suspected the second he stepped behind her. They were bloodshot and unfocused. The harder she breathed, the more the remnants of juniper-forward gin crowded out her orange-blossom scent.

Ann was drunk.

Drunk and angry and trying to squat 275 lbs.

Zane waited, silent. He wasn't about to answer for her, though an intrinsic part of him wanted to tell this meathead to shove off.

"We're good, thanks." Her arctic words were accompanied with a hard stare.

The man side-eyed Zane and shrugged before walking away.

Two seconds after he left, Zane felt Ann's focus shift to him in the mirror. She still hadn't let go of the bar, her fingers flexing.

"Are you going to let go?" Her tone was still icy, but Zane didn't feel any of its bite. All he could hear was the word "we're."

Her question wasn't a challenge. It was a test.

"No." He kept his voice soft, open.

Her chest expanded in a long, slow inhale. "I can do this."

Ann's gaze still hadn't left his, hadn't blinked, almost like their normal prolonged eye contact was now some Wild West showdown.

"I have no doubt."

Those mesmerizing eyes surveyed him for three thick heartbeats before her fingers loosened and flopped to her sides.

Then Ann was ducking under the bar and misjudging how much space was open behind her. Space *he* was currently occupying. When her body flattened against his, Zane barely kept a hiss trapped behind his teeth. His right arm wrapped securely around her waist. Zane could argue that the movement had been instinctual, to steady her, but that didn't explain the satisfaction that swept through every single one of his cells.

"You okay?" It was automatic the way those words were husked over her ear, how his chin dipped to breathe her in.

The shudder that racked against him should have set off the part of his brain that usually was in control, but some unknown part of him had taken over. Rationality sat in a cage somewhere far away. States away. Continents away.

Zane didn't have to guess what her visceral reaction had meant. The same steady thrumming that pulsed through his body vibrated over her skin. He knew it, just like he knew *this* was the reason they avoided each other at all costs.

"Cold? Do you want my hoodie?" Zane could hear his deepest timbre in those questions, the one he'd begun to intentionally infuse during certain scenes in his home studio.

Never one he'd weaponized against a living, breathing woman.

Ann's mouth slacked open with a halting exhale as her eyelids fluttered. Zane immediately amended his complaint about the mirrors. They allowed him to see everything, to drink her in—the beauty of such a snug garment wrapped around her strong frame, the way her impossibly long hair swept over her slight chest, the freckle under her jaw when she tilted her head back.

Zane hadn't allowed himself to admit that he'd wanted this, this moment, this closeness with Ann since the second she walked away from him in the hallway that first time. But now that she was here, pressed against him, *melting* against him, Zane wanted to live here.

Free weights clattering to the ground from the corner of the gym snapped Zane back to reality.

This wasn't him. He didn't seduce innocent teachers by the cover of darkness.

Caroline's teacher.

Zane's stomach twisted into four distinct knots, prompting him to step back. While Ann's brow pinched over her unfocused eyes, Zane stooped to pick up her shoes and clutch.

"I—" He adjusted his glasses with one hand while outstretching her possessions with the other. "I couldn't help but smell the gin. Did you drive here?"

It was painful watching loose, pliable Ann return to her organized self, but that was where they needed to be. Where they could safely interact with each other. It didn't matter that he'd never felt a stronger pull toward a woman in his life.

"No." Ann grabbed her belongings without touching his fingers. "My car's at a nearby bar. Since my date wouldn't let me talk, too obsessed with the sound of his own voice, I made a game of taking a sip of my martini every time he said, 'BitCoin.'"

"Oh, no."

When Ann smiled at him like they were sharing *the best* secret, his abs clenched. He almost reached up to touch the curve of her lips.

Almost.

"Oh, yes. When getting sloshed didn't help make him less of a chauvinist,"—Ann shrugged like she genuinely thought that would work—"I told him I was going to the bathroom but walked here instead."

Zane tried to ignore the burning around his ribs. It was definitely there because her date had been a massive jerk, not because he wished *he'd* been the one sitting across the table from her—been the reason for Ann to put on those pencil-thin heels.

"It's just another failure. J for Jerry." She shuddered, but for an entirely different reason than she had before. "I should have known it wasn't going to work out when most of his profile pictures were of him holding fish. There's not even any water around here. We live in a desert."

"Not the fish pics," he said.

The alcohol was likely to blame for Ann's loose lips. She'd never said anything other than necessary, school-related words to him before.

"I know." Ann ran her hand through her hair, sending a curtain cascading down her back. "I should have known better."

Zane tried to stop his eyes from tracing over her body when her spine arched as her fingers sifted through her hair, but he failed miserably. He didn't even *notice* he'd failed until his gaze landed on her toenails.

Stifling the thoughts and impulses bombarding his body took tremendous willpower, but Zane reminded himself who they were. Her entire whiteboard might as well have *OFF LIMITS* printed in all caps. Even with that, there was no way Zane wasn't going to be absolutely certain Ann made it home safe.

"Can I give you a ride home?" He tugged his lips up into a friendly grin. "I'd hate for something to happen to Caroline's favorite teacher."

There. Boundary set.

That should balance everything.

So why did the way her face crumbled make Zane want to snatch his words out of the air and swallow them?

Ann blinked at her bare feet for a few seconds before she moved to open her clutch. "Thank you, but I'll call a car."

His hand covered hers before he'd noticed his movement, before he could stop himself. "It's no problem."

It was impossible to miss the controlled way she inhaled. "Okay."

Though the gym was only a few miles from the school, Ann's condo was twenty minutes away, near Sabino Canyon Recreational Area.

Twenty silent minutes.

Except for when Ann muttered, "The sky tastes like spaghetti right now," to the passenger window and the whisper of The Allman Brothers Band's debut album playing in the background. Normally, he'd have kept the conversation flowing, but a niggling part of him whispered warnings over learning more about the woman with whom he was already enamored. Seven hundred conversation starters whipped through his mind, but he only allowed himself one.

"Do you hike there all the time?" Zane asked after she'd given him the code to the entry gate to her neighborhood—a code he memorized, though he was certain he'd never need it again. "My friend Rowan and his family love Sabino Canyon."

Ann seemed to slump in her seat. "I'm not . . . outdoorsy. I know I should go because it's so close, but—" She shrugged.

"You shouldn't feel guilty. If it's not for you, then it's not for you. No matter how close it is."

A smile flirted with the corner of her mouth, and Zane focused back on the three-way split of the neighborhood street. "Which way?"

When they were settled in the driveway of her single-story condo, Ann rotated in her seat with a noisy inhale. Zane's hands clenched the steering wheel, waiting for her to wedge more space between them, to complete the action he'd started back at the gym—the thing that *needed* to happen between them.

Because the way his skin had been coated in lightning by her sheer presence in his car was dangerous. Now that he had a tactile memory of what Ann felt like, it had been a gargantuan feat to not let some part of him touch her again—to have his forearm brush hers over the center console, to let his fingertips drop to her exposed kneecap . . .

Zane struggled to keep his breathing even as he shut off that intrusive thought.

At least Ann was going to fix this by saying goodnight and getting out so they'd only interact with each other when in regard to Caroline.

But the next words Zane heard were, "How do you feel about weddings?"

Chapter 7

It took four heaving seconds for Ann to realize that it wasn't a cinching rattlesnake cutting off her air supply, but the excess fabric of her peasant nightgown twisted around her ribs. When she bolted upright to reshuffle the fabric, it felt like a cast-iron frying pan had whacked her on the forehead.

"Oh." An inhuman groan left her lips as she grabbed her throbbing skull.

Her dehydrated brain finally caught up enough to remind her of the two martinis she'd chugged at the bar last night. Since Ann rarely drank, and her date had rudely dismissed the server before she could order food, today's hangover was scoring extra credit for its effort.

Water, her abused body reminded her. *You need water.*

Ann's metal water bottle wasn't in its usual position on her nightstand, so she stumbled toward the kitchen. Her clutch, keys, and shoes were discarded in the short entry hall instead of put away in the coat closet where they belonged, but hydration took priority. As much as her reckless mess made her eye want to twitch, she could clean up after she drank a gallon—maybe two.

Bits and pieces of last night filtered in with each soothing ounce slushing down her esophagus. By the time she'd finished two large glasses, Ann had to dart to her phone. Just to make sure her mischievous brain was playing tricks on her.

No such luck.

Her screen was open to a text message stream.

Ann: *My cell*

Ann: *Thanks again for doing this.*

Zane: *No problem*

The memory of her suboptimally brushing her teeth and sending the second message assaulted her. She'd given Zane her number by sending the first message before she'd exited his tidy SUV, but the next message confirmed that her huge lapse in judgment hadn't been a dream.

Everything from last night came slamming back in painstaking detail.

Her behavior at the gym, warring with herself on the ride home, how she'd opened her mouth with a question and everything else had just . . . fallen out—her sister's impending wedding, the parameters of the bet, a play-by-play of each miserable date, asking Zane to be her fake date to save her from future trauma.

Everything.

"Ugh," Ann groaned. "You are a crazy person. You are a lunatic, unfit to teach children. And you're probably going to lose your job because of this."

She wasn't certain what the parent/teacher dating policy was at Hillcrest, but it was probably frowned upon. Rushing to pick up her belongings and set them in their proper places, Ann fired off another text.

Ann: *Sorry to bother you, but do you have a moment for a phone call?*

When her screen flashed with Zane's incoming call, this desperate choking sound escaped her dry lips. Her heels clacked on the tile floor as they slipped through her non-functioning fingers.

"Hello?" Ann had planned on answering with a professional, "Good morning, Mr. West," but her shaky greeting was already loose.

"Hey."

It was unfair how delicious his voice sounded over the phone. Usually, a phone call distorts a person's voice, making it ugly and digitized, but Zane's sounded even huskier. The memory of it, sliding into her ear accompanied by the warmth of his breath, sent a shiver through her. Ann clicked the speaker button, subconsciously wanting his timbre to infiltrate the space around her.

She fiddled with the lacy edge of her sleeve, stalling. "About yesterday—"

"When you were of sound mind and body and simply took a ride home from the parent of one of your students?" Zane supplied. "Because if there was anything else, I don't remember."

He was making this easy on her. Ann got the impression Zane made everything easier.

"Yeah." Her relieved answer was more of an exhale.

"If you'd prefer to imagine that you transported Star-Trek-style directly to your condo, that works for me too." That smile he always wore infiltrated his words. "I'll pretend I never saw you. It was a fluke that I was at the gym myself."

His admission rolled around in her mind. She'd noticed Zane's tall, limber build but now wondered if he earned his muscles passively through activity instead of building them for the purposes of having them.

The second that thought drifted into her mind, Ann tried to suppress it. Just like she did with every other fact she'd learned about Zane since the start of the year. It was obvious he was an attentive, caring father, raising an amazing child. Though Ann and Zane tended not to speak unless it was academically necessary, everyone—absolutely everyone—from the front office staff to the custodians, loved Zane.

Plus, single dads were always a hot topic in the teacher's lounge. Especially single dads who'd lovingly nursed their ex-wives back to life before being asked for a divorce. It wasn't something the staff at Hillcrest should have known, but home-life details had a way of trespassing at school. Only, Zane wasn't the scorned lover the school busybodies had hoped he'd be. Amicable warmth flowed between Caroline's parents.

"You don't mind?"

"Not at all."

A brief pause hung over the line, and in the space where Ann should have counted her lucky stars and wished him a good day, the sound of a deadbolt sliding open deafened her ears.

There was only *one person* who would enter her condo without knocking.

"Did you forget that you had a dress fitting this morning?" Rene's cutting eyes scrutinized her disheveled appearance. "Why are you still in those ridiculous pajamas?"

Ann glanced at the timestamp on her phone—11:00 a.m. She should have been at the tailor's thirty minutes ago. "I'm sorry. I overslept. I'll—"

Rene's gaze zeroed on the glowing phone in Ann's upturned palm. "Who are you talking to?"

"I'm Zane."

He didn't even hesitate, just launched himself in front of her sister. Reckless, foolhardy man.

"Zane, huh?" Rene winked in Ann's direction and lowered her voice. "Went straight to Z? You rebel."

"Who's this?" he asked.

"The blushing bride to be." Rene tossed her shoulder-length hair with a coy sigh.

"Rene. Right." A slight edge crept into his tone. "Ann's told me all about you."

Rene's lips dropped open in an exaggerated smile, missing the nuance beneath his words. "Aww. She's the best big sister."

"She is." There was an assuredness in his answer that made Ann straighten.

A pause reverberated between the narrow walls of her entry before Zane's voice detonated like a bomb.

"I look forward to meeting you, Rene."

No, Zane. Run. You're supposed to run.

"Meeting me?" That flirty, sticky quality laced her sister's question. "So, you'll be Ann's plus-one at the wedding?"

"I will."

What? They'd just agreed that they hadn't seen each other last night. That all her drunken mumblings never happened.

A perturbed look wrinkled Rene's brow before she smoothed out her flawless skin.

So many words pummeled Ann's already throbbing forehead, but as usual, Rene spoke over her. "Why don't you meet me today? Beyond Bread on Speedway, in an hour?"

"I'll be there."

The phone be-donked as Zane hung up, and it took Ann several slow blinks to register what had just transpired and that all Zane's usual warmth had drained from his voice with his last answer.

◊◊◊

Ann rubbed her left ribs. The seamstress had poked her twice after muttering, "Too much muscle," while fitting the side zipper of her strapless maid-of-honor dress. Though Ann had repeatedly apologized to the matron for missing their appointment, she had a strong suspicion the pin pricks were a not-so-subtle retaliation for tardiness.

When Rene pushed open the glass door to Beyond Bread, reality mimicked the blast of air conditioning rushing over her face. Ann had been swimming in a stuffed-olive hangover for the last hour, but Zane standing across the restaurant was a strong slap to the cheek.

She'd only seen him wear a surprisingly extensive collection of loose-fitting band shirts, like the Silversun Pickups one he'd had on last night. The white of his snug T-shirt was almost blinding, but she couldn't look away. It was too perfect atop his jeans. What was it with men in white T-shirts and jeans? It was some sort of kryptonite for common sense.

Zane's gaze found hers like Ann's thoughts had been shouting his name.

Had the din of the bustling restaurant been muddled, Rene would have heard Ann's shaky inhale.

Four frozen seconds passed between them. Seconds in which she subconsciously took in the way his warm brown eyes held a determinedness she hadn't seen before, and how today, his black frames didn't provide any respite from their power over her.

Then it was like everything was entirely too loud. Bile splashed the back of her tongue when what was about to occur slammed to the forefront of her mind.

No.

This can't happen.

She couldn't throw this kind man onto the railroad tracks of her dysfunctional family. She couldn't do that to anyone. That was another reason she was single.

Ann shook her head, trying to tell him to pretend he didn't see her, to leave before it was too late.

Run, Zane.

Zane's gaze never left hers as he strode toward her. The intensity in his eyes and his purposeful movement in her direction drew the attention of several onlookers.

"Oh," slipped from her sister's lips as Zane swallowed Ann in a firm embrace.

Her heart was a zipping hummingbird, thrumming in her chest for the brief seconds she spent wrapped in Zane's arms. Ann wanted to spend the next hour there, maybe the next three. The softness of his shirt brushing her bare arms, his subtle sandalwood scent, and the way he held her deserved more time to be thoroughly relished.

"Hey." He dropped the low, quiet word over her ear before leaning back. "You look amazing, as always. And you"—he turned to her sister—"must be Rene." Zane didn't offer his hand, but a brief hug. One Rene enjoyed a little too much.

"So nice to meet you." Caustic acid burned Ann's breastbone when Rene squeezed his upper arm and let her fingertips linger. "Ann, you didn't tell me your new beau was so handsome."

"You ladies hungry? Lunch is on me." Zane turned with an easy smile, efficiently freeing himself from Rene's grip.

Though the swirling ceiling lights and blue accents of Ann's favorite sandwich shop usually brought her happiness, a galvanized lead ball was rolling in her stomach. Zane, on the other hand, seemed completely comfortable conversing with an over-the-top Rene, ordering their sandwiches, and securing them an open high-top table in the busy eatery.

Honestly, all those activities were basic. It's not like Zane was performing heart surgery on the moon, but Ann kept waiting for something to implode, for Rene to figure out that Zane didn't really want to be here.

That this whole thing was *fake*.

Once their meal had been delivered, the mouth-watering scent of her roast beef and green chili sandwich reminded Ann that she hadn't eaten since yesterday's failed lunch date. She was so hungry she took a huge bite without even opening her sandwich and loading it with her pasta salad side dish like she usually did.

"Ugh. Could you be a little daintier when you eat? You're going to chase Zane away," Rene scoffed with a twist of her lips.

Zane mirrored her bite with a humongous one of his caprese sandwich. "This is so good. How's yours, Rene?" he asked over his full mouth.

Ann had to cover her grin with her hand when Zane's eyes flashed to hers with a quick eyebrow bounce. A flooding sensation that they were a team swept down her spine, settling her. She swallowed, letting her hand fall as her lips lifted higher.

When his gaze stalled on her mouth, they both snapped their focus to their lunches.

Rene threw personal questions at Zane like they were grenades, while Ann marveled in his ability to keep her sister off balance. For one, he didn't tell her who he was—thankfully. He instead took on the alias of a part-time scuba-diving enthusiast, part-time investment banker. Zane was halfway through a riveting story of the time he'd recovered from the bends in a hyperbaric chamber and had almost fallen in love with the doctor treating him when Rene's fiancé, Denis, called, and she excused herself from the table.

"Where are you getting all this?" Ann had long since finished her lunch and had spent the last ten minutes listening to Zane's vivid descriptions with her chin on her knuckles.

A small smile lifted the corner of his mouth before he took another bite of his half-eaten sandwich. "I read a lot."

"That's right. You're an audiobook narrator."

Caroline had told the class before winter break that her dad put the voice behind books. Ann *might have* searched his name and listened to three sci-fi audiobook samples before her doorbell had rung with a package, prompting her to slam her laptop closed.

A quizzical expression wrinkled his dark-blond brows.

"Caroline mentioned it once," Ann said.

Zane nodded, continuing to shovel food into his face like it was his only chance with Rene gone.

"Thank you for what you've done today, but you don't have to do this—to keep doing this," she clarified.

"I know," he said, after lifting a palm to shield her from mozzarella and freshly baked focaccia.

"Seriously." Ann straightened and smoothed out the skirt of her tiered peach sundress. "There's no good reason for you to help me. You're not getting anything out of it."

"I have a hero complex," Zane said, holding up the last baby carrot from his side dish. "If I don't save at least one person or animal every day, I go into shock."

A chuckle burst from her, followed immediately by swelling unease.

Don't make me laugh. Don't give me another reason to like you.

Surprised delight washed over his face before he tucked it away.

"I don't mind." Zane folded his thick paper napkin into fourths before placing it in his empty basket. "Me going to one event will help keep the peace between you and your sister. And what you plan on doing with your winnings is admirable."

"You *should* mind," Ann said, completely ignoring how his second sentence warmed her skin like the afternoon sun. "Rene is just the tip of the maladjusted iceberg."

"Denis needs me, so I'll see you later." Her sister grabbed her purse from the back of the cafe chair and was a step away before remembering Zane. "Oh, it was good to meet you. I look forward to seeing more of you."

Ann had to keep her fingers from clenching when Rene sent him a loaded wink.

They both watched her exit before Ann sighed loud enough to be heard even in the noisy restaurant. "See. It's not worth the trouble."

Chapter 8

It was impossible not to hear the implication in Ann's words—*she* wasn't worth the trouble. Zane had to take several deliberate breaths and focus on clearing the table to allow his surging anger to dissipate. For as confident as she'd always been at school and at the squat rack last night, Ann seemed to crumble in her sister's presence. With each passing minute, it was like floodwater stripping away another layer of sediment.

When he turned around, Ann was hugging her elbows, a frown resting on her gorgeous lips.

"I'm guessing your sister drove you here." *And then abandoned you*, his mind fired off before he could stop it.

Ann's eyes snapped into focus before her head tilted back. "Yeah, but it's okay. I'll just—"

"Come on," Zane said, stepping toward the door. "I parked in the back."

Gratitude flushed his muscles when Ann didn't fight him. He was already fighting the impulse to wrap her in his arms until her shoulders slid away from her ears. As Zane opened his passenger door, he forced his eyes not to watch her. They drifted over to the line of creosote bushes along the painted brick wall separating the back lot from the neighborhood behind it. Yellow blossoms were interspersed between miniscule, fluffy, white seed capsules.

"We need rules if this is going to happen." Ann hadn't lowered herself into the car. Instead, she stood beside the open door with a determined jaw.

Yes. Rules. Clear boundaries. Good.

"Sure. What are you thinking?"

Ann pressed her lips together, and the air in his lungs condensed.

"First, I want to thank you for not telling Rene who you really are and for concealing your connection to the school. I don't think either of us wants this . . . arrangement affecting our real lives."

"Right. Of course."

Even though he'd been mildly—okay, more than mildly— intrigued by Ann since the beginning of the school year, Zane would rather cut off his left hand than cause Caroline more distress. It was obvious that Caroline was struggling with the idea of moving from her grandparents' home to Isaac's for the weeks she stayed with Tessa. Zane couldn't throw another variable into his daughter's life.

Not right now.

The joke at Rowan's expense yesterday had been like a tectonic shift beneath Zane's feet, signifying that his cheerful girl was returning to him.

But even with his daughter at the forefront of his mind, Zane couldn't stop himself from helping Ann. Not when she'd drunkenly given him every messy detail of her relationship with her sister. Not when she was trying to improve the lives of children less fortunate than the ones she taught at Hillcrest. Especially not after hearing she'd been on ten tortuous dates.

It'd been challenging to listen to Ann being mistreated by men who didn't deserve her, knowing that he wanted nothing more than to be the one across a table from her. For months, Zane had reminded himself that he just needed to wait out the school year. Once Caroline was no longer in Ann's class, there wouldn't be the barrier to asking Ann out. But knowing she was out there looking for Mr. Right changed things.

A cool sensation slithered up his spine. Zane didn't want her to meet the man of her dreams before he'd had a chance to see if there was something beyond their intense chemistry. With him acting as a fake placeholder, Ann wouldn't be dating others.

Zane's ulterior motives for helping Ann out of this situation made him a complete jerkwad. But only if he acted on them.

Just don't act on them.

His grip tightened on the door jamb.

"Rene's never cared about my job and doesn't have any connections to the school," Ann continued, "so I don't think it will leak back from her. Assuming there's no one else on the guest list that could connect us to Hillcrest, I think we'll be okay. Obviously, *we* won't tell anyone."

Zane nodded, subduing how his shoulders wanted to physically shake off the irritation caused by Rene's indifference.

"Rene will think that we've been dating the whole time between now and May 29th, when we see her next, so I'll compile a basic facts spreadsheet, fill in my side, and share it with you to supply your answers." She pulled out her phone, typing a reminder into her to-do app. "That way, when they ask us questions at the wedding, it won't be weird."

It was bad that he liked Ann even more when she was being hyper-organized.

"And we should probably come up with some sort of endearment for each other. Pookie. Sweetum." Her nose wrinkled even as she said those suggestions.

"I want to call you Ann." The sentence held more gruff than he'd intended, but he'd just gained access to her first name and wasn't about to trade it for Pookie.

"Oh." Her mouth parted with an unsteady exhale. "Okay."

This was such a terrible idea. It was taking all his fortitude not to lift his hand and feel the fluttering fabric of her sundress over her waist. His mind had been on a loop of pondering what her lips would taste like since last night. Presently, they probably tasted like vinegar from her pasta salad and green chilies, but that combination sounded more heavenly than anything a Michelin-star chef could come up with.

Zane pushed his fingers into his jeans pockets. "What else?"

"Um. We shouldn't be seen in public, except for school events where we'd act like our normal selves, until the wedding."

"Makes sense." His neck was going to crick from all the nodding.

Her shoulders bounced. "I guess that's it."

"Easy enough." Zane gestured toward the still-open door and waited for Ann to lower herself before shutting it.

"Where's your car?" he asked after taking the slowest steps possible around the back of his SUV to collect himself.

"Bluey's." She adjusted her sunglasses.

Normally, Zane would have espoused how he loved the Australian eatery and pub. He was a sucker for a good zucchini slice. If Ann had been anyone else, he would have been deep in conversation with them within minutes, but doing so with Ann felt like violating the unspoken rules they'd set alongside the declared ones. They were here to fool her sister, to know facts on a spreadsheet, not to really get close.

"This isn't going to work," Ann said after ten minutes of silence.

"What do you mean?"

Her intertwined hands tensed in her lap. "We can't even make idle conversation. How are we going to convince my sister we're dating?"

Zane wanted to tell Ann that every time they were in the same room, he wanted to ask her four thousand questions. Like, what made her lie awake at night? What was her happiest memory? What did she find comedic? Because Zane not only wanted to hear that raspy chuckle again, he wanted to record it and play it back whenever he wished. Instead, Zane focused on answering Ann's question.

"Do we need to convince her we're dating, or do you need a body beside you at her wedding?" Ann winced, and Zane regretted his harsh words. "I didn't mean it like that. It's just that she only seems to care about appearances, not that you're happily dating. I got the impression that she half wished we weren't dating so she could have a run at me."

Ann slumped like she had last night when he'd asked her about hiking Sabino Canyon. Zane hated being the cause of that motion. He wanted to be the person to fortify Ann, not tear her down like her sister had done throughout lunch.

"I was hoping you hadn't noticed."

"Ann, she touched me as much as she possibly could." Zane barely restrained his instinctive shudder.

When Ann buried her face in her hands, searing pain ribboned its way through his stomach again. He was generally more careful with his words—because you never know when the last thing you say to a person will be the last words they'll hear from your lips.

Zane's eyes were on the road, but his memories were spinning a chaotic spiral around the car. He swallowed hard, forcing them away.

What was worse was the things Zane wanted to tell Ann— that she was incredible, that he was already captivated by her, that he wanted nothing more than to see where this went—had to stay trapped in his throat because this was an *arrangement*.

He was here to fulfill a role.

Nothing more.

"I'm sorry." Ann lifted her face with a pained expression. "I told you—"

"Let's think about it as a game," Zane said, reshuffling his emotions. "Like a game show where you and I have to behave in a certain way for a short period of time and the prize is four thousand dollars for underfunded classrooms. I think I can dust off my *Introduction to Acting* skills I learned sophomore year for such a good cause."

In truth, Zane used those skills, and others he'd acquired over the years, each day he recorded. He could be dozens of different characters at once. His voice would twist, slow, bite, smile, or rasp to effectively express the author's intention. Taking on *this* role, pretending to be Ann's boyfriend, would be effortless.

Zane let his smile lift his cheeks. "What do you say?"

A doubtful look scrunched her forehead. "You're sure?"

He rolled to a stop in Bluey's parking lot and let himself fully take her in. It wasn't until this moment that Zane noticed how little her expressions had shown in front of Rene, how little he'd seen of them during school, even when she was chatting with Tessa or another teacher. Her body had always been perfectly postured, her words thoughtful and even.

It was only when they were alone that her guard came crashing down. Ann probably didn't even know she was allowing her expressions to show, that she was letting him—only him—in.

A barricade in his body broke, and warmth flooded his veins.

"One hundred percent."

"But—"

Zane's fingers were lifting her sunglasses atop her head before he could stop himself. He needed to watch understanding soften the green of her eyes. "I'm here for as long as you need me."

His breathing sounded like a screaming wind tunnel in his ears as he waited for Ann's acceptance. Her gaze bounced around his face, uncertain for several eviscerating seconds. Zane had offered to help hundreds of people in his lifetime, but the idea that the one woman he desperately wanted to stand beside might refuse him pummeled his bones.

When Ann exhaled and relief splashed across her face, it was like a gentle rain pittering on the roof of his car. A sound he'd waited months to hear. The life-giving force that allowed the Sonoran Indian mallow to soften its tiny, peach petals toward the sky. The only thing that returned the slight green to the arid landscape.

"I'm here for you," he repeated.

Ann nodded, a small smile lifting her beautiful lips, and Zane had to ignore how his heart was attempting to escape through his throat.

"Okay, fake boyfriend."

"Okay, fake girlfriend." His mirrored sentence was slightly huskier than hers.

Her fingers scratched at her neck as Ann's gaze fell to her lap. "I should go."

"Yeah." He cleared his throat. "See you at the wedding."

Ann nodded, returning to her organized self, and Zane couldn't bring himself to watch her walk away. Instead, he kept his eyes on the corrugated metal half-wall surrounding one of his favorite restaurants, ignoring how much he wanted to edit out "fake" from his newly acquired moniker.

Chapter 9

"We have a problem," Ann said, the second Zane picked up her call.

Mid-day sun warmed her flushed cheeks as she shifted her weight while watching her students through the windowed door that separated her classroom from the small courtyard. Any regular third-grade teacher could have leaned out their room but probably wouldn't have dreamt of closing the door to make a call, but Hillcrest students were different. They were self-motivated to a fault.

Often, she'd have to plan playful endeavors into their day to remind them they were still eight-year-olds. Since it was Friday, Ann was going to hold a contest of who could count and pop the most bubbles in the courtyard before pickup. The winner would get their pick of miniature candies from the oversized fishbowl on the class bookshelf. At least half of her sixteen students were going to roll their eyes at the frivolity of the exercise, but they were still young enough that candy would ensure their participation.

"What kind of problem?" Zane asked.

It'd been almost two weeks since their lunch together, and Ann hadn't seen or spoken to Zane since. Their only interaction had been when she'd sent out the spreadsheet to fill out that Sunday. Each topic had its own row: birthday, allergies, parents' names, siblings, friends, where you grew up, and schools attended. He'd filled it out overnight and added the categories of pets, coffee order, and favorite food, band, movie, and color.

Comparing the two columns, Ann had felt less intriguing. Her answers were short, one-worded, or vague. Ann didn't have a favorite band—she listened to whatever was on the prefab playlists on her streaming app. Though, after their lunch, Ann had searched for playlists with the names of bands she'd seen on Zane's shirts. She didn't have a pet, or a favorite movie, and didn't think 'anything breakfast' technically counted as a favorite food. Weren't you supposed to list a cuisine?

Meanwhile, some of Zane's answers had been paragraphs. "*I know I should say my favorite movie is* Citizen Kane *or* The Godfather, *but it's* The Mask of Zorro. *I spent four solid Halloweens in a mask, cloak, and sombrero cordobés.*"

That had made Ann smile. She liked imagining a boy-sized Zane triple-slicing the air with a rapier.

"*Honestly, it's hard for me to enjoy movies like the average person. Every time I watch a movie, all I hear is what went into it. My mom is a Foley artist. That's the person who makes the sound effects for a scene, like when a character is walking, drinking, the rustle of clothes in a fight scene, etc. When a film is shot, the sound is concentrated on the actor's dialogue, so sound effects are recreated in post.*

After years of sitting with her coworker, the sound mixer, watching her use a million unexpected things to make a sound, like swathing a plastic decapitated baby doll head with sopping paper towels to approximate the sound of a person stuffing a turkey, I can't separate the behind-the-scenes efforts in my mind. If I ever told her that, it would crush her because that's the exact opposite of what Foley artists are trying to accomplish."

Ann had spent an evening lost in a rabbit hole after searching 'Foley artist' online, having no idea what went into sound. She watched video after video, marveling at what behind-the-scenes object had actually made Superman's cape snap. Another artist had run in place through unwound and piled magnetic tape from several cassette tapes to mimic the actor on screen running through leaves.

"Rene told my parents about you," Ann continued. "She embellished our relationship, stating that we were 'an item.' Now, my dad wants to meet you and for you to join us tonight at our dinner with Denis's mother."

When silence—absolute, endless vacuum of space silence—met her ear, Ann backpedaled. "I'm sorry. I don't know why I called. There's no reason—"

"I have Caroline tonight."

Her focus snapped back to the classroom. Caroline's tongue was currently pressed against her upper lip as she bent over her lined page, perfecting the sloppy-copy of her persuasion essay.

Ann loved all her students equally—officially. But every year, there was a tiny light that snuck through, that shined brighter than the others.

This year, that was Caroline.

Which made this agreement with Zane even more problematic.

Ann winced. "I understand. I'll tell them you've got a spring cold and can't make it."

She was an imbecile for even calling in the first place. If only she could think on her feet like her sister could, instead of needing six sloppy-copies of her own words before coming to the right ones. Ann should've made an excuse for Zane with Rene and never informed him of the invitation.

But it'd been the way Rene had emphasized Dad's joy over hearing that Ann had a boyfriend that had cascaded to this conversation. It was her sister's vivid descriptions that had slid the long icy needle in between Ann's ribs.

Knowing Rene, she'd probably done that on purpose.

You're such a fool.

Though a teensy white butterfly weightlessly flitted from one lantana bloom to the next, Ann felt an anvil against her throat.

"Sorry for disturbing you," she said, pressing her eyes closed and shutting out the overbright courtyard.

Why was her voice so meek? Her voice wasn't meek. It commanded the attention of—albeit, generally attentive—children most moments of the day.

"Ann, wait."

It was disturbing how much those two little words produced an overwhelming swell in her chest.

"Tess and I switch weeks on Saturdays. Let me see if she can pick up Caroline today instead. Just—" An exhale blew over the phone, and Ann's mind raced to determine the emotion beneath it—annoyance, irritation at this inconvenience, wishing he'd never sidled up with the likes of her in the first place. "Just let me call her."

Ann took a second to even her breathing before returning to class. The bright orange-yellow poppies and multi-colored lantana of the courtyard could usually brighten Ann's mood. She loved flowers in any capacity—florist-prepped, grocery-store-purchased, garden-nurtured, side-of-the-road-wild-grown. Today, their cheerfulness mocked her. Nothing good was going to come of this.

◊◊◊

Ann had felt sick for the rest of the school day, particularly after informing Caroline of the change in plans. Obscuring that *she* was the reason Tessa had called the front office staff to inform them that Zane wouldn't be picking her up today had made Ann's stomach feel filled with embalming fluid.

It was slight, but Ann caught how Caroline had suppressed her displeasure at a deviation from her routine. It made sense. Caroline had no control over the events she'd lived through, so she clung to what was constant.

Ann understood a version of that desire from her own childhood.

Mounting tension sequentially tightened Ann's muscles as the seconds dwindled down to the dinner with her parents. She wouldn't be able to breathe easily until this night was over, which was why she'd worn her favorite dress. A supple, drape-sleeved, snuggish wrap dress in a pink that almost matched her nail beds. The color highlighted the natural tan of her skin, her rich brunette hair, and made her feel pretty.

Rene was undeniably gorgeous. She'd even done a short modeling stint before deciding that being told what to do wasn't for her. Ann knew she was essentially her younger sister's duplicate, but she'd always felt . . . off. Like how animators fell into the uncanny valley before they started making computer-generated characters with oversized eyes and small chins. Her proportions weren't quite right.

Regardless, Ann was proud of what her body could accomplish. It lifted massive amounts of weight. It allowed her to teach, to move as she wished. It was healthy and sound. Was it the feminine ideal? No. But that didn't matter because Ann wasn't trying to impress men. And tonight wasn't any different because this wasn't a real date.

Everything about this was fake.

Still, Ann couldn't help checking her makeup in the parking lot of the upscale restaurant. "The children," she reminded herself. "You're doing this for the children. That's it."

Her car door swung open before she'd put away her lip gloss.

"Hey, sis." Rene stooped at the waist to smile at her. "Just wanted to let you know that the parameters of the bet have changed."

"What?" she asked, trying to shake off how easily Rene had made her feel caged.

"In addition to the wedding, you have to bring *Zane*"—Ann hated the way Rene purred his name—"to a couples weekend with Denis and me in two weeks."

Even though Ann wanted to protest that you can't change a bet once it's set, her brain zipped through the calculation. In two weeks, Caroline should be with her mother for the weekend, assuming check-in was on Saturday.

"I've rented two gorgeous suites at that new wellness resort outside of Oracle. It would be some great bonding time for the four of us." Rene had never, in her life, wanted to *bond*. "That is, if you think he'd be interested." Venom dripped from the edges of her smile.

"Interested in what?"

Ann didn't have to look up to know it was Zane's deep timbre that had voiced that question.

"Zane! We were just talking about you."

When Rene moved out of the way to probably squeeze the life out of her reluctant date, Ann kept her eyes on the recently resurfaced asphalt as she stepped out and locked her car.

"My, you clean up," Rene drawled.

"I just came from work. Hopefully, this'll be okay for meeting your parents." There was an affable charm in his voice. A cheeriness.

Ann drew in a silent, deep breath before raising her gaze. She'd expected Zane in some sort of business-casual attire, khakis and rolled-up collared shirt. What he was wearing spun her brain like an unmanned carnival ride, careening out of control.

Tucson was a casual city. Only weddings garnered the need for such formal attire. Even then, it was up to the couple getting married. The immaculately tailored, navy, three-piece suit Zane was wearing belonged in Manhattan, and even then, only in specific boroughs. The silky black tie tucked beneath his vest seamlessly accented his glasses.

"Hey." When Zane hugged her hello, he pressed a possessive hand to the small of her back before releasing her. "That dress . . . " He smiled and bit the corner of his lip. "Wow."

Ann could only manage to blink. Breathing was beyond her right now. None of this made any sense.

Zane rubbed his knuckles over his still grinning mouth before visibly remembering his surroundings. "Sorry, Rene. You look lovely as well."

Still frozen, Ann could only rotate her stunned head in her sister's direction.

An emotion skirted over Rene's face faster than a roadrunner silently racing through the underbrush, but Ann caught it.

Envy.

Bald, blatant envy.

Ann felt her shoulders slide back and her spine straighten.

"We should head inside." Rene was already six steps away, leaving them behind in the dwindling twilight.

"I thought this might befit an investment banker." Zane lifted his lapel as his normal smile returned to his face—the playful, friendly one. Not the bone-melting, seductive one he'd pinned her with a second ago. "You ready to get this show on the road? I'm making a side game of how many times I can put

Rene in her place. If I get to ten, you owe me an eegee after dinner."

When his eyes flashed with devious delight, Ann wanted to kiss him.

It was that simple.

She wanted to slide her hands over his smooth vest, tuck them behind his back, and pull his lips to hers.

No one had ever shown up for her like this. Ann was always the one to be there for her family, her coworkers, but she rarely asked for help because she'd grown accustomed to being let down. It became easier to do everything herself.

But today . . . all she'd done was *ask*.

Ann had asked Zane to come to dinner, and he'd shown up like this—ready for battle. She blinked again, but this time it was to cover how her eyes were misting over.

"Yeah. Let's go," she said once she could trust her voice.

It became obvious as Zane swirled his Manhattan glass that he had *severely* underplayed his acting abilities. The entire table was eating out of his palm. At one point, Priscilla looked like she wished Denis was a Denise so Zane could marry into her family.

But Zane didn't seem to notice because he acted like he could only see Ann. He'd bounce his gaze to whoever was speaking, laugh along with everyone's jokes, but it was like *she* was his attention's natural resting place—where it preferred to spend its time.

It was intoxicating.

And Ann had only had a tiny sip of the three-hundred-dollar congratulatory champagne Priscilla had purchased for the table to flex her wealth.

Over and over, Ann kept saying *this is fake* in her head.

This is fake when Zane draped his arm around her shoulders and leaned in to whisper, "That's four. I can almost *taste* the Piña Colada."

This is fake when his arm remained, and his fingertips played with the flowy fabric of her sleeve.

This is fake after they finished their salads, and he slid his fingers through hers and kissed them while bragging about how proud he was of her teaching accolades. Ones she'd never shared with her family and that Zane must have researched, like receiving the Hillcrest Teacher of the Year award last spring.

This is fake. This is fake. This is fake.

Ann repeated it so often that semantic satiation settled in, and the words lost meaning.

She was in such a mental whirlwind that when her entree arrived, Ann automatically slid the medium-rare, petite filet to the side and began swirling her sauteed onions and mashed potatoes together before remembering her surroundings.

Her mother's not-so-subtle throat clearing halted her fork's mindless spirals.

"That looks amazing. Can I try some?" Zane's fork was already halfway toward her plate. "Mmmm," he hummed after swallowing the potato mixture. That bone-melting smile was back. "Your culinary prowess never ceases to amaze me."

Was he serious? She was mixing her veggies like a four-year-old. If he'd spent more than two minutes with her, he'd learn that dipping cold, crispy bacon into peanut butter wasn't dietary sophistication. It was a quirk. One of many she possessed. Several of which people found irritating.

The charade abruptly became intolerable. Heat swept beneath the V-neckline of her dress and pin-pricked down her legs, stinging her exposed toes. Being on the receiving end of affection that wasn't genuine was suddenly more heartbreaking than her sister's casual attacks. Vise-like squeezing worked its way through her insides until it reached her stomach, and Ann's appetite vanished.

"Please excuse me."

Zane rose as she pushed back from the table. Ann knew he was doing it out of politeness, to stay in character, so she kept her gaze and her artificially placid smile on Priscilla.

"I'll be right back."

Ann didn't bother trying to hide in the bathroom. Rene would track her down, corner her again. It was the perfect place because Zane couldn't act as a shield. Instead, her wedges clicked down the marble-tiled entryway until cool spring air met her tight lungs.

The posh, open-air shopping complex held a gelato shop, an upscale consignment boutique, and a fine jewelry store in addition to the restaurant. Though the soothing sounds of the three-tiered fountain in the center courtyard drew Ann's attention, she kept to the artfully bricked wall until it bent around the boutique. Her fingertips found her forehead as she allowed herself to sag against the building.

"What on earth am I doing?"

Chapter 10

Zane wasn't sure how he knew Ann would be outside, but it took exactly two pulsing heartbeats to find her tucked out of sight, beside a closed storefront. He had allowed sixty seconds of conversation to continue before excusing himself from the table to follow her.

"Hey," he said once he was close enough.

Ann looked at him like his soft greeting had been a gunshot to the liver. When she trailed her fingers through her hair and straightened, Zane could feel the shift. He'd been on the receiving end of that look too many times. Bad news was coming.

"Your dad . . . he's . . . he's gone."

Zane pushed the memory of his mother's shocked words out of his mind to focus on Ann.

"I can't do this," she said.

It shouldn't have been surprising how much those words stung, but Zane's breath punched out like he'd received a slamming tackle.

"What are you talking about?" he asked once he could speak, adding an affable grin—one Zane hoped was convincing. "We've almost won."

The rapid way Ann shook her head made his shoulders tense.

"I can't have you"—her fingers ran through her hair again—"saying things like that. I'm *particular*, and it's not cute, and you pretending that it—"

"Particular? You mean like exclusively using bubblegum sparkle toothpaste?" Zane asked, deadpan.

Ann leveled a *Be serious* look, and he splayed an affronted hand across his chest.

"You think I'm kidding? I'm not. I'm kind of a snob about it. Once you go bubble, you don't go back."

After modeling good teeth-brushing technique to a then eighteen-month-old Caroline, using her toothpaste, Zane had switched permanently. The flavor was far superior to mint.

She tilted her head with a nasally exhale. "Zane, I mean it. I'm the type of person who has people's birthdays auto-populate into my calendar long after I'm no longer friends with them. You seem about as easygoing as it gets, and I'm . . . not."

Zane shrugged, trying not to get irritated that she felt a few idiosyncrasies made them incompatible. "I have to kiss my fingertips and touch the ceiling if I drive through a yellow light. Otherwise, I might as well be asking for a car crash the next time."

Ann mulled that one over for a breath. "I rinse out and take my yogurt containers home to recycle them. I can't just put it into the trash. The thought gives me hives." She shuddered, and a strand of her hair slipped in front of her shoulder.

He made a dismissive noise. "That's just being an earth-conscious citizen. Honestly, I'm surprised Hillcrest doesn't have recycling service."

"I get almost violently angry when my nails are too long." Her gaze fell to her trim fingernails. Today's polish was a nearly imperceptible lavender.

Air was expanding beyond the capacity of Zane's ribs. Each fact Ann shared was adorable, not annoying. "I twitch when people say niche without the French pronunciation. It's like a record scratch for me even though I know both pronunciations are valid and I'm being pedantic."

The corner of her mouth lifted in the loveliest way. "I can't sing."

"I can't dance." Zane smiled, watching those green eyes flicker with light. "I love music, but I'm incapable of moving along with the beat. My friends tried to teach me once, but I was deemed hopeless. If there's music playing, you'll find me against the wall or seated, enjoying it with an uncoordinated head nod."

Ann let out a long, slow exhale, and Zane thought he was in the clear, but then her lips dove into a deep frown.

"But Rene wants us to do this couples getaway in two weeks, and—" She cut herself off with a headshake. "And if Dad thinks this is real, he'll want you to come over for family dinners and—" Another dropped sentence. "I can't bring you to my parents' house." Ann wrapped her arms around herself. "None of this is fair."

His mind was tumbling in chaotic somersaults, trying to follow her train of thought, until the last sentence. That he could sturdily stand on.

"What's not fair is the way your family treats you." Zane could hear the clip in his voice but was well past being able to subdue it. "It's like your mother and sister are trying to see how much of you they can chip away. Do you know how many times I fisted my hand under the table over the last hour?"

Ann's head shook again, but this time, her eyes widened.

His hard exhale blew between them as he collected himself. "Too many, Ann," he said, softening his voice. "Way too many."

The helpless way Ann shrugged tattered his chest.

"They don't deserve you." Zane couldn't help that he shifted closer.

"Dad does," Ann whispered as her gaze fell to the knot of his tie.

The way she'd said those two words made his automatic counterargument to her father's inattention to Rene's cruelty halt in his dry throat. Her father *had* spent half of the evening away from the table after Ann's mother shooed him when sips of water wouldn't clear his nagging cough. Perhaps he wasn't fully aware of the situation between the women in his family.

"Okay, but that shouldn't mean that Rene and your mom get to make digs at you," he said, his fingertips framing her elbows.

Jumbling thoughts crowded his mind the second he touched Ann. He'd intended the action to be comforting, but now Zane felt turned inside out. It was the first time that evening that he'd touched her without it being part of a role.

This differentiation shifted everything.

Ann seemed to recognize the stark contrast as well. Her halting exhale drew his attention and every contemplation dropped away until one clamoring thought remained.

He wanted to kiss her.

He wanted to kiss her more than he'd ever wanted to kiss a woman in his existence. If Zane was honest, he'd wanted to kiss her the second her green eyes had locked with his in the school hallway that first time.

This desire was insensible and demanding, like something beyond him was taking control.

"Ann."

Zane didn't know what he was asking for when her raspy name fled his lips.

Permission? Confirmation?

All he knew was that he didn't want to fake this anymore. They'd barely begun this artificial dalliance, but he already wanted *real*. He wanted Ann to be with him because she wanted to be, not as a part of her ruthless sister's manipulations. Not because she needed him to run interference.

If Ann wanted this—wanted him—Zane would sort everything out. He'd pulverize whatever obstacle they came across if Ann was feeling this ripped-out-of-your-skin sensation too.

Ann looked up, and her beautiful lips parted with an inhale, but Zane would never learn the words she'd planned on saying because another voice interrupted.

Two voices.

At the same time.

"Dad?"

"Z?"

Tucson was one of those strange places. Though its population hedged just over half a million, each corner of the city held its own mini culture. Within those, there'd often be small-town moments like this, when you'd run into the last two souls you wanted to see.

Zane pressed his eyes shut. He should have thought of this possibility when he discovered that the restaurant was within three miles of his home and this complex held Caroline's favorite dessert spot.

Ann had the wherewithal to step back and drop her hugged arms with a semi-steady, "Caroline. Ms. Liske. Good to see you."

"What is—" Tessa's eyes bounced between them, a blue star-designed cup of gelato in her clenched hand. "I thought you were out with Rowan."

"I—" Zane began.

"I was eating with my family and saw Mr. West and his friend leaving the restaurant." Ann's voice was sure, convincing. "I stopped him to discuss Caroline entering the Arizona Young Writers Contest."

Tessa wasn't buying any of this—Zane could tell—but Caroline quickly swallowed her spoonful of pink bubblegum gelato with an uninhibited smile. "Really?"

Ann had just dangled the juiciest carrot in front of Caroline, because aside from drawing, his daughter relished in competition. She was already the third-grade checker team captain and after winning second place at Hillcrest's art contest last semester, Caroline was inspired to trade portraiture for more mathematically balanced drawings, studying artists like M.C. Escher. The last sketch Zane saw was of saguaro cacti receding and expanding out of each other.

His daughter's artistic talent had been stumbled upon during Tessa's cancer treatment. Too often, Caroline would have to fend for herself while he helped Tessa deal with bouts of vomiting or intractable pain. Whenever Tessa's parents or his friends couldn't help watch Caroline, their next-door neighbor did.

Gwen was a breast cancer survivor and talented etching artist. After she and Caroline were done hunting for horny toads in the gravel of her backyard, Gwen would show their then five-year-old daughter the intricacies of perspective and scale. He and Tessa had been forced to let go of their worry that their young daughter preferred to create art with a fifty-year-old on the weekends than play with kids her own age. Whenever they went to the oncologist's office or to the infusion center, Caroline carried her sketchbook the way another child would hug a stuffed animal.

"If that's something you'd be interested in," Ann said, directing her attention to Caroline.

"Oh, yes." Caroline's grin stretched even wider.

Though Caroline had been awarded a spot at Hillcrest because of her artistic ability, she had been working hard to keep up with the advanced curriculum.

"Great." Ann's smile was sincere. It always was when Ann talked to Caroline or any of her other students—something

Zane had noticed from day one. "Applications start April 1st but aren't due until the 15th, so you've got time to consider what you'd like to submit."

"I'll submit my persuasive essay." In true Caroline fashion, she didn't waffle.

"Excellent. It was great to see you all, but I should be getting back." Ann gave them a quick nod before striding toward the restaurant.

"Caroline, why don't you see if I have change in my wallet and make some wishes about the contest." Tessa slid her oversized purse off her shoulder and slung it over Caroline's.

"I don't need luck." Caroline rolled her eyes but trotted toward the fountain, spooning another mouthful of gelato. She stopped halfway, turning back. "You look nice, Dad. Did Uncle Rowan get all dressed up too?"

Zane hated that a lie was going to come out of his mouth. During Tessa's treatment, there'd been times when they'd decided it was better to keep the truth from their daughter. She'd been so young at the time. She was still young, but lying about this made acid spill over his muscles. Regardless of how Zane felt, there wasn't a good way to explain how he was faking dating her teacher.

"We thought it'd be fun."

Caroline bounced her brows once—an expression she'd learned from him. "I like it."

The stuttered pause that hovered between Tessa and him sounded like the ever-climbing anticipation sound layered into movies to accelerate the viewer's heartbeat. Zane kept his gaze on their receding daughter, waiting.

"This is so great."

It was the breathy honesty in Tessa's voice that snapped his head in her direction. "What?"

"I'm so happy you found someone. And Ms. Powell is incredible. I *love* her." Her blatant joy sent shame spiraling down his spine. "But . . . I get why you'd want to keep it from Caroline so there wouldn't be any doubt about favoritism or anything in the classroom. That makes sense. But why didn't you tell me?"

"It just, sort of . . . happened." The second those words fled his mouth, a sledgehammer smashed his sternum.

He never wanted to use that particular expression in regard to Ann. Zane wanted being with Ann to be the opposite of happenstance. He wanted to pursue, to ensure, to nurture a relationship between the two of them. But as much as he was certain that Ann was attracted to him—her melting at the gym was proof of that—Zane still wasn't sure if she liked him as a person. They were still getting to know each other. Zane couldn't risk upending his delicately balanced life—his daughter's life—without knowing if this was more than playing pretend.

"We're still figuring things out." At least that sentence was true.

Tessa nodded, a smile flirting with her lips as she squeezed his forearm. "I'll keep it between us." She paused, her grin growing until it overtook her face. "Enjoy your date. I'll distract Caroline so she doesn't see you going inside."

Wet concrete soaked Zane's suit pants and made every step toward the table a struggle. Reality had quite literally burst the fictitious bubble he'd been languishing in over the last hour. Zane tried to use the walk back to the restaurant to organize the difference between the two.

But that was the problem.

Everything he'd done since he'd hugged Ann in the parking lot . . . he'd wanted to be real. He *wanted* to be able to drape his arm around her, to hold her long fingers in his, to touch her just because he could. Zane even enjoyed coming to Ann's rescue time and time again and seeing gratitude flicker in her eyes. He'd meant what he'd said outside. He'd only seen a fraction of her family life, but already, Zane wanted to whisk her away from it.

Maybe he really did have a hero complex.

"There you are." Rene's honey-toned voice clashed through his thoughts, snapping him back to the room. "We were worried that you'd run for the hills."

Zane paused behind Ann's chair, holding the top rail. "I'm not going anywhere."

Then he allowed himself to have what he'd wanted for eight months.

He kissed Ann.

Just her cheek, briefly, before whispering, "That's seven," in her ear and covertly inhaling a steadying breath of orange blossom.

"Not when this amazing woman is right here." He lowered himself into his seat as Priscilla's bejeweled hand spread over her heart.

Zane hoped that Ann understood the truth behind his declaration. It might be tortuous at times, but he wasn't going to abandon her.

He picked up his fork, affixing a charming smile to his lips. "Something about this dinner just reminded me of a trip I took. Did I ever tell you about my run-in with a shiver of hammerheads off the coast of Fiji?"

Chapter 11

"The children," Ann muttered under her breath after saying goodbye to Priscilla, Mom, and Dad. She held onto her father's frail, wheezing chest longer than usual, prompting him to pat her gently and whisper, "It'll be fun. You'll see."

Except, there was nothing fun about this twist in events. Especially when it was so obviously a trap. A dropping sensation corkscrewed through her intestines. Rene had picked this restaurant for dinner because its snug lounge area hosted piano karaoke after nine p.m.

"You're doing this for the children."

"What?" Zane whispered, leaning into her as they walked from the separated dining area to the dark and intimate bar.

"Nothing."

This night was already exceeding her capacity. When Zane had brushed his lips to her cheek earlier, Ann had had to remind herself for the sixteen-millionth time that he was acting. This was all an act. The moment outside before Tessa and Caroline had stumbled upon them couldn't have been real either. Zane was an exceptionally kind man, taking pity on her situation. That was all.

Textured golden walls, teardrop chandeliers, and dark wooden furniture made the space effortlessly trendy and classic at the same time. The pianist that had been heard playing delightful mood music throughout dinner was now pounding the keys as a chorus of voices belted "Great Balls of Fire" from the slightly elevated stage.

Zane's hand slipped up her spine, his thumb and forefinger pressing the sides of her neck in a way that was unexpectedly effective. "You don't have to sing."

An incredulous laugh burst from her.

The whole reason they were *here* was for her to sing, to humiliate herself.

"I'll meet you at the table." Rene nodded to a wooden roundtop in the corner before jogging over to speak to the person that was organizing the song list.

Beside the baby grand piano, a sleek stand held a black tablet that provided the lyrics to those crooning into the onyx microphones. Ann ran a shaky hand over her stomach as she sat in the chair farthest away from the sonorous instrument.

"What if you do 'Twinkle Twinkle Little Star' or something really short?" Zane asked, finally understanding that Ann wasn't going to get out of the night unscathed.

"Hi," a bubbly server with flickering false eyelashes greeted them. "Can I get—"

"Gin," Ann interrupted. "All of the gin."

"Okay," she said with a light chuckle, unfazed by Ann's rudeness.

"I'm sorry. I didn't mean to snap." She ran her anxious fingers through her hair. "It's just—"

"No worries." The server waved a hand, her glittery nails catching the faint light. "A little liquid courage is necessary on karaoke night. For you boys?" She smiled at Zane and Denis.

The server left with their orders, Rene returned to the table, conversation was made, drinks were delivered and sipped, but Ann was surviving by imagining the joy on the faces of students who would get their own personal box of brand-new markers when they'd always had to use the half-dried communal ones before.

That thought took her to the squat cinder block library in which Ann did her free tutoring. She'd chosen that location because the building was central to several Title 1 schools. As much as it could be challenging to alter her curriculum to meet the needs of the varied advanced students in her classroom, there was nothing like helping a child who either didn't have an adult at home or whose caregivers were too busy to help them succeed in school.

After each session, Ann would offer something little. Stickers. A fresh composition notebook. Slap bracelets. A pristine 24-pack of crayons.

It never felt like enough.

Winning this bet meant Ann could supply each of her tutoring students with their own books, in addition to the reading passages she printed out for them.

The steady pressure of Zane's fingers between her locked shoulder blades brought her back to the room. Despite herself, Ann leaned into his palm. Though she generally didn't drink—overindulging during the "J" date being an exception—tonight's martini nicely blurred the edges of tension pulsing at her temple. The downside was it made fighting the desire to be near Zane more challenging.

The lone spotlight springboarded off of Denis's closely shaved, balding head as he performed an endearing version of "Can't Help Falling in Love." Upon returning to the table, he shared a kiss with Rene so genuine that Ann blinked, her expression shuddering. Rene had always kept an air of casual disinterest with Denis, which somehow made him pursue her even harder. Seeing that tender moment made Ann feel like she was trespassing.

A few songs later, Rene's sultry voice made the room explode after she finished her version of Frank Sinatra's "My Way."

"What if I sang first?" Zane dipped his head to ask against her ear.

Heat from his lips seared her skin, but she kept herself from flinching. "I'm not sure how that would help."

"Ann Powell! Come on up," the organizer called.

It was strange that relief coursed through her stagnant veins. Being led to the guillotine was surprisingly better than being at the mercy of a suspenseful ticking clock.

Zane grabbed her hand as she rose. "Let's do a duet, snookempants. Wouldn't that be fun?" He was on his feet, tugging her toward the small stage before Rene could protest.

"Snookempants? I thought we weren't using pet names," Ann whispered.

"Not my best work, sorry, but I have an idea." The corner of his mouth twitched, highlighting a jawline that would make a Hollywood hopeful weep. "Do you know the songs from *Frozen?*"

Her forehead scrunched. "Of course. I teach third grade."

Even though the popular animated film had come out a decade ago, it was still a fan favorite on the movie-and-pizza-party half-day before winter break.

"Could you talk/sing your way through 'Love is an Open Door?' It's short and largely conversational."

Ann's mind flooded with the memory of the song she often tapped along to in her darkened classroom while the kids splayed themselves on blankets brought from home. There was no way she was going to be able to hit most of the notes, but maybe she could say the words and let Zane carry the tune.

"I'll try."

"That's my girl." A squeeze of her fingers accompanied his words before he released them to grab the proffered mic.

It was the possessive pronoun in that casually used idiom that seized Ann's brain, making her numbly fumble through receiving her own microphone as Zane requested the song change.

My.

There was no version of the world in which she should have been Zane's.

The din of the noisy bar sounded like a jet engine directly above her. When the pianist began the short, bouncy intro to the song, Ann froze. Her mouth opened, but nothing but stagnant air escaped.

The intro ended, and the pianist looped it again, unfazed. The lyrics on the tablet shuttered and restarted from the top, counting down to the beginning of her part of the duet. Ann was two seconds from setting down her mic and leaving the bar when Zane wove his fingers around hers again, leaned over, and whispered, "You can do this," before brushing her temple with his lips.

It was halting, the way she started the first line while turning to face him, but Zane's smile made it worth it. He grew even more animated as he began his lines, playing his part perfectly while never letting go of her hand. Her voice cracked as she tried to hold onto the phrase, but Zane's grin only broadened, easily carrying the complementary line for her.

The back-and-forth nature of the lyrics slowly began to feel natural and fun. The piano thundered beside her, and electricity sizzled in her veins as they jokingly sang to each other. Every other sound fell away as she focused on his voice, helping her through. Ann even grew a bit more confident, trying to stretch out and hold out-of-tune notes with him. Zane rewarded her with an eyebrow bounce that shouldn't have made her as giddy as it did.

She even giggled.

Ann was *not* a giggler.

When they got to the last "With you!" section, they released hands, saying each iteration louder with pointing finger guns. Ann laughed so hard Zane had to finish the last line without her.

Roaring applause deafened her ears as Zane leaned into her with a wink, their foreheads nearly touching before he tilted his toward the audience. "Hear that? Just more proof that you can handle anything."

Ann was laughing and about to argue that it'd been his rendition that had earned them their applause when a single word was lobbed like a rotten tomato onto the stage.

"Kiss!"

Rene's command threw ice water over the buoyant moment. Zane blinked, his face faltering as other audience members took up the chant, repeating the word.

The microphone at Ann's side suddenly felt like an anvil.

Why hadn't she thought of this? Prepared for it? Prepped Zane for its possibility? It was unbelievable that Rene hadn't demanded this display of affection already. All evening, she'd been asking probing questions about their relationship, almost as if she could smell the deceit.

Zane's light-brown irises darted between hers before his chest heaved with an inhale. His breath was tinged with bourbon and cherry as it puffed over her lips. It was nearly imperceptible, the subtle lift of his eyebrows, but Ann understood the question beneath. Zane wasn't going to kiss her without permission, even if it was just for show.

Her free hand found his chest, his silky vest searing her palm as her chin dipped in an invisible nod. Then his thumb was framing her jaw, the rest of his long fingers burrowing into her hair. Everything was too much all at once. Her eardrums pounded, her heart decided to sprint a marathon with absolutely no training, and every single inch of her skin itched.

Ann barely had enough time to process those overwhelming sensations before Zane's mouth slid over hers, and the world stilled. Just . . . stopped. They were no longer complying with social pressures amid dozens of alcohol-emboldened people in a cozy bar. They were just *them*. Two people who shouldn't have fit together, but undeniably did.

The relief was incapacitating.

Just as a sigh was softening every cell in her spine, Zane's lips left hers. Ann didn't think. She only reacted, clenching his tie and pulling them back together. His grip on the back of her head tightened as a low rumble left his throat. Ann was tone-deaf, but the frequency at which her body was vibrating undeniably matched Zane's. Three blissful seconds suspended before reality came smashing in.

Raucous hoots and hollers jolted Ann back to her surroundings. Relinquishing her grip and leaning back was in exact opposition to her body's thundering commands, but she forced herself. Zane's wild-eyed stare was momentarily interrupted by flickering eyelashes. Their golden hue captured the stage light like a hundred rays of sunshine. Astonishment—unguarded and raw—swept across his freckled cheekbones.

Several thick heartbeats pounded before he adjusted his glasses and turned to the audience with an easy smile. Ann barely registered the organizer taking the microphone from her stunned fingers or her feet moving automatically behind Zane's toward the table.

"That was quite a performance," Denis said with his affable grin, not a trace of malice in his words.

Pain started at the base of her neck and spread to every extremity as the truth struck like a supersonic blast.

Performance.

Of course the kiss had been fake. Just part of the act. Zane was simply ensuring that Rene believed they were truly dating. He must have picked up on her cynicism as well.

"Thanks." Zane sent another jovial grin Denis's way and took a gulp of his nearly untouched Manhattan.

Ann's teeth ached from their clenched position as she distracted herself with the condensation rings left on Zane's black paper napkin.

It didn't matter that that had been the most breathtaking, soul-rearranging kiss she'd ever had. *This is fake.* It didn't matter that the way Zane had looked at her afterward made her feel simultaneously seen, understood, and inexplicably gorgeous. *This is fake.* It didn't matter that, even with its numerous pitfalls, she'd had more fun tonight than she'd ever had with a man.

This is fake. This is fake. This is fake.

With another patron beginning "Proud Mary," Ann shouldn't have been able to hear the controlled exhale coming from Zane, like he was trying to slow his breathing. Her gaze darted up. When their eyes locked, flicking energy sizzled up her forearms.

Denis asked a question, and Zane's attention struggled to deviate from hers. When it eventually did, Ann swallowed, her shaking fingers taking up her empty martini glass and helplessly bringing it to her lips.

This is fake, her mind feebly repeated.

Chapter 12

"Where's my nugget?" Kevin pouted after plunking himself down at their usual outdoor table at Ground Street Coffee the following morning.

"Tessa picked her up from school yesterday." Zane blew on his purple mug of coffee, impatient to get resurrecting caffeine coursing through his weary system.

At least the air was cool today, helping rouse him. The cottonwood trees that towered over the burnt-orange building had just regained their viridescent foliage. Each waxy, heart-shaped leaf shimmered as it spun in the breeze, splintering the sunshine into fluid patterns.

"How dare she," Kevin said, affronted by missing his bi-monthly dose of Caroline. Each of his friends had taken turns caring for Caroline in various ways over the years, but Kevin took on his role as uncle with the most enthusiasm.

Rowan simply snickered while Kyle asked, "Why'd she do that?"

It was killing Zane not to explain the arrangement with Ann. Particularly because it would have helped him grab at least an hour or two of sleep had he been able to process last night's kiss with another person. Instead, he'd lain atop his comforter, staring at the lazily circling fan, concerned he was misremembering the night's events.

They'd been forced into that first kiss, but the way Ann had grabbed his tie and brought her mouth to his the second time . . .

Zane shifted in the metal cafe chair, trying to dislodge the impending what ifs. What if that kiss hadn't been so public? What if they'd had the discussion Tessa and Caroline had interrupted? There was likely a set of rules against dating the parent of one of your students, but if they were good at keeping it hidden, maybe this fake relationship could bloom into something else.

"She wanted a little extra girl time. Tess will be moving in with Isaac in two weeks." Zane hated how good he was getting at lying.

Each of them had known the intimate details of each other's lives for over a decade. Obscuring the truth felt treasonous, but the less people who knew about the situation with Ann, the better.

His friends nodded along, sipping their various drinks. Discussion moved along to Rowan's newly installed outdoor pizza oven, and Zane felt wistful of times when their most worrisome conversation topics were passing midterms and what pizza toppings to order.

"Are we getting a showcase?" Kyle teased.

"How about next Friday?" Rowan brought his mug to his lips, the dangling green tea tag twisting freely.

"I'm game." Zane was always up for whenever Rowan wanted to flex his culinary muscles.

His friend would drive miles out of the way to get the freshest produce from local farmers and responsibly sourced meats but was never snobby about his foodie preferences. What Rowan did love was cooking for a group. His stepfather, Augie, had been the one to make most of the meals growing up, and Rowan had inherited Augie's love of a good pozole and how food could bring people together.

"Can I get sourdough crust on mine?" Kyle ran his fingers through his thinning brunette curls. "With your walnut pesto and prosciutto . . . ." His sentence dropped off in a blissful groan.

Zane chuckled that the conversation *had* dissolved into pizza toppings, though duck and roasted pine nuts were items that hadn't graced the pies they'd ordered in college.

Several minutes later, Kevin jumped up as his wife, Becca, strode to the table in her chef's whites. He'd been wigglier than usual, his knee bouncing against the table and shaking it subtly.

"*Here she is,*" Kevin sang the phrase.

Even though Becca was a part-owner of Ground Street Coffee and could create her delectable pastries in a T-shirt and jeans, she always wore her uniform.

"Hey, guys." She swept a strand of auburn hair behind her ear, already blushing.

The action zipped Zane's mind to the minute flush that had danced over Ann's cheeks when she'd leaned away from him onstage last night. His eyes pressed closed in an attempt to focus, but that only intensified the image.

"You know I'm no good at keeping a secret," Kevin began.

Kevin and Becca's secret workplace romance had caused a bit of commotion when they'd been juniors at the University of Arizona. Kevin had been working for Becca's father as a barista and making out with his recently graduated pastry-chef daughter during breaks. But they'd seamlessly weathered any initial objections to their relationship and have been happily married for a little over five years.

"We're going to be parents!" Becca gushed.

The table exploded in congratulations as every man shot up to hug the soon-to-be parents. They'd all known Kevin and Becca's adoption process had been a long and complicated one.

Onlookers craned their necks to see what the commotion was about. Liz and Tina, two regulars who usually shared tea and treats while their three white bichons grumbled at their feet, looked at Zane inquisitively. Knowing news like this would reach every awaiting ear anyway, Zane pointed to Kevin and Becca and then cradled his arms like he was rocking a baby. The two women jumped up as quickly as their aging bones would let them and made their way over.

Becca and Kevin took turns being enveloped by every regular patron, which at Ground Street Coffee was quite a few. When things calmed down, Ethan was video-called, and Haley cried sloppy tears over the news. She promised Kevin and Becca she'd embroider a dozen onesies for the baby. Then Kevin made a joke at Ethan's expense, causing Haley to laugh so hard she hiccupped.

Eventually, the hubbub subsided, Kevin disappeared to the kitchen with his wife, and Kyle excused himself to meet with Dani, his fiancé, to finalize things with their wedding photographer. Zane and Rowan remained, coming down from the excitement of their friends' announcement.

"I forgot how infectious Haley's laugh was," Rowan said, smiling and rubbing his chin.

"Yeah," Zane agreed. "I can't believe Caroline's getting a cousin." A twinge of uneasiness that he'd kept her from learning that information directly from Kevin ribboned down his spine.

"Our group is expanding again. First with Haley. Now with a baby."

That offhand comment brought Ann to mind—though it didn't require much effort for her to zip to the front of his every waking moment. If things changed between them, Zane could bring her to group get-togethers. Dinners at Rowan's house on the outskirts of town, as coyote song rivaled their laughter at his friend's long, outdoor dining table. Holding her hand as they chuckled or cried, watching whatever theatrical masterpiece Kevin and Kyle were producing. Searching for Ann at the sidelines of his city-run games, that smile of hers tugging at her lips.

"What is it?" Rowan asked, leaning back in his chair.

It took two seconds to realize he was rubbing his knuckles against his breastbone. Zane should've tried harder to mask the action, because now he was toast. Rowan's ability to see through a person had been eerie *before* he'd gotten his PhD in clinical psychology. His troublesome early childhood, before his mom had moved him and his sisters to Tucson, had influenced

Rowan's career choice. Now he spent his days helping male clients understand their emotions, so they didn't turn into the type of men that ruined families.

Since Zane couldn't tell his friend the full truth, he settled on something close. "Do you ever feel a little left behind? Ethan found Haley. Kevin and Becca have always been rock solid. Kyle and Dani are finally tying the knot. And I'm . . ."

. . . in some ridiculous limbo with the woman I want more than anything.

"Stuck?" his friend offered.

Goosebumps at Rowan's perceptiveness crept up his neck. "Yeah."

Rowan thumped his thumb twice on the table. "You're in a transition phase. Tessa moving in with Isaac might be making you feel restless about your own future."

If only his friend knew the half of it. Zane was debating breaking his agreement with Ann not to tell anyone just to get a tiny respite from the limestone boulder sitting on his chest.

"Or you could just be a jerk because, up until recently, you were married with a child." His friend quirked a single eyebrow.

There was an established rule among the five friends that Rowan wouldn't clinically evaluate them. He'd simply help as any friend would. Sometimes, though, he'd drop intense psychological knowledge on you and then cover it with a ribbing jab.

Zane shook his head with a smile, knowing Rowan's words weren't spiked. They'd all been incredibly supportive of him with Tessa's illness, caring for Caroline whenever they could.

Then they called, took him out, and sometimes just showed up at his house during his separation and divorce.

"Selfish Zane." He grinned. "That's me."

"You're a real piece of work." His friend stretched his impressive shoulders—ones he'd acquired by rock climbing almost every day. "I can't believe I'm still friends with you."

Tugging at the collar of his The Black Keys T-shirt, Zane recalled something Kyle had said right before they'd received their drinks. Something he'd yet to address with Rowan but now could since they were alone.

"On the topic of being a jerk, should we talk about who's coming back?" Zane asked, wanting to address the rumors of Rowan's first love returning to Tucson this summer.

It was slight, but Rowan's expression faltered. His friend was always in control, like he held some kind of vise grip on zen. In the history of their friendship, Zane had only seen that calm waver in two instances—when watching football and when talking about Claire Winesett.

"There's nothing to talk about." A tendon popped in his friend's neck.

"Really? You, the shrink, not wanting to talk? That's rich."

Rowan grimaced at the slang term, just like Zane knew he would.

"She's just Meg's best friend."

Zane knew she was more than that. Though Claire was Rowan's sister's best friend, she'd also been the unofficial sixth member of Rowan's family. They'd grown up together. There were mountains of history between them.

"So we're doing this the hard way. Okay." Zane stretched until his spine cracked like a glowstick.

A noisy breath blew over the table as Rowan pushed his half-finished mug toward the center. "I know there will invariably be a family dinner when I'm there and she's there, but it won't matter."

Rowan hadn't said Claire's name since she'd left, almost like saying those letters together would conjure her from the ether.

"To her, I'm nothing more than a brother. That's the way it is."

Zane's mind flew to the memory of the only time he'd seen Rowan drink more than two beers. At their end-of-junior-year party, Rowan had come clean that he'd been hiding his feelings for Claire since high school. He'd admitted that earlier that evening, when he'd told Claire that he'd loved her, she had ruffled his hair and casually parroted the sentiment. She'd obviously taken his admission as one of familial affection. Then Claire had left, as planned, the following day to thru-hike the Pacific Crest Trail and hadn't been back to Tucson since.

"She shouldn't be here longer than a few weeks. Maybe you'll only have to see her once. Maybe not at all," Zane said, trying to highlight how Claire's wanderlust might benefit his friend.

Since leaving Tucson nine years ago, Claire had transitioned from recreational hiker to solo-travel influencer. Zane followed both of Rowan's sisters on his personal OnlyApp account, and occasionally, Meg would tag Claire—and her immensely popular travel account—in one of her posts.

"I just know it's not going to be easy seeing her again, and I want you to know I'm here for you. We all are."

Rowan ran his hand over his pulled-back hair. "I know that, and I appreciate it."

Quiet in which Liz's and Tina's staccato chuckles could be heard over a saxophone-heavy version of "S'wonderful" stretched between the two friends.

Zane had only wanted to let his friend know that he supported him, but the sorrow etching into the subtle creases around Rowan's eyes made unease volley between Zane's collarbones. As complicated as his situation was with Ann, there was at least the chance that she felt the same way. Rowan wasn't that lucky.

"Or you could pretend she doesn't exist," Zane suggested.

The tightness in his stomach lessened when Rowan's hearty laugh spilled over the patio.

"I don't usually condone living in denial, but this is one of those instances where protecting my peace might be worth going against my own advice."

"Well"—Zane drummed his fingers on the edge of the table—"since we're going with avoidance, want to hear about the space opera I'm recording next week?"

"Heck yeah." Rowan had a very analytical mind, which was why he and Ethan had always clicked, but apparently, he was desperate enough to let Zane indulge him with a fictional distraction.

Even if Zane hadn't had to read for work, he always had at least five books stacked on his nightstand and loved going through premise and plot with anyone who would listen. In this instance, recapping the book would do double duty in pulling his thoughts away from Ann as well.

"This one has cyborg zombies in it," Zane said through a growing grin.

"Of course it does." Rowan chuckled, his tense shoulders loosening as he allowed Zane to distract them both.

Chapter 13

Ann struggled to focus on her computer screen. Her kids were at their morning resource class for the hour, which meant she should have been catching up on work emails, planning, or grading, but her brain was a gauzy ball of mush.

Hillcrest prided itself in having an extensive arts and science curriculum. In addition to the advanced third-grade lesson plans, each student received in-depth instruction in art, music, technology and robotics, science lab, and mental and physical wellness. Once students matriculated into fifth grade, they were able to specify which resources they preferred to pursue. Every student had to attend wellness class once a week, but they could spend the rest of their resource time writing computer code or composing music.

Ann had just left a jubilant Caroline and the rest of the class with Ms. Schneider, the art teacher, before being presented with a task she didn't want to complete. Staring at the simple online check-in form from the oral surgeon made Ann wish she'd skipped her iced hazelnut latte. The earthy flavor syrup wasn't half as delightful crawling up her esophagus.

Niggling pain over the weekend had forced Ann to see her dentist on Monday afternoon. Even though she'd crossed her fingers at her sides, her worst fears had been confirmed. Her lone, impacted wisdom tooth was potentially infected and required extraction. Lucky for her, the surgeon had an opening Friday afternoon. Joy!

Ann only had the lower left one—the others had thankfully never developed. Since that tooth hadn't caused her any issues until recently, she'd convinced her dentist not to remove it. Anesthesia—even partial sedation—wasn't something Ann walked into unless absolutely necessary.

She craned her neck to the ceiling, focusing on the cutout flowers she'd hung from translucent strings to transition her classroom into spring. *It'll be okay. It won't be like last time.* Even with those reminders, Ann shuddered, hugging her belly and caving into herself.

An unsteady breath filled her lungs as Ann's phone vibrated with a text.

Zane: *I added some topics to the spreadsheet. I think it would be a good idea to go into next weekend's trip prepared.*

Memories of last Friday night swarmed her. They'd been haunting her every waking moment that her tooth pain wasn't commanding attention. Zane standing outside with her, his featherlight touch on her elbows. Zane's lips brushing her cheek, declaring he wouldn't leave her. Zane onstage, his face slacking with reverence after their impromptu kiss.

Giving herself a firm shake, Ann opened the document. Knowing more about each other was a very practical step, especially with Rene already wary. Ann chided herself for not thinking of it first.

Surging anticipation swept through her, efficiently blocking out her anxiety over tomorrow's appointment. It was slightly embarrassing, the way Ann gobbled up each tidbit about Zane like syrup-coated flapjacks after a good workout. The impulse to ask for seconds had been oppressive, but unlike last time, when the prompts had come with his answers pre-filled, Zane's column was blank.

Seven new topics were listed in the spreadsheet, but the message was clear. If Ann wanted information, she'd have to respond first.

Some of the questions were easier to answer than others. Two pet peeves? *School zone speeders and those who break the rules and get away with it.* What did you want to be when you were small? *A teacher.* What are your hobbies? *Weight-lifting and tutoring.* What's your favorite holiday? *New Year's Eve.* But not for the traditional reasons.

She'd typed that in with the intention of letting Zane assume she liked to party and kiss someone at midnight—something she'd never done. Ann's favorite part was sitting on the patio of her condo, bundled against the desert chill and seeing the world turnover a new year. People would be cheering, and sometimes illegal fireworks would blast into the sky, and Ann would exhale a warm breath with a smile. A new year was like freshly minted dollars that still stuck together, a blank notebook with a pristine spine, or a brand-new whiteboard that didn't carry the ghosts of lessons past.

There was such simplicity and beauty in something clean.

Ann's cursor blinked over the last three questions. What is your biggest fear? *Scorpions*—which was unfortunate since the desert was crawling with them. If you were a superhero, what powers would you have? Ann didn't see the purpose of such fantastical thinking. That didn't help her live in the real world. A world that came with limitations that were fixed. Before macabre thoughts could overtake her, Ann typed *Flying* and read the next one.

What's the best gift you've received?

A defeated breath blew over her keyboard.

It was so incredibly sad that Ann wanted to type *This fake relationship*, but Zane being at last Friday's family dinner had beautiful ripple effects. For the first time in years, Ann's mother had been reaching out and showing an interest in her life. A part of her knew that she shouldn't accept that her mother's attention only came with the encouragement of a man, but a malnourished part of Ann's soul didn't care. Her mother had even offered to drive her to and from her oral surgery appointment tomorrow so Ann wouldn't have to ask Kennedy to also take the afternoon off.

When her gaze rose, it rested on the small wooden apple. Ann felt her lips lift. The green-painted apple had been a gift from her favorite student her first year of teaching at Hillcrest and was the perfect placeholder answer for Zane's last question.

My wooden apple, she typed.

Ann knew she didn't have to detail it further. Zane would know what she was referring to.

The uneven number of questions irked her, so she added, *What is something that always makes you smile?* Ann got lost in the memory of Zane's enamored grin as she butchered karaoke lyrics like she was trying to win a prize for worst songstress.

"Ann, quick! Come see this!" Kennedy slid into her open door and then back out before Ann could push up from her chair.

It was a little overzealous how fast she ran to catch up with her friend—*No running in the halls!*—but Ann would have taken a shoebox of scorpions as a distraction at that moment.

"What's going on?"

Kennedy and her kindergarteners were pressed against one of the many floor-to-ceiling glass panels that lined the hallway, designed to allow in as much natural light as possible. Most of them showed the sidewalks, parking lot, or the playground, but this part of the hall edged along a short portion of natural desert left by the school's designer.

Her friend was bouncing almost as much as her students, five-year-old energy in a twenty-two-year-old body. Kennedy was very much the adult she needed to be when around parents or other teachers, but she let herself be unguarded and enthusiastic with her students, which they *LOVED*.

"Baby javelinas!" one of the girls squealed.

Ann grimaced. The medium-sized, pig-like peccary was not her favorite desert dweller. Most people feared rattlesnakes when they first moved to Tucson. Each Hillcrest staff member was under strict instruction not to prop open their doors open to the outside, lest they be welcoming a serpentine guest. It was true that you could occasionally be surprised by one sunning itself on your welcome mat, but for Ann, javelinas were the stuff of nightmares.

At her parents' house, the stout, scruffy animals would rub themselves against the stucco under the window of her and Rene's bedroom. Rene had slept through their gruff snorts, dead to the world, but Ann had often been jolted awake by the sounds of heavy breathing and shuffling next to her pillow. Once, she'd peeked out the window to see two males bare their tusks and fight. Ann used to dream of them chasing her, or that Rene and her mother would abandon her with a pack of them.

"Aren't they adorable?" Kennedy asked, hands clasped in front of her alphabet-block dress.

Ann leaned over her friend's head, catching sight of the mama javelina with two babies in the shade of a mesquite tree. One of the little ones paused in nosing the ground to sneeze and shake its tiny ears.

"Awwwwww." Twelve kindergartners—and Kennedy—cooed in perfect synchrony.

Kennedy's brow wrinkled when she glanced at Ann. "How are you not affected?"

She shuffled her shoulders. "They're kind of cute."

Objectively, Ann could see how the tan babies with a soft, dark line down their back resembled sweet little piglets, but she'd had too many negative experiences with their bristle-furred, hard-hooved adult counterparts. Though javelinas were generally harmless and kept to themselves, every once in a while, you'd hear a news story about them attacking a dog they mistook for a coyote. Like most creatures in the desert, they were wild and should be left alone.

"Oh, no." Kennedy slung a dramatic wrist over her forehead. "Friends, I have bad news. Ms. Powell is sick. She can't see how adorable these little cuties are."

At least half of her class spun their attention away from the window, with murmurs matching their overzealous instructor.

One little boy laid his hand on hers with desolate doe eyes. "I'm sorry you sick."

The inside of her cheek stung from how hard Ann was biting it so she wouldn't . . . 1) roll her eyes at Kennedy, 2) laugh at the ridiculousness of being pitied by a group of children, and 3) undermine the boy's kind gesture.

She and Kennedy held a quick, wordless teacher conversation that went along the lines of:

Kennedy: *Now look what you've done.*

Ann: *Me? You! You started this.*

Kennedy: *If you'd just admitted they were cute, we wouldn't be here.*

Ann: *I DID admit they were cute.*

Kennedy: Kinda *cute.*

Ann: *Ugh. You're ridiculous.*

She bent to get eye level with the boy whose pinky was still wrapped around hers and rested her other palm on his shoulder.

"Thank you, but I'm going to be okay."

The boy's face brightened. "Oh, good. I don't wike being sick."

"Me neither." Ann returned his smile.

Kennedy clapped. "Okay, friends, let's line up and head back to our room."

While the kids assembled into a disjointed queue atop the powder-blue line on the ground, Kennedy leaned over with a whisper. "You sure you don't need me to drive you tomorrow?"

Though Ann had shared the details of her dental appointment and the terrifying, pending surgical appointment, she'd excluded last weekend's events—including the breathtaking kiss with Zane—from their twice-weekly gym sessions. Confiding in Kennedy about this whole situation would make it easier, but the fewer people who knew the better, especially since Kennedy was also a Hillcrest employee.

"No." A ghost of a smile lifted her lips. "My mom's got me."

Kennedy squeezed her arm before calling to her kids, "Quiet coyote."

Instantly, her wiggly class stilled and placed their two middle fingers on their thumb. Many of them puffed out their cheeks as they sealed their lips, and several others wiggled their hand coyote's ears. It was a hand gesture used by teachers throughout the country, but Tucsonans had the added bonus of actual coyotes as their neighbors.

"Bye, Ms. Powell." Kennedy began skipping at the start of the line.

A gaggle of giggling five-year-olds copied their teacher's salutation before following her like hiccupping ducks. Ann smiled at the scene, checking her watch—ten minutes before she needed to pick up her class. A resolute breath left her nose as she straightened her shoulders. Enough procrastinating. Time to fill out the pre-op check-in. Everything with tomorrow was going to be fine.

Chapter 14

Zane's abs were on fire. There was no better way to describe it. They were an insatiable, blazing inferno. All from laughter.

"I'm glad you think this is funny, because let me tell you, I wasn't as delighted." Tessa's voice echoed on speaker from his phone's location on the kitchen counter.

"You didn't shut her down, did you?"

"No, of course not. You should have seen the devious little smile on her face. Your smile, you trickster. I loved when she inherited your blond curls, but I could have done without this." Tessa's teasing tone held zero bite. "I can't believe when you called to say goodnight last night that you were giving her battle instructions."

Zane spread mayo on his toasted, sprouted-wheat bread. "I wasn't about to discourage her when she wanted to pull a few harmless April Fools' jokes."

"Urine was *everywhere*, Z. Saran-wrapping the toilet is not harmless. It's disgusting."

He shouldn't have laughed again. There had undoubtedly been a mess that Tessa had had to clean, but he was too thrilled that Caroline had wanted to do something deviant.

"The googly eyes on my morning banana? Now that's the kind of joke I can get behind. The bubble wrap under the kitchen mat? You know I can't function until I've had a kiddie pool of coffee. I thought someone was setting off fireworks outside."

Zane laughed a third time, layering thinly sliced cucumbers, onion, roasted red bell peppers, havarti, lettuce, tomato, and sliced black olives onto his bread.

"I will decrease your blood pressure by letting you know those were the only ideas I gave her, so you should be safe now."

"Thank goodness," Tessa said through an obvious smile.

A short pause settled over the line before his ex-wife's voice dropped several pitches.

"Hey, so . . . I did call to complain, but I also wanted to let you know that if you don't have plans for tonight, you can join us for dinner here. I'm making my mom's five-layer mac 'n' cheese."

Last year, on April first, Tessa had come home even though she'd been living at her parents' since she'd moved out in January. She'd left Caroline with her mother and brought over a twelve-ounce bottle of Bulleit since she knew Zane never drank alone. They'd silently sat on the wicker loveseat in the backyard with his record player murmuring in the background through the open screen door. Just like they'd done for years.

The anniversary was one of those things that you'd think would've lost its sting over time. Today was fifteen years. Zane had officially spent an equal amount of his life without his father than he had with. More if you consider that he couldn't remember the first four years. But time didn't seem to be able to fade this wound.

The worst had been that Zane hadn't believed it at first.

It was his dad that had started the April Fools' prank war. There wasn't a time Zane could remember waking up on the first of April and not having his entire bathroom filled with balloons, or wrapping paper over his door, or tape over the remote sensors. Over the years, the pranks became more elaborate, so when his mother showed up at his friend's house, where he'd been spending the night, in the early hours of April Fools' and told him his father had died, Zane had laughed.

The memory of laughing in his mother's tear-streaked face was one that haunted him at odd intervals. It splintered his heart into sliver-like pieces, bringing breathing to an abrupt halt. At the grocery store. While recording pick-ups. When putting Caroline to bed.

Teenage Zane had slid right into anger after the shock had worn off. Raging indignation that his dad had ended his coastal drive at a local bar had kept Zane from eating and sleeping. Dad was the adult. He'd lectured Zane about alcohol at parties, about the dangers of getting into the car if someone had been drinking, and had instructed Zane to call home if he ever needed a ride—no questions. Why hadn't Dad followed his own advice? Why had he gotten behind the wheel drunk?

Then outrage wore away and regret moved in permanently. Because what if Zane could have stopped the accident from happening? What if he hadn't said no when his dad asked him to take that long drive up the coast in favor of attending a sleepover?

His father's screenplay—his baby, the big one, *the* story—had just fallen through after being optioned by one of the biggest producers in Hollywood. Zane had known that his father had been upset, but show business was fickle, and this hadn't been his father's first rejection. He assumed Dad would bounce back like he always had and decided to hang out with his friends, anyway.

Zane had made a choice. A choice that left a vacant hole between his ribs. A spot ripped open so violently that no amount of doing, helping, or living could quite stitch up.

"Z?" Tessa's voice pulled him back to the present.

"No. That's okay." Zane swallowed and pushed away his freshly made sandwich, leaning his elbows on the countertop. "I'm going rock climbing with Rowan, and then we're grabbing dinner."

"Okay, good." Tessa let several seconds pass before she asked, "Are you really going out with Rowan, or is Rowan just Ms. Powell's code name? I feel like I should know so I don't say the wrong thing to Caroline."

A short exhale left his nose as he straightened. "No, it's actually Rowan, though that's not a bad idea." Zane said that sentence like he and Ann routinely spent time together, keeping the ruse for Tessa. In actuality, he wouldn't see Ann until next

Saturday morning when he'd pick her up to drive to the resort together.

"How about I'll use Micah for Ann?"

Zane rarely hung out with his football team's captain and coach, so it would be the least confusing.

"Sounds good." Tessa paused again. "So . . . how are things?"

It was obvious she meant with Ann.

The *non-existent* relationship with Ann.

"I don't—"

"No, you're right. I didn't share details about me and Isaac." A sigh accompanied Tessa's nervous pen clicking. She always did that. At one point in their marriage, he'd wanted to remove all the clicking pens in the house and replace them with capped ones. "I'm just happy you're happy."

"I am."

He wasn't. Not even close. Not in regard to Ann.

"How's pool construction?" Tessa gracefully changed the subject.

Zane had contracted with a company to put in the only thing this house was missing, a respite from the summer heat. But every time they wanted to start construction, he'd have another deadline. It was bad enough that Zane had to work around his next-door neighbor working on his car in the driveway, the air wrench slicing into his recordings.

"Um," he hedged.

Tessa snort-laughed. "You keep pushing them back. Why don't you rent studio space while they do the really noisy stuff?"

"That's a good idea." Zane nodded, making a mental note to look up if any studios nearby had any availability.

A quick silence slipped between them.

"Okay, well, I should get back to work." His ex-wife's tone dropped with compassion again. "I just wanted to check on you."

"Thanks, Tess. I appreciate it."

After hanging up, Zane let himself stretch and put his sandwich plate in the fridge before dialing his mom's number. They often chatted every day, just to say hello, if nothing else, but today's call would be longer and more somber. Though they'd always been close, having to work through the grief of losing the only other member of their family had cemented their bond.

"I love you," was his answer to her, "Hello."

That pulsing, runaway sensation that often haunted him had sent the syllables sprinting from his tongue.

"I love you too." His mom's voice was sad before silence stole the line for several seconds.

Zane collapsed on his light-gray, streamlined couch and propped his feet on the rustic, reclaimed-wood coffee table. His cat, Marley, jumped into his lap and began purring the second Zane scratched his black ears.

He'd spent most of the morning in this position, prepping the book he'd begin recording later this week, drinking lemon-ginger tea, and giving his voice a rest. While he'd been marking breath points, thinking up different character voices, and finding words he'd need to email the author about proper pronunciation, Marley had been his companion.

"I love hearing that from you," his mom continued, "but I feel like that's another thing his reckless mistake took from me."

His brows pinched. "What do you mean?"

"You used to smile at me and tell me you loved me, and—you'll laugh—but it was like a stage light warming my skin. My golden boy, all full of light and affection. So emotive." His mom sighed. "As time went on, you returned to that, but sometimes, it's like today. You love me, but it's out of fear you'll lose me. It's not the same."

Broken shards of glass ripped down his arms because she was right. "I'm sorry."

"You don't need to be sorry, Zane. I just wish you'd trust that I'm not going to leave you."

Even though he knew what his mom meant, the truth was she would leave him, eventually.

Everyone did.

That was why he couldn't be the first one. That's why Tessa had to be the one to ask for a divorce. Zane would have stayed in a loveless marriage to his best friend because he couldn't be the one to leave. Not when his father had left him and his mother.

Since it was a hard day for them both, Zane didn't want to argue. "I trust you."

"Good." She let several heartbeats rest between them before asking about his day.

◊◊◊

After lunch, Zane tamped down the guilt over leaving Marley to lock himself into his home studio. Unfortunately, Marley's gleeful noises would have destroyed today's recording. Staring unseeingly at the gray acoustic foam paneling the wall beyond his small desk, Zane listened to yesterday's recording in preparation for today's session. It was important to be in tune with each character's voice and recall the tone and speed he'd read at yesterday.

Everything was set up. He should have started, but Zane opened his silenced phone and checked if Ann had updated the spreadsheet after receiving his text this morning. He'd reasoned that learning more about each other would help them as a couple.

As a *fake* couple.

It was important to remind himself of that operative word. He, of all people, understood that words held meaning. Zane would simply have to ignore how each fact about Ann slid effortlessly into a cavern in his soul he hadn't known needed filling. He'd have to brush off that he was looking forward to the weekend away with Ann more than he'd looked forward to anything in over a year. Understanding Ann was necessary research to perfect this act.

That was all.

Even as that rationality whipped through his brain, Zane tried to ignore how his chest thumped in opposition.

The dopiest smile tugged at his lips, seeing that Ann had answered his questions. Zane quickly read her responses, trying not to flush over the idea of kissing her at midnight. Leaning back in his chair, he used voice-to-text to give his answers before adding five more, knowing that she'd even the sheet with a question of her own.

Discovering information via spreadsheet instead of over a series of dates was unconventional, and it vaguely reminded him of the international pen-pal he'd had in fifth grade, but the end results were the same. The only problem was, the more Zane knew about Ann, the harder he fell for her.

Chapter 15

"Wow, these drugs are good," Ann said, blinking at the mirage in front of her. "They're making Mom look like my fake boyfriend."

Ann knew she'd have some trouble coordinating her body after coming out of the anesthesia—similar to being drunk—but she hadn't expected full-blown hallucinations.

The dental assistant laughed. "Ain't nothing fake about him, honey. He's standing right here."

"No—Never mind." Ann waved an uncoordinated hand, remembering that she shouldn't be saying the F-word.

Her mom thought her and Zane's relationship was real. It'd been all she'd talked about a few hours ago when she'd picked Ann up for her dental surgery appointment. Ann's stomach had been twisting as Mom carried on about how proud she was that both her daughters were dating such successful men.

"She'll be out of it for a few hours as the meds wear off," the assistant was saying. "Most people just wanna sleep, so don't be surprised if she passes out in the car."

"Okay," Mom said, while collecting the outstretched paperwork.

Huh. The drugs even made her mom's voice deep like Zane's. "Are auditory hallucinations part of this whole—" Ann waved her hand again before using it to catch the drool trickling down her chin. "Ow," she said once it made contact. "My face hurts."

The dental assistant laughed again. She had a nice laugh. Light and tinkling. Tinkling. That's a funny word. Like amoeba. Ammmoooeeba. Amoeba's a funny word too.

"Amoeba does have a ring to it," Zane/Mom was saying, trying to suppress a chuckle.

"I said that out loud?"

Huh.

"I'm not gonna lie. This right here is the best part of my job." The assistant was wheeling her to a car, and then Ann was weightless and buckled into a seat.

"Huh," she said again, this time confused as to how her body had moved on its own.

"Y'all have a good weekend." The dental assistant put Ann's purse in her lap with two hearty pats and a squeeze to her shoulder.

"You're nice," Ann told her. "We should be friends."

"This one's a sweetheart," she said through a smile. "Take care of her."

"I intend to."

Ann blinked at the rearview mirror for two minutes as guitars strummed a bluesy melody in the background. Mom's car didn't have a mini stuffed cat hanging from the mirror.

Huh filtered through Ann's brain before the car's movement lulled her to sleep.

◊◊◊

What is *that?* That was the first thought that smacked—no punched, throttled, whatever was the better adjective—Ann in the jaw. Her mouth tasted like cotton and sawdust had a very ugly baby. When she sat up in bed and saw she was wearing black joggers and a tank top instead of her work clothes, everything came flooding back. The dentist appointment. The surgery. Being driven home.

Ann glanced at her closed bedroom door, getting her bearings. It was nice of her mother to draw the curtains. Knowing Mom, she'd left the second Ann's head had hit the pillow. Which was fine. Ann could take care of herself.

After shuffling to her en suite bathroom to find her fuzzy flip-flop slippers, Ann looked around for the post-op instructions to care for her throbbing mouth.

"They're probably in the kitchen."

That was what Ann tried to say, but it came out muffled. Gently, she laid her hand over her partially numb left cheek and looked in the mirror. Her jawline could rival Batman's—at least on that side.

When Ann stepped into her main room, she had to swallow twice and blink a thousand times to make sure she wasn't still hallucinating.

Her boho-chic-on-a-budget-designed room was soft and comforting, as usual. A well-loved peach throw was tossed over her powder-blue couch tucked against the wall. Above it, several whimsical prints of animals in topcoats layered on a narrow oak picture rail with two spilling pothos plants bookending the frames. A designer, hand-me-down leather chair rested opposite the couch, grimacing at the squat IKEA coffee table in the middle. Her postage stamp but cozy backyard was graylit through the sliding glass door—the sky unusually cool and dreary.

Everything was in its place.

Except for the man sitting on her couch.

Zane was snuggled into the corner against two of the four neutral-toned decorative pillows. He had his jean-covered ankle crossed over his knee, a tablet on his lap, and a spiral notebook sitting beside him. A warm, caramel knit sweater sat in place of his usual rock band shirt, pushed up to expose his forearms. And he was barefoot. *Barefoot.* Like he belonged here.

Even after pinching her inner arm a third time, Zane remained.

Ridiculously, unnecessarily, devastatingly handsome.

It didn't make sense how he was more attractive while reading, but when Zane adjusted his glasses at his temple and then used two fingers to turn a virtual page, this desperate, involuntary noise escaped her throat.

"Oh, hey. You're up." He clicked the tablet a few times before shutting the cover and setting it aside. "Do you want some water or an ice pack?"

"Both." Ann headed toward her oversized water bottle. She could sort out why in the world Zane was in her condo after liquid had flushed this garbage taste from her mouth.

"Wait. Don't drink that." Instantly, Zane was crowding her. His arms boxed her against the counter as one hand tugged her bottle from her fingers a second before the straw hit her lips.

Then everything went a little fuzzy when Ann heard the near-silent, masculine hum that followed as Zane lightly pressed his chest to her back. She froze, bliss over the sensation warring with her lingering confusion. When Zane cleared his throat and vanished, the sink running sounded like Niagara Falls' deafening roar.

"Here." Zane set a glass of water in front of her and leaned his back against the counter. "You can't use a straw for a few days. The suction might cause bleeding and dislodge the clot. They said you didn't bleed much, and the site looked really good, but let's not chance it." Ann blinked from the glass to Zane's face, and he tapped on the instructions beside him on the counter. "It's all in here."

She didn't add sound to her quiet kitchen, only stared, prompting Zane to tug at his ear. "They said you should drink lots of fluids and eat something soft that's high in protein." He gestured to her multiple pre-workout, protein, and creatine powder bottles on the counter. "Want me to make you a smoothie?"

"Why are you here?"

Zane's facial muscles flickered briefly before he smoothed out his expression.

On some higher-functioning level that wasn't in control of her mouth, Ann recognized the sharp tone of her question. But her writhing emotions disemboweled any ability for civil conversation. Her fingertips twitched against the pearly quartz countertop as an aching, racing flush scratched up her forearms.

"I . . . I drove you home and wanted to make sure you didn't need anything when you woke up."

Yes. Obviously. Higher-level Ann had already figured that out. But physical Ann simply turned her body toward Zane's, fisting her hands at her sides as her quad muscles tensed.

"Why isn't my mom here?"

"She—" Zane adjusted his glasses again, averting her piercing gaze. "She had to leave the dentist's office."

Higher-level Ann launched into a very reasoned monologue. *You didn't expect Mom to stay after driving you home. You expected to wake up alone. Why are you snapping at Zane? Kind, wonderful Zane, who stayed to make sure you didn't need anything, who just offered to make you a smoothie. He doesn't deserve this attitude. Knock. It. Off.*

But physical Ann wasn't listening to reason right now and snapped out another question. "Why?"

Zane stepped forward, hands lifting as if he wanted to frame her upper arms but then thought better of it. "Why don't we get you something to eat? I think you'll feel better. Do you have a favorite soup? I can go get it for you."

"Why, Zane?"

His broad chest rose with a deep inhale, and it was the empathy in his eyes that did her in before his words mutilated what was left.

"Priscilla rescheduled the cake tasting at the last minute, and your mom didn't want to miss it. She called me on your phone and asked if I could take you home so she could go to the bakery with Priscilla. I assumed that since you were unconscious at the time, you'd want me to keep up the ruse. A boyfriend would certainly do that for his girlfriend." He palmed the back of his neck. "But that doesn't matter. You have every right to be angry. She should be here now. Not me. I'm sorry I'm the one that's here."

Stagnant saliva struggled to slide down her tight throat as a single tear singed her cheek. "My mom would have left the second my head hit the pillow."

That sentence was absolutely true. Her mother wouldn't have nurtured her past the point of necessity. When she'd been a little girl, Ann was often relegated to far corners of the house the second she showed signs of a sniffly nose to prevent anyone else from the infection. Dad would be busy at work, unaware that she'd be fending off a cold or the flu on her own.

But this time, her mother should have known better. It'd been impossible to miss how unsettled Ann had been before she walked back with the dental assistant earlier this afternoon. Her mother knew *why* Ann would have been nervous upon waking up, how it would have reminded her of that horrible day that changed everything.

Her mother should have stayed.

It didn't seem possible that Zane's light-brown eyes could

contain any more compassion as his head subtly shook.

Her body spun one-eighty before Ann pawed at her face. Her left lower jaw was on fire, but it was a tempered, tolerable pain compared to the one crushing her chest. Tears streamed as anger swiftly transitioned into shame. She should have seen this coming. She was a fool for thinking that her mother would have considered her feelings. The only reason she'd taken on the task of driving Ann to her appointment had been to obtain information about Zane.

"I'm sorry," husked over her ear as Zane wrapped his arms around her.

With him standing behind her, Ann could allow the contact. He wasn't watching her break down—something she didn't do in front of others. Zane couldn't see her crying, even though he could certainly feel her body heaving with each heart-wrenching sob.

The steady cadence of *I'm sorrys* whispered in a deepened timbre made her sag against him. Before Ann realized what she was doing, she'd turned and burrowed her good cheek into his chest, hugging Zane back. He shifted them, leaning back against the counter and taking on her full weight. The chorus of *sorrys* was replaced by the rhythmic beating of Zane's heart.

Which was preferable.

Ann didn't want his pity, his apologies, or for him to know that in the short month they'd been fake dating, he'd treated her better than anyone she'd ever met.

Behind her, the gray light deepened as, far across the city, the sun slipped under the horizon. The sweet evening bats would be heading out to feast soon, their soft wings adding a subdued undertone to the orchestra of crickets. On a normal Friday, she would've just finished a solo workout, made herself a meal, and settled on her teak patio daybed to eat in the peaceful quiet. So much of her week was encompassed with other people's—often children's—voices, that silence was the respite Ann needed at the end of it.

"I want to go outside."

"On your patio?" The question was accompanied by a tender hand flowing over her hair and down her back.

The sensation was so unexpectedly comforting and lulling that Ann sighed, sinking deeper into his embrace. "Yes, please."

After a few seconds, Zane loosened his arms. Ann kept her gaze low as she stepped back. Even when he sat on the cushioned daybed and she settled next to him, Ann kept her eyes from his.

Rationally, Ann knew Zane stayed at her condo because he was a decent human being and wanted to make sure she was safe when she woke up. Her trainwreck of a family life had triggered his compassionate heart. He was collecting her back into his arms right now because, moments ago, she'd freaked out on him and burst into tears.

But he'd broken something by being here, by taking care of her. Something Ann didn't want to admit to. She was willing to walk barefoot over the splintered shards of the truth than to admit that she *wanted* Zane here. Alone with her. Not fulfilling a role because he'd agreed to.

After sixty more heartbeats, she'd politely ask him to leave.

Zane staying was dangerous.

Because suddenly, this all felt too real.

Chapter 16

It's creepy to "bump into" a woman at a place you know she'll be. Right?

Zane stared at the drafted text message in the 'dorm bro' group chat for seven seconds before growling and deleting it. Raising his chest from his hunched, elbows-on-knees position, Zane stretched until his collarbone popped. Not being able to talk to his friends about what was going on with Ann was giving him heartburn, especially after how vulnerable she'd been with him on Friday.

When Ann had asked him to leave her condo, he'd reasoned that she probably wanted to take a pain pill and drift back to sleep. Though Zane had wanted nothing more than to stay and take care of her, he'd respected Ann's request. After having an oral surgeon drilling in her jaw and her mother's careless abandonment, it hadn't been the time to see if *fake* could be dropped from their relationship title.

The desire to check on her had pulsed like a beat in his chest all weekend, so he'd done the only thing he could think of. Sunday morning, he'd initiated another round of getting-to-know-you questions in the spreadsheet. What Zane hadn't expected was Ann texting him, stating in overly formal sentences that perhaps they should come clean to Rene and abandon the plan. The idea of not being able to be close to her, even in a false capacity, had punched the breath from his lungs.

Zane: *When we're so close to victory? Never.*

Ann: *I'm not sure it's worth it. The weekend with her and Denis is going to be terrible.*

Zane: *I'm sure. Let's finish this.*

Zane: *What's your favorite flower?*

Ann: *What? Why?*

Zane: *Because a good fake boyfriend knows his fake girlfriend's favorite flower.*

So much time had ticked between his answer and hers that Zane had worried he'd permanently pulverized their delicate non-relationship relationship.

Ann: *Stargazer lilies.*

Zane: *Why are those your favorite?*

Ann: *They're beautiful and have this captivating fragrance. When I graduated high school, my dad bought me a bouquet, and Rene said she could taste them in her cereal. It's petty of me, but that made me like them even more.*

Since that conversation, they'd been texting off and on every day, often for a few hours each night under the pretense that knowing more about each other made them better prepared for Saturday.

Zane's tapping toes splashed in the small puddle beneath the plastic pool bench as he toggled from the group chat back to Ann's messages, scrolling up to last night's conversation.

Zane: *The worst smell in the world is rotten eggs. You can't change my mind.*

They'd somehow stumbled down the offending-scents rabbit hole after talking about their worst summer jobs.

Ann: *I'm pretty sure the compounded sweat and feet smell at the gym has that beat. They should seriously invest in a diffuser for the weight room.*

Zane: *Yeah. I noticed that, and I've only been there once. You're there all the time?*

Ann: *Monday, Wednesday, Friday after school and weekends.*

Zane didn't bother reading his subsequent answer, joking about his fetid football teammates. Instead, he took an uneven breath of muggy, heavily chlorinated air and looked up at Caroline. His daughter was doing a semi-successful backstroke with her swim instructor at the far end of the lane. Caroline wouldn't care if he stepped out of the indoor pool area for a moment. Usually, Zane sat and chatted with the grandmother of Benny, the other child in Caroline's semi-private lesson, but they hadn't shown up today.

The fact that Ann could be in the weight room at the far end of the building was like a sink drip. It dominated his attention, demanding to be dealt with.

Zane punched to his feet, giving the swim instructor a universal *I'll-be-right-back* hand gesture, and pushed through the side door to the gym lobby. Having to patiently wait for the family of six to toddle down the hall in front of him was tortuous. Everyone in Tucson seemed to be trying to get their Wednesday workout at the same time.

For as abandoned as the weight room had been a month ago, it was almost breaking fire code today. Quickly eyeing each piece of equipment and coming up empty was like dropping a fresh roll of toilet paper into the toilet water. A resigned sigh left his open mouth as Zane turned to leave.

"Don't I know you?"

The bright voice didn't sound familiar, but Zane had a million friends in various places, so he rotated around. Coming down the stairs that lead to the cardio machinery was a small woman whom he vaguely recognized. Strands of her black hair were plastered to the sides of her sweaty, flushed face, but her dark-brown eyes held a nurturing warmth.

"Hey. Good to see you."

"Kennedy," she supplied, with a smile. "I teach at Hillcrest. You're one of our parents, right?"

Zane grinned as the pieces slid into place. "Yes. My—"

It was a little ridiculous the way the rest of his sentence evaporated faster than a drop of water in summer. Time no longer obeyed natural laws as Ann descended the stairs. It might as well have been a campy going-to-prom scene from a teen movie. Slow-mo. Soft focus. OK Go's "Here It Goes Again" popping in the background.

Makeup smudged below her eyes, her toned arms were slick with perspiration, and her shirt was dark with sweat stains. Zane had never seen anything more captivating in his life. The way that Ann casually flipped her long ponytail over her shoulder as she arrived beside Kennedy made a shudder sprint down his spine.

For the love. Pull yourself together.

"My daughter's in third grade." Zane put all his focus on Kennedy while finishing his sentence.

"Oh." Kennedy brightened even more. "Ann teaches third grade."

"Yes. She's actually Caroline's teacher. Hello, Ms. Powell."

Zane grinned affably, keeping up the impression that they only knew each other through school. He pretended that he didn't have intimate knowledge of what her lips felt like, that his heart hadn't shattered while she'd sobbed against him a few days ago, that their secret, fake relationship hadn't started in this very room a month ago.

"Mr. West."

Ann's loose-fitting gray T-shirt billowed over her black joggers. Her outfit was similar to the one she'd worn to the dentist's office. It was in such contrast to anything else Ann owned, to the way she decorated her classroom. Zane wanted to know why. As a shield? To blend in? The desire to understand each of Ann's decisions intensified. He'd never wanted to fully comprehend each nuance of a person's thought process before.

"Are you here for a workout?" Ann asked, pulling him back to the room.

Anyone else would have missed the mischievous lift of Ann's mouth, but Zane had spent the last month becoming an expert in her microexpressions. If there'd been an official Ann dictionary, Zane would've already had it memorized.

"No." He smiled at Kennedy to ground himself. "Caroline is having a swim lesson, so I thought I'd check out the facility."

Lies.

Ann knew they were lies.

He'd been caught red-handed, looking for her.

"Oh?" There was a slight, flirty challenge to Ann's question. An undertone that, again, no one else would have noticed, but Zane heard like it'd been shouted through a loudspeaker.

Kennedy launched into a detailed explanation of the two workout areas, an obvious extrovert like him, happy to offer information. Zane nodded along at all the right places as relief tiptoed across his forehead. Ann wasn't upset that he was here, being a slight creeper. She was . . . entertained? Happy, maybe?

Zane tried not to give that idea too much leash as he relaxed into the conversation with Kennedy. Somehow, they ended up on the topic of skydiving as Kennedy recounted her experience of flinging herself out of an airplane with her husband over Christmas break. While chatting, Zane only allowed himself three glimpses in Ann's direction. That way, he wouldn't get caught in a tangle of soul-quenching green.

When his phone pinged with a text, Zane pulled it out of his pocket.

Samuel: *We're all set. Return to the pool when you get a chance.*

Zane glanced up, let a rueful smile lift his lips, and gave his goodbyes to both women. He was halfway to the pool when the crisp, order-up sound of his text dinged again.

Ann: *That was close.*

He tucked into an alcove, prepared to pen an apology, when another message came through.

Ann: *Don't let it happen again.*

His breath hitched in his throat until a winky emoji followed the previous sentence.

Zane wasn't one to use emojis. Ann hadn't used them in their conversations thus far, and something told him she wasn't one to use them with other people, either. Her school-related emails were also devoid of unnecessary exclamation points. Something he found odd at the beginning of the year because Ms. Thompson from last year couldn't finish a sentence without at least one.

Zane: *Yes, ma'am.*

Zane: *I'll be sure to be on my best behavior from here on.*

Three dots hovered, then paused, hovered, then went away completely, but it didn't matter. Fizzy seltzer water had replaced the blood in his veins. As quickly as he could without running, Zane returned to the indoor pool, trying to cool the warmth that was slipping over his skin. Only two more days until he'd have Ann alone to himself for the weekend.

Chapter 17

Zane drummed his fingers on the steering wheel in time to the Blues Traveler song streaming through his speakers. Though it was only mid-morning, the day had already warmed to a toasty eighty-five degrees. He was running the air conditioning inside of his car, partly to counteract how he felt even warmer with Ann sitting beside him.

When he'd picked her up a little over fifteen minutes ago, Zane had stood at her door with his friendliest grin in lieu of the bouquet of flowers he wanted to give her. Ann had returned his smile with a shy one and asked if she could finish up some work while he drove. Since then, she'd been grading.

Which was adorable.

There was no other way to describe it.

Ann had curled herself into a hunched ball in his passenger seat, shuffling through papers. She murmured words of praise while reading over her students' sentences. When she wasn't using her red pen, it sat between her teeth. Halfway through, she grew impatient with her hair and efficiently knotted it into a ball, secured with a second pen.

Tapping the steady bass rhythm of "Hook" was the only thing keeping Zane from tucking away the wispy strand at her temple.

He didn't have to wonder what would happen if he reached out. Ann had kept something physical between them since he'd picked her up—her luggage, her work satchel, her papers. Though Zane had felt something shift between them, Ann still had her guard up.

That should've pushed a barbed thorn into his ribs, but Zane had been waiting since August, had been prepared to wait until the school year had ended. Time was almost irrelevant at this point. When Ann was ready, he'd be here.

"Oh, no."

A quick glance was all Zane needed to recognize that it was his daughter's loopy cursive atop Ann's legs.

"What is it?"

"Caroline's essay used to be about banning personal lawns to promote water conservation." Zane nodded. He'd read her most recent draft Tuesday afternoon. "But she's changed topics."

"To what?" Zane returned his gaze to the dusty, flat landscape on either side of the six-lane road as a souped-up truck zoomed past.

"Divorce should be illegal."

It was as if that truck had pulled in front of them and stopped, smashing the steering wheel into his chest. When Zane had met Tessa this morning before he kept driving east to pick up Ann, Caroline had been less than enthused to leave his side. Tessa had spent the last week, while Caroline had been with him, moving her things out of her parents' house and into Isaac's. Zane feebly hoped that Caroline's surly attitude had been due to the fact that they'd met Tessa an hour earlier than usual, not the change in her part-time residence.

The ragged sigh that left his mouth carried the weight of the last fifteen months with it.

"Can I ask what happened?"

Zane kept his eyes on the road. "We weren't working. We hadn't been working for some time."

That was what outsiders didn't understand. Why they looked at him and couldn't comprehend why he wasn't livid. They thought Tessa had used and then betrayed him, but that wasn't the case. They were best friends who should have never gotten married. That was why their divorce and co-parenting was so easy. There was no passion in a dissolution when there hadn't been passion in the first place.

And both he and Tessa had had those antsy moments in their relationship. Each time they should have called it quits, duty and loyalty had pressed those thoughts out of their minds. They both had been doing the best with the circumstances they were presented with, tempering their disappointment and moving on with their day.

"We got married young because we thought it would be the best thing for Caroline, but once our heads rose out of the water of graduating, starting our careers, and taking care of a toddler, we realized that as much as we worked as partners . . ." He let another breath blow over his hands. "Then Tessa got sick."

His eyes flicked to Ann's, her gaze open and compassionate. Zane already knew that Ann didn't fill the air with unnecessary words, that her silence didn't mean indifference. Often it was laced with focused intent, as it was now.

Zane rarely spoke about how hard it was to watch his pint-sized, spitfire best friend be reduced to a fraction of herself. At five-three, Tessa was a full foot smaller than him. During the worst of chemotherapy, her one hundred and fifteen pounds had become a dangerous seventy-eight. That was when he'd begged her to eat, knowing it wasn't her fault that she couldn't tolerate anything.

"I'm sorry." Ann's words pulled him out of the astringent-stained memory.

"Yeah." He swallowed against his rough voice. "I would have been there for Tessa the same even if we'd been divorced beforehand, but it hit her so fast. And then there were days we both genuinely thought she wasn't going to make it."

Ann's fingertips landed on his forearm, and Zane jolted from the unanticipated contact. His mind had been swallowed up in Tessa's sallow face, her jawline and cheekbones too prominent.

"Sorry," she whispered. When Ann tried to slip her hand away, Zane covered it with his left palm, securing it.

"Don't be sorry." He squeezed her fingers before returning his hand to the steering wheel.

Ann's palm lingered for two beautiful seconds before she tucked it under her blue canvas shorts.

Zane swallowed. "It's just . . . for the first time in eight years, we're putting our lives first, and Caroline is having a hard time adjusting."

"You both love her so much."

He nodded to the road. There wasn't any trial he wouldn't take on if it would guarantee Caroline's happiness.

The car hummed as the wheels turned over the road for several minutes before Ann broke the lulling quiet. "What should we do about Caroline's essay? The submission deadline is next Thursday."

Zane adjusted his frames. "Edit it and let her submit it. That's how she feels right now. I don't want to discourage her from speaking her mind, from saying what's on her heart."

The irony in his words picked at his temple. He couldn't tell Ann that he wanted this to be real, that he hoped she saw him as more than a solution to an unwanted problem.

"You're a good father. Sometimes, I wish . . ." When Ann's voice tapered off, Zane kept his eyes on the road. He didn't want his attention to disrupt her, not when she was opening up on her own.

"That's one of the reasons I spend so much time with children, teaching them, nurturing them when I can. Not everyone has a parent like you at home." She paused. "At least with me, they can see they are valued for who they are."

Ann shifted in her seat, a paper flitting to the ground. "You'd think that Hillcrest students would be set because they have the income to be sent to a private school, but some of those kids come from an emotional wasteland. Their entire worth is chained to their output. Just the other day, I got a scathing email because a student received an eighty-nine percent on their geography test." She shook her head. "Their parents expect perfection as if they don't matter as people."

She hugged herself, staring out the passenger window.

"I'm glad you're there for them." Zane couldn't imagine treating Caroline the way Ann had just described.

"School can be the safest place for a child sometimes," she said to the window. "For some emotionally, for others physically, which is devastating, but true." Ann sighed. "We're not just teaching our students. Sometimes, we're the only ones to love them."

An extended quiet settled as each of them receded into their own thoughts. Blooming Palo Verde trees preened as they zipped past. The vivid green bark of their crossing branches broke into a spectacular show of thousands of tiny yellow flowers, their brightness rivaling the ever-present sun.

"Sorry."

When Ann shifted, Zane glanced at her. It was a challenge not to get caught in the sorrowful turn of her lips and return his gaze to the road. "What for?"

"I can be too negative at times. There are just so many moments of the day. It's hard to be positive for all of them."

That sentence pierced through him because Zane understood it better than most.

Ann released an audible exhale. "I know there are a hundred better things you could be doing with your time. I shouldn't make this experience worse by being broody."

Zane's hands squeezed the steering wheel. "What's irritating is your inability to take my words for face value."

Instantly, he regretted the snap in his voice.

"I'm sorry. For what little I've seen of your relationships, it seems you've been taught to not trust what people say, but I'll make this easy on you. If I say I want to be here, then I do. Do you think you can wrap your head around that concept?"

Out of the corner of his eye, Zane caught Ann shaking her head before she stopped herself.

His jaw tightened.

If you let me, I'd love you like you've never known.

A shaky breath entered his open mouth as pinpricks ran down his legs in response to that automatic thought. As much as he wanted things with Ann to be real, the consequences now seemed catastrophic. He'd already lived through the torture of watching his best friend almost die. Only a fool would voluntarily walk into a situation where the risk of heartache was intensified. When Zane ran over his dating history, one common thread stuck out like the hi-hat pulsing beneath most modern music releases.

He'd always *liked* the women he was with—or, in the case of Tessa, loved like his closest friend—but he'd never let himself tumble head over feet down the steep, rocky cliff that was falling in love. The way he felt about Ann was already stark in its demarcation from his previous relationships. And they weren't even dating—not really.

There was too much potential here.

The potential to have his heart ground into a fine-grain sand that slipped through his fingers.

Maybe they shouldn't be doing this, baring their souls to each other, discovering the gritty inner workings of the other person. What Zane already knew about Ann was going to make her leaving him behind so much harder.

Zane let out a controlled exhale.

He needed to lighten this conversation, to imbue ease and warmth back into the sun-soaked interior of his car.

"Hey," he said, brightening his tone. "Let's just make the best of this, okay? I've never been put up in a fancy wellness resort, and I looked it up. Nice restaurant. Hiking trails. Full spa. Pool. Hot tub. I think two friends can have a lot of fun at a place like that. What do you say?"

Ann reached down to pick up the discarded essay, then straightened the stack on her lap. "I guess."

Even though those words felt like an actual jab to the chest, Zane stabbed his heart with his clenched fist, infusing his voice with playful hoarseness. "That hurt."

Ann's tortoise-framed sunglasses swung toward him. "Are you okay?"

"No." He coughed. "I'm bleeding out internally because being on vacation with me is worse than having your nails pulled off by pliers. I'm not going to make it." He heaved with a cinematic wheeze. "Quick, take the wheel."

The most delightful scrunch twisted Ann's brow. "Very funny."

"Goodbye, cruel world." Zane slumped his body against the window while keeping one hand low on the steering wheel.

"Knock it off." Ann pushed his shoulder. "You know you're the only thing making this weekend tolerable."

Though her slightly forced admission made his collarbones swell, Zane kept his limp posture against the door.

When an irritated growl came from the passenger seat, his lips twitched. "What if I buy you an eegee? Will that make it better? There's one right before we get to Oro Valley."

"Eegee's makes everything better," he admitted.

"Okay, then. My treat." Ann watched him until he dramatically revived himself, gasping and running his fingertips all over his heart as if he couldn't believe he was alive.

That was when Zane received it, the chuckle he'd be subconsciously aiming for. He needed to keep his head straight this weekend. The best way to do that was to pal around with Ann the way he would with anyone. They were trying to make the best of a weird situation, and while doing so, Zane was going to aim for hearing that raspy laugh as much as he possibly could.

Chapter 18

"You'll have a bit to get settled," Rene said, leading Ann and Zane down the hall. "We're having a couple's massage. I'm sorry we didn't think to book you one." Though her sister pouted, malice sparkled in her green eyes.

"Afterward, we're all going to do the three-mile hike that surrounds the property before dinner." Since Denis said the sentence into his phone, he missed that she and Rene grimaced at the word *hike*.

For as little as Ann shared with Rene, their dislike of the outdoors—with the exception of experiencing it via a well-manicured patio—was one of the few things they could agree upon. Since Denis had spent their check-in process espousing all the "magical" and "breathtaking" trails that surrounded the resort's property, Ann was left with the deep, sinking suspicion that everything she owned would be covered in dusty sand by the time they left Sunday afternoon.

"Oh, babe. I'd forgotten. I only brought flip-flops and heels." The saccharine lacing Rene's words would've cost a diabetic their foot.

"Not a problem. They've got a shoe section in the gift shop," Denis said while typing a text message. "I think I saw hiking boots there."

"Great." Rene's artificial smile contorted into a wicked one as she pushed the keycard against the door sensor. "I'm sorry about them giving you a basic room, but you have a private balcony and a *king bed*. All the necessities."

Her heart drummed against her ribs because there was only one reason Rene would have intentionally booked them the smallest room at the resort. She must know that her and Zane weren't real.

"It's perfect." Zane dropped a kiss on Ann's head on his way toward glass balcony doors overlooking the cactus-speckled mountains in the distance.

The second they had arrived on the property, Zane shifted effortlessly into his boyfriend role, tending to her luggage, opening doors, placing his hand at the small of her back as they navigated through the lobby.

"Thank you again, Denis, for accommodating us." Zane turned around. "You're sure I can't cover our costs?"

Denis was about to refuse Zane again, like he'd done when they'd arrived, when a chirping alarm noise cut him off.

"Oh, that's our reminder. We've got to go. See you *lovebirds* later." Rene gave a finger wave before sashaying toward the door.

"Meet us in the lobby in an hour and a half," Denis said with a smile before following his fiancé.

Zane and Ann stared at the closed door for several seconds.

It was safer to keep her gaze there than at the imposing king bed. The pristine white linens and southwestern-patterned throw pillows didn't soften their impact on her psyche. Like most tourist destinations, the room was peppered with strategically placed hints of their surroundings. Burnt-sienna chairs bookended the unnecessary gas fireplace as artistically distressed furniture rooted the turquoise-enameled lamps.

There was barely enough room to walk around the bed, let alone space for them to spread out. When she'd been anticipating a suite, there would have been a door separating the bedroom from the pull-out couch she'd intended on making her oasis from the onslaught of pretending they'd have to do during the day.

Ann's shoulders army-crawled toward her ears. Point to Rene. She was sufficiently rattled.

Zane cracked open a complimentary water bottle and drank half of it before rummaging in the small closet. "Perfect."

"What?"

"There are extra linens and pillows in here." He closed the door with an armful and strode into the bathroom.

The mischievous smile on his face prompted Ann to follow. It made sense that they wouldn't share the bed, but why was Zane heading into the bathroom?

"When we were in college, my friends and I didn't have a formal room. It was a study hall they crammed some extra beds into. The University of Arizona had miscalculated the size of our freshman class. Rowan and I were the last to arrive, so the three single beds had already been claimed by Kevin, Kyle, and Ethan." Zane dropped the bundle on the floor and began spreading sheets into the jacuzzi tub. "We stood back to back to see who was taller, reasoning that the taller person should get the top bunk." Next came the blanket. "But I'm only an inch taller, which we all agreed didn't matter . . . until Kevin reminded us that an extra inch only mattered in certain areas."

A surprised, nasally snort spilled from her nose.

Zane grinned. "We were teenage boys away from home for the first time. There were bound to be some dirty jokes every once in a while. Anyway"—he fluffed the pillow and set it opposite the tap—"this will be just like the bottom bunk."

"There's no possible way I can let you sleep in the tub. You won't fit."

"Oh, I won't?" He kicked off his leather flip-flops and stepped in, settling against the edge with his hands behind his head. It was impossible not to notice how his snug blue T-shirt stretched over his broad chest, or how his biceps popped with his arms in that orientation. The same spray of tiny freckles that crossed the bridge of his nose danced down his neck. "See. I fit. And Rowan won't be snoring above me."

Ann folded her arms, trying to cool the unexpected heat that had just tumbled through her. "Sitting in the tub isn't the same as sleeping in it."

Zane scrunched down, his bent knees nearly knocking his glasses off his face, and closed his eyes. The action made his shorts ride up. Inky black edges of a geometric design over his right thigh peeked out.

"You're ridiculous."

His eyelids popped open. "You're smiling."

Was she? Ann straightened her lips. "Be reasonable."

"I refuse."

What?

"I can't be fighting with you and my sister all weekend."

"Then don't fight me." He bounced his eyebrows.

"Get out." Ann used her sternest teacher voice.

"Nuh-uh." Zane dropped his head to the side, closing his eyes and pretending to snore.

Seriously? Nuh-uh?

Ann rooted her sneakered feet against the tile floor, bent at the waist, reached into the tub, and grabbed his wrist off his chest. "I said get out."

Zane simply tensed a bicep, and her movement jolted to a halt. He didn't even open his eyes.

Annoying. So annoying.

She'd always suspected that he was strong, but at that moment, Ann wanted to heave him out of that tub like she'd dead-lifted a half-dozen plates. Ann changed tactics. Sitting on the edge, she positioned her feet against the other side, wrapped both hands around his wrist, and heaved. His hand wrenched away before Zane pulled it back, his eyes still closed.

A satisfied smile lifted her lips.

Progress.

"You're the one being ridiculous now," Zane said before resuming his fake snoring.

"Zane—whatever your middle name is—West, get out of this tub!"

"Anthony," he said, still successfully resisting her efforts.

Ann rolled her shoulders, switched her grip, and tried again. "Zane Anthony West, think about how destroyed your spine will be in the morning. We're not twenty anymore. At least sleep on the floor."

She'd secretly loved knowing that he was exactly six months older than her. Ann liked fantasizing about them both inhabiting the same buildings at the University of Arizona years ago. Maybe they'd even sat in the same two-hundred-plus-seat auditorium of one of the general education classes without knowing it.

"Ann—whatever your middle name is—Powell, you need your space, and I'm giving it to you."

"Opal." She tried again, pulling his hand away, just for him to regain control over it. "You think you are, but what happens when I have to pee in the middle of the night?"

Zane's eyes popped open. "That would be awkward."

She stopped pulling but didn't let go of his wrist. "Okay. So now that we both agree this is a bad idea, can we make you some sort of second bed with the comforter in the main room?"

"Fine," he huffed like a sullen teenager.

As much as Ann's face reflexively scrunched, a smaller version of Ann rose on tiptoes, whispering, *Let's play.*

"Unless you want to contend for the bed. How much do you weigh?"

"One-ninety," Zane rattled off before he pinned her with a look. "I don't know what you're thinking, but there's no possible scenario where I'm letting you sleep on the floor. It isn't going to happen."

Ann nodded, ignoring his protest. "Oh, I'm taking the bed. After I deadlift you out of this tub."

"Ann, you can't—"

"You're right," she interrupted. "You'd need to be on the ground. Otherwise, your weight would be distributed wrong. Come on"—she motioned for him to get out—"cross your ankles and your arms at your chest so I can get a grip."

Zane was already climbing out of the tub. "No. This is ludicrous."

"Fine. Lie on the carpet. It will be more comfortable." Ann strode out of the bathroom, rolling her shoulders.

Every cell within her was sparking. Muscles stiff from the hour-long drive shimmied with anticipation. Even though she didn't love the idea of dusty sand sticking to her skin, the hike after she showed Zane she could easily lift him sounded kind of nice.

When she spun around, Zane was standing with his arms crossed, but instead of blatant refusal on his face, a hint of a smirk tipped the corner of his mouth. "On the floor?"

"Yes, please." Ann bounced a bit, setting her stance and rocking from foot to foot. "Keep yourself as rigid as you can."

Zane followed directions flawlessly, and she gripped the wrist of his crossed arm closest to her. Then Ann realized she'd have to slide her hand between his knees to get her other hold. Her breath staggered a moment before the athletic part of her brain took over, and she tucked her palm beneath his leg, just above his kneecap.

Ann took a quick inhale, setting every muscle in place before she lifted. She was used to a barbell, not the uneven distribution of a human man, but by the second rep, Ann had gotten the hang of it.

"What do you say I go for three?"

"I'd say you proved your point." Zane's voice held that amused quality, but Ann kept her good form, looking out over the rocky mountains through the glass door instead of down at him.

"Three it is," she said, her voice showing the strain of her effort.

When Ann finished her final rep, she placed Zane on the ground as evenly as she could, releasing her grip and resting her forearms on her thighs.

"See, I told—" The rest of that braggy sentence died in her throat when her gaze linked with Zane's.

She'd expected his eyes to reflect the teasing quality of his previous words, but they focused on her with that bone-melting intensity.

But . . . Rene wasn't here.

There was no reason for him to look at her like he wanted to pull her atop of him and devour her whole. Ann's chest was already heaving from her effort, but now each labored breath became more scattered.

A drop of sweat sliding from her temple to the fabric over his abs jolted Zane into action. He rolled away from her, crouching for several seconds before standing.

"I'd say you won the bed fair and square."

Ann noticed that he kept his frame turned slightly away from her, that he didn't meet her gaze again.

Zane swiped the ice bucket and key card from the bureau that also held the mini fridge. "I'm going to grab some ice for my Camelbak."

"Oh . . . sure."

All the insecure thoughts were automatic. *You shouldn't have shown him you could lift him. Men don't like strong women. You've disgusted him.* Ann was already wrapping her arms over her torso when Zane looked over his shoulder.

Even over the twenty-foot distance, Zane's expression obliterated her ruminations. He wasn't leaving because he was revolted by her—quite the opposite. His twitchy hand paused at the door handle as he bit his lower lip, his gaze flitting unevenly over her body.

Time stalled for several beats along with her heart. Blood was trapped uselessly in her veins, waiting for Zane's next movement, for his decision. When his eyes returned to hers, a shaky breath escaped her vibrating chest.

Then everything sped up again as Zane opened the door, tossed, "I'll be right back," her way, and left her alone and confused.

Chapter 19

I'm glad Rene is here. It was the most impossible of thoughts, yet it scratched around in Zane's skull as he followed Denis's shoulders through the narrow, brushy section of trail. Both Ann and her sister were tromping behind them, displeasure more obvious on Rene's face. Denis seemed oblivious to Rene's disquiet, but Zane was zoned-in to Ann's—every tweak of her cheek, wrinkle of her forehead, shuffle of her shoulder.

He hadn't felt right leaving her before, but the alternative would have been cataclysmic. If he'd walked across the room, framed her jaw with his hand, and tasted her sweet lips, they wouldn't have made it on this trail. He'd never seen anything more attractive than Ann's focus as she tossed his weight around. And after hearing her labored breathing, Zane wanted that sound to come from the result of *his* efforts, not hers.

Zane's boot caught on a rock, distracted by the subsequent cascade of images. The misstep nearly sent him into a nearby hedgehog cactus.

"Careful, Zane." When Rene quietly purred her sentence, Zane automatically renounced his previous thought about her company. "We wouldn't want you getting hurt."

Her nails scratched down his arm, and Zane stepped to the side, motioning for Rene to pass as he pulled the mouthpiece part of his hydration pack from its fastener. It had been intolerable the first several hundred times Rene touched him without his consent, but now each caress made him want to vomit up the peanut butter protein bar he'd taken from the lobby.

Rene stopped in front of him, whispering, "I'm thirsty too."

"Are we taking a water break already?" Denis turned around from his position far up on the trail and slung his backpack forward. "Babe, I brought that cucumber-mint spa water you like."

"Oh." Rene took her eyes from Zane's and blinked at her fiancé. "You did?"

The act faltered as a small, genuine smile lifted her lips. Rene continued, almost distractedly, toward Denis.

"I'm sorry," Ann murmured when she trudged up to him, spraying little rocks over his ankles. "It's not too late to fake pink eye or leprosy."

Zane chuckled. "Leprosy?"

"I don't know." Ann shrugged, defeat sagging her otherwise strong shoulders. "I'll take anything to get out of this."

His hand reaching up to tuck a strand that had escaped her long Dutch braid was reflexive, and because Zane was within thirty feet of Rene and Denis, he could allow it. That was another reason it was better when they were around. He could touch Ann when he wanted to.

Zane didn't react to the way her eyes fluttered half-closed when his thumb brushed her neck. Instead, he pointed to the metal water bottle hanging from her fingers. "Have something to drink. It's hot out here. I have no idea why Denis would want to hike during the hottest part of the day."

"Or after a massage." Ann took a long drag from her bottle. "I'd want a glass of wine and a nap after that."

"Yeah." Zane moved his body as a barrier between Ann and her sister and noticed that her features softened with every rested second.

"Something occurred to me after the room 'mix up,'" Zane said, using finger quotes. When Ann's lips curled up around her water bottle straw, he forced himself not to focus on them. "Rene is probably being extra ruthless because she's about to lose a great deal of money." He leaned close, whispering even though they were far enough away. "That means we're winning."

"All right." Rene clapped. "Let's keep going."

"You heard the drill sergeant," Ann said with a rueful twist of her lips.

"Hey." He caught her fingers before she continued on. "Look."

Just beyond the ring of hedgehog cacti, a desert cottontail loped forward from its position behind a rock. Its speckled tan and brown fur blended seamlessly with its surroundings. A little nose twitched in the air twice before taking another hop toward the ring of magenta flowers topping the spiny plant. The rabbit was just about to nip a petal when Rene called out again, scaring it off.

Ann deflated with a sigh.

"Maybe sometime we'll come back here on our own and do this trail without the banshee leading the charge." Zane squeezed her hand before letting it go and walking ahead of her.

It only took him three steps before his heat-fried brain recognized the two major holes in his suggestion—Ann didn't like to hike, and there might not be a future when the two of them would be traveling here for a getaway.

The foursome trudged along for another five minutes before Rene stumbled, drawing in a strained breath.

"You okay?" Denis asked, crossing back over his gained distance to her side.

"Yes." Rene offered a tight smile. "I'm sure it's—" A horrible hissing sound ricocheted off the nearby rock as she attempted to put weight on it.

"Oh, babe. You might have sprained it." Denis was crouching at her side, feeling her leg and ankle.

"You think so?" Her theatrical doe-eyes were evident even through her sunglasses.

When his hands pressed the inside of her ankle bone, Rene's red nails clenched on Denis's shoulder. "That hurts."

"Should we pop popcorn for this show?" Zane let his whispered words brush over Ann's shoulder, delighted when her hand flew to her mouth to stifle a laugh.

"Oh no, Rene. How could you possibly carry on?" Zane made sure his face conveyed the appropriate amount of sympathy. He definitely didn't smirk when Ann wheezed from behind her fingertips.

"Yes, we'll have to turn back," Denis said. "Shoot. We were just a quarter-mile from the overlook."

"I'm *so* sorry, babe." Rene was really selling it. Give her an Oscar.

"It's not your fault." Denis stood. "Here. Put your arm around my waist and lean into me."

"Ann, you go ahead." Zane motioned toward the trail back toward the resort.

Behind them, a cacophony of miserable moans followed them down the moderate decline.

"This isn't working," Rene huffed. "Someone will have to carry me."

Someone.

Not *you'll*. Not *my darling fiancé, please pick me up.*

Someone.

"You know I can't with my bad back," Denis said.

There it was.

"Oh, that's right." Rene's voice was pure syrup. "Zane, could you manage?"

He barely kept his hand from fisting. Zane didn't want anything to do with Rene, let alone schlep her frame back to the resort. Ann's eyes were obscured behind her dark sunglasses, but her downturned lips were a reflection of the grimace staining his mouth.

"Sure." He unfastened and handed Ann his Camelbak, noting that she sighed again when her fingers clasped the shoulder strap.

Everything in him recoiled when he took on Rene's weight, and she wrapped her arms around his shoulders. Zane was usually game to help anyone, but this wasn't helping. This was another one of Rene's schemes. Plain and simple.

Zane was prepared to shoulder her the rest of the way down—the same way that he'd shouldered each sucky event he'd had to weather when things should have been good. Hard, marching steps brought him closer to the buildings, trying to get this over with as quickly as possible. But then, Rene leaned to purr into his ear, and an alternative idea shot up like a flare in his brain.

◊◊◊

"So sorry for almost dropping you, Rene. You're more solid than you look." Zane twisted his face with believable remorse, leaning heavily onto Ann, his human crutch for his own sprained ankle.

The lobby split to where he and Ann would continue in the direction of their lowly room and Rene and Denis would head to the area with the vista suites.

Rene's lips lifted in a fake smile.

"This wasn't how I expected the afternoon to go," Denis said, and Zane felt sympathy for the man. It wasn't his actions that'd tainted their foray into the desert.

"Sorry, Denis." Ann's voice held the remorse Zane hadn't expressed. "Hopefully, dinner will be less eventful. You want us to meet you there at six, right?"

"Yes." He perked up. "See you, then."

Zane continued to baby his ankle until they arrived at the long corridor to their room, well beyond the view of the lobby.

"I'm sorry about having to use you as a support," Zane said, glancing back to double check. "I guess it's safe now."

"Safe for what?" She turned her face to him.

With his arm around her shoulder, her flawless skin was right there. Zane wanted to lean down and brush his lips over her cheek, but they were alone now. So instead, he let her crutch-walk him a few more feet until they were closer to the room.

"This." He spun away from her with a goofy step-ball-change, finishing in a stumbly side slide before leaning cross-armed on their door. Zane was a terrible dancer, but that little ditty would have made his theater-owning friends, Kevin and Kyle, proud.

Ann's gaping mouth morphed into a luminescent smile. "You faked the whole thing?"

He mirrored her grin as he nodded. "Sure did."

"But you put your full weight on me." She rolled her right shoulder.

"I had to make it look real." He bounced his eyebrows once. "Plus, I knew you were strong enough to carry me."

"You—I can't believe—" Then Ann broke into a throaty laugh that sent sparks shooting over his skin. She shook her head, stepping over. "I could kiss you." The sentence was meant casually, to express gratitude, but then her face slacked.

Shuttering silence snapped down the hallway, all sound absorbed into the patterned carpet.

"I could kiss you."

The second time Ann said that, everything about it changed—the intonation, the volume, the awe filtered within. It escaped breathlessly, almost like she'd been considering it.

This charged sensation ran backward through Zane's body—from the soles of his feet upward until it singed his scalp. A swallow somehow managed to squeeze down his throat as he waited.

And waited.

Time was a tortuous, deviant thing, trying to see if it could break him.

Yes. Go ahead. Break me.

That was the clamoring answer pulsing from his chest. Whatever fear he'd had on the drive here, whatever worry he'd had that Ann could crush him, hadn't decreased. It'd intensified.

The difference was that now Zane didn't care. Chew him up. Spit him out. He'd take what he could get and then ask for more if it meant he could have this moment, this time, with Ann. If it meant her lips on his again.

Her gaze fell to his mouth as she sucked her bottom lip between her teeth. Ann's hands drifted up, and she glanced at them as if she was surprised they'd moved. But then her fingertips were smoothing over his jaw, securing his face in her hands. Zane fell fully against the door, taking her with him, his hands flat against her shoulder blades. A shocked puff of air accompanied her gaze, momentarily bouncing down before her eyes were back on their task, focused.

Zane never wanted to stop watching Ann deciding to kiss him. Each careful step was its own aphrodisiac, holding its own blinding pleasure. He didn't want to miss a nanosecond, but when her eyes fluttered closed, his did as well. Ann hesitated for one breath, two. Then the softness of her lips on his felt like nothing he'd ever experienced. This was different from their first kiss. Every cell in his body was firing, spiking with sensation, scrambling to understand why this, this slight touch in this way, felt more significant than anything that had come before it.

The cool AC hit his lips when Ann pulled away, but before Zane could open his eyes, she kissed him again. This time it was familiar—hungry, insistent—like when she'd grabbed his tie at piano karaoke. Her fingers slid into his curls and tugged at them. A growl rumbled from his chest as he met her intensity, sliding his tongue into her sighing mouth, banding her body to his as his arms wrapped around her back.

Everything was messy, fervent, and Zane's brain was struggling to keep up with each new touch. One of Ann's hands left his hair, and the sound of unlocking registered before a weightlessness replaced the solid door behind his back.

"Inside." Zane's brain exploded, hearing her rushed words. "Now."

Chapter 20

The heaving slam of the hydraulic door shutting into place sliced through the air of the small hotel room like a punctuation. Outside was her life before—careful, guarded, alone. Inside, with Zane's lips on hers, Ann was walking into wild and unfamiliar territory.

They'd flipped after tumbling through the door. Zane now pressed his muscled body against hers with ideal pressure, his mouth exploring hers in a way that was equal parts sweet and stunned. When her fingers smoothed down his sides and snuck under the hem of his shirt, his breath drew in sharply before this indescribable hum vibrated from his throat. Zane's chin tilted away long enough for Ann to witness his eyes roll back.

All from a few fingertips on skin?

Drunken power surged in Ann's veins, and she flattened her hands against his abs, using the wall at her back as leverage to push up his chest. Her motion set him into overdrive again, and Zane quickly ripped his shirt off before returning both hands to her face and pouring himself into her. The kiss was endless, circling and looping, over and over. Months of pent-up potential traded between their bodies, an overdue conversation come to fruition.

Zane leaned back to momentarily gather his breath, and a flash of black along his side prompted Ann to explore. A long quill tattoo stretched down from the feather tip, nearly tickling his left armpit to a sharp splash of ink at his lowermost rib. Like the one she'd glimpsed on his right thigh earlier, it was solely black. The quill almost seemed to dance with each irregular seesaw of Zane's ribs, like an invisible hand was writing this moment, their story, in onyx ink.

Ann was overwhelmed by the impulse to twist his shoulders around to see if any other designs accompanied the miniscule freckles over his upper back. Instead, she satisfied herself with watching Zane shudder as her fingers traced the quill until her hand rested on that masculine dip over his hip, her thumb slipping slightly beneath the waistband.

Zane was shaking his head. "I—We can't—I didn't think—I didn't bring—"

"I did," she rasped, eyes still trained on the sharp V indentation.

Zane collapsed forward, his head over her shoulder, his forehead pressed to the wallpaper. One hand braced the wall while the other found her waist and squeezed. It was like her words had stolen the energy from him. Like the idea of her at the grocery store, putting condoms in the cart with cantaloupe and kale, thinking of him, of this potential moment, was incapacitating.

But Ann had thought about it—extensively. They wouldn't have been here had she not. They wouldn't have been pressed against each other if she hadn't calculated each possible option, each potential outcome. Every interaction with him since last Friday had only pushed Ann toward the idea that maybe this—this fake arrangement between them—could be something more.

Something real.

Zane lifted his head with an inhale and softly kissed the corner of her jaw. "You're sure?"

When Ann nodded, Zane framed her face and brought his lips to hers again, tenderly nudging her toward the king bed. Certainty over her decision bathed Ann in shimmering light as she fully let go and trusted him.

◊◊◊

As they walked hand in hand to dinner, Ann's mind was on a cycle of Zane's fragmented compliments. The ones he had muttered into her skin earlier. *'Sweet orange blossom,'* when he had breathed her in. *'So beautifully strong,'* after kissing her shoulder. And when coherent phrases were beyond him, *'Ann,'* laced with wonder, had simply sung on repeat.

She had no idea it could be like this.

Unlike that one disastrous time in college, being with Zane had been like the love stories she didn't believe in. Even getting ready for dinner had had an ease to it—sharing the mirror as they each styled their hair, him zipping her into her long-sleeved shift dress, her buttoning his suit vest. Somehow, the addition of clothing had been just as revolutionary as the removal of it.

An unsteady breath stumbled into her lungs, and Zane looked over, smiling, his cheeks still holding onto the flush that had brightened them before. Ann never wanted those two cherry spots to fade.

"There you are," Rene's voice crashed into the tender moment as her limping feet caught up to them. She was still nursing her fake injury, though Zane had abandoned his. "Your ankle's all better?"

Zane squeezed Ann's fingers. "Just a little tweaked now."

Ann was pretty sure her sister hadn't meant to let the petulant *humph* out of her mouth, but she was rescued by Denis kissing her cheek. "Don't worry, babe. You'll be back to normal soon."

As drinks and appetizers were delicately placed on the crisp table linen, the conversation between the two couples unfolded at a surprisingly enjoyable pace. Ann could feel the tension in Zane's forearms loosen as he and Denis stumbled upon their mutual love for classic rock. Even Rene ceased her petty attacks for the first thirty minutes of their meal.

Zane touched her about the same as he had during their first dinner out, but this time, every caress felt different. When his fingers slid up her neck, aimlessly tracing figure eights as he debated which band had the best harmonicist, Ann's mind automatically replayed the way he'd joined her in the shower earlier. Zane had shyly asked if he could wash her hair, and a different kind of pleasure had swept through Ann as his soapy fingers reverently massaged her skull.

Her attention snapped back to the present when Rene cleared her throat.

Caution should have been screaming in Ann's mind, but she'd been distracted by the way Zane glowed when he spoke about the various subgenres of rock. He looked incredible in yet another three-piece suit, this one a deep, absorptive black. Curious thoughts over why an audiobook narrator owned so many pristine suits were interrupted by her sister's rough voice.

"So, Zane, what kind of future do you envision for yourself?" Rene asked as the server slid a mouth-watering pasta dish in front of Zane.

The golden-seared filet of salmon settled beneath Ann's gaze was OnlyApp-worthy, but Ann was examining the artful presentation of French peas and roasted potatoes to keep her stomach from bottoming out.

Zane's fingers gathered hers under the table. "One with Ann in it."

Ann couldn't even enjoy the swelling sensation between her ribs because Rene was up to something.

Her sister struggled to keep the delighted wickedness out of her smile. "What else do you imagine about the future?"

The casualness in which Zane brought his glass of Cabernet to his lips, swallowing before speaking, obviously irked her sister. "Normal things."

"This lamb chop is perfection. Babe, why don't you try a bite?" Unlike at the dinner with his mother, Denis seemed to be picking up on the looming tension.

"Like children?"

Ann's head snapped up, her gaze zeroing in on her sister.

Rene didn't know about Caroline, didn't know that Zane already had a daughter. So this line of questioning only meant . . .

She wouldn't.

There had to be a limit to how far Rene would go to win this bet.

Rene's eyes flashed with victory, and Ann clenched Zane's hand like she'd gripped the bed rail on the stretcher in the ER before everything changed, before she left the hospital different.

Ann's mouth opened, but a strangled sound replaced her objection. Then Rene dropped the sentence that stunned the table to silence and caused the server to pivot mid-stride and retreat.

"Ann can't have children, so if that's something you want, she shouldn't be in your future."

The din of the restaurant was a deafening scream boomeranging in Ann's skull. Her throat tightened as the memory of the conversation that a sixteen-year-old version of herself overhead as the aftereffects of anesthesia wore off automatically played in her head. The words used to replay so often they should've been deemed inhumane. Like the way an interrogator shouldn't be able to play "Baby Shark" on repeat to crack their subject.

"No one will want to marry her now," Mom said. *"It's bad enough that she's so sporty and tall, now this."*

"Not everyone wants children." Her dad's voice was calm. *"It's not like she's ruined."*

Mom's words held a steely quality that tore through Ann's spine. "That's exactly it. Now she is."

Her father had already been asleep when a teenage Ann had approached her mother, complaining of abdominal pain. Mom had blown her off, citing premenstrual cramps, and told her to go back to her room. By two a.m., Ann had been crying and lying face down on the cool kitchen tiles, trying to get some relief. Once her father had found her, the rest of the early morning hours had been a whirlwind.

The darkness of her family's kitchen had been replaced by the blinding lights of the ER as doctors ruled out appendicitis, cholecystitis, and ovarian torsion. Before Ann knew it, she had been wheeled to the OR in the hopes of repairing a twisted ovary. The doctor's expression had sobered as she explained that if the organ had already undergone necrosis from lack of blood flow, she'd have to remove it. With torsion, she'd said, *time* is a primary factor in outcome.

Once Ann had fully regained consciousness and observed her parents' sullen faces, the doctor had returned. A prickling pause had settled over the noisy PACU as the doctor pulled in a breath.

"Unfortunately, I had to remove the ovary. And . . ." The doctor's *hesitation tightened an invisible grip on Ann's throat. ". . . your other ovary seems to be malformed and potentially nonfunctional."*

Then the doctor had launched into a litany of questions and tests that had revealed that Ann's inconsistent menstruation wasn't caused by her athleticism, but because she'd only possessed one functioning ovary. The one that had just been emergently removed.

"Excuse us." Denis almost wrenching Rene's arm out of its socket as he dragged her from the table was shocking enough to keep Ann's tears from dropping on her turquoise cloth napkin.

Ann stared unseeing at the space they'd vacated as Zane's fingers flexed irregularly around hers. After what felt like thirty minutes—but was merely seconds—the hostess arrived at the edge of their table with an apologetic grimace.

"Mr. Gannon and Ms. Powell say to send their regards, but they won't be returning to dine with you. Mr. Gannon has covered the bill and encourages you both to enjoy your meal."

Violas tangled in the background as a table across the room burst into laughter. Forks tinged and scraped against stylistically speckled ceramic plates. A bartender shook a stainless-steel shaker, slushing the ice and liquor.

That was one of the hardest things to accept about life.

Something can shatter you, but the world ruthlessly goes on turning.

Chapter 21

"I'm not broken," Ann blurted. Heat flushed over her skin as embarrassment swiftly replaced the shock still buzzing through her system.

Logically, Ann knew she wasn't broken. She knew that, even though she'd undergone surgically induced menopause at sixteen and had been on hormone replacement therapy ever since, she wasn't any less of a woman. She'd spent years processing her diagnosis and finding ways to deal with potential triggers, but the blatant way Rene had announced it to the table had knocked Ann's rationality off balance.

Because sometimes you can't logic your way through things. Sometimes, the emotional response bubbles up and demands to be dealt with. Even though Ann addressed this subject all the time—as it was a natural topic that came up as friends and coworkers had their own children, even though she reminded herself that she was lucky enough to nurture sixteen little souls every day, and even though Ann was grateful for everything she *did* have—that didn't mean that sorrow over what could have been didn't occasionally bludgeon each of her organs.

That was why she'd sobbed in Zane's arms last Friday. She'd wanted her mother to understand *why* going under dental anesthesia would be hard on her, that it would remind Ann of the night everything shifted. Mom not being there had been like working through the trauma of that day all over again.

"No, you're not." The compassion in Zane's voice was nearly intolerable.

The heavy seconds that passed were infiltrated with overstimulating restaurant noise. Because Ann had never dated, discussing future children had never been an issue. They'd barely begun a real relationship, but now that Zane knew kids weren't in the cards, she should give him a chance to leave.

Ann swallowed to keep the drowning feeling at bay, to not succumb to the pain sweeping her collarbones. Her dry lips parted, and she forced herself to say the words. "I understand if this changes things."

"*Ann.*"

Her chin dropped at the tortured way Zane said her name. Ann didn't want it to sound like that. She wanted it to sound like it had when he'd husked it into her ear before kissing his way down her neck.

"This doesn't change anything. Not for me."

Ann should have expected his immediate acceptance. He'd been that way with everything. But surprise reverberated her bones with a ferocity that made her teeth ache. When she finally felt strong enough to search his eyes, they mirrored the veracity of his words.

"Come walk with me." Zane brought her fingers to his mouth for a kiss. "It'll make it better. I promise."

It shamed her how much she leaned into Zane as her heels struggled over the pristine southwestern-patterned carpet. Ann didn't even have it in her to fight when Zane led her outside to the flawlessly constructed stone path, rambling from one part of the property to the other.

The temperature had dropped significantly, and sucking dry, chilly air into her lungs lessened the tension between her brows. The rhythmic sound of their shoes accompanying the evening sounds of the desert was surprisingly lulling. They were midway through their third circle of the path when Rene's sharp voice broke the steadying silence.

"You!" The poison-laden word was followed by the aggressive clicking of well-coordinated heels. "This is all your fault." Rene pushed her way between them, her eyes smoldering as she got within inches of Ann's face.

"How is any of this Ann's fault?" Zane's chest rose with his barked question.

"This isn't funny anymore," Rene said, ignoring Zane. "I know you're faking this whole thing so you can get the money from me, and it has to stop now." Rene punctuated that sentence with a pointed finger. "This mess is starting to affect my *very real* relationship." Her sister's voice quavered, fear sprinting through her expression before she tucked it away.

"It's not fake," Ann countered. Even if it'd started that way, it wasn't anymore.

"Come on." Rene's palm dug into her hip. "I can tell when you're lying about something. So what is it? Did you hire him?"

"No one hired me. I'm dating her," Zane growled. "In fact, I—"

"Sure," Rene interrupted with a dramatic eye roll. "Sure, you are. Whatever. It doesn't matter because the bet was never real. You never had a plus-one. You were always going to sit with Denis's great aunt."

Ann's cheeks burned as boiling oil incinerated her intestines.

Of course.

Of course, the bet had been fake. It had all been a plan for Ann to go on date after humiliating date, purely for her sister's sick enjoyment. Rene had anticipated her failure from the start.

This was usually the point where Ann would lock her knees, say whatever was needed to get out of the situation, and find a quiet, private place to cry. But instead, she was caught in a rapid slideshow of her life.

Across the inky, star-speckled sky, flickers of her childhood slashed in saturated colors. As each image pierced her retinas, it was like tectonic plates shifted beneath her. Her left foot staggered to the side against the earthquake jolt only she was experiencing. Zane's hand steadied her elbow as understanding solidified.

In the short month she'd been fake dating Zane, he'd shown her more compassion than Rene had in a lifetime. Ann had expected each revealed layer of her personality to repulse him, but it had only drawn him closer. Even now, the worried way his eyes surveyed each beat of her eyelashes was breathtaking.

Ann expected sorrow to accompany the spiky revelation streaking through her soul, but only exhaustion resonated.

Three thousand ways to react slipped through her bloodstream before only one remained. It was time to defend the tender softness that lived within her the same way she'd protect one of her students.

Ann swallowed the boulder crushing her windpipe. "Please apologize to Denis, but I won't be able to make it."

Zane's hand gave a nearly imperceptible squeeze on her elbow.

"You what?"

"I—" Her voice cracked, her first attempt at self-preservation stumbly. "I'm not coming."

"You—" Rene blinked, her head shaking subtly. "You can't do that. You can't not come. What will Priscilla think?"

Ann fixed a serene look on her face even though scorpions were stinging down her spine. "You should have thought of that before you used me as a pawn."

She took a shaky step away from her sister, and Zane was there, his arm banding around her shoulders.

Sputtering resounded before Rene spurted, "This will *crush* Dad."

Zane's arm tightened.

When Ann glanced up with a minuscule nod, he let go, stepping back.

"I think what would crush Dad is knowing that his youngest daughter is a snake." Ann halted her advancing steps, calming herself with an audible breath. "But I'm not going to tell him any of that because I love him, and he needs to focus on his health and not our squabbles."

"I love our father too," Rene countered.

"Like you love Denis? As someone to provide for you and then toss aside? Like you've done with your previous husbands?" Her sister's cheeks flushed like she'd been slapped.

"What's going to happen is I'm going to walk away. I'm done with you always pointing out that I'm less than you. You win, okay? You're prettier. You're better. You're the prize that everyone wants, but I was never trying to compete with you, Rene. I was just trying to be your sister."

Ann spun and strode away. Saying no to Rene felt like there were six needles pushing beneath her pinky nail, but she kept moving.

Zane was at her elbow in an instant.

"I was wrong." He blew out a large breath when they re-entered the building. "I thought the most attractive thing you could do was deadlift me, but nothing beats watching you stand up for yourself. That was . . ." A hushed expletive left his mouth. "That was magnificent."

Zane was trying to lift her up. Maybe even trying to get her to smile, but numbness was already spiraling through her muscles.

"I want to go home." Her words were barely a murmur as adrenaline crashed swiftly into fatigue.

"Of course," Zane said. "Let's pack up, and we're out of here."

◊◊◊

Zane's thumb on the steering wheel was twitchier than it'd been on the drive up. When they reentered Tucson city limits, he cleared his throat.

"I know you wanted to go home, but I hate the idea of you being alone right now. If that's truly what you need, I understand, but I'd prefer you come back to my house."

"Completely platonic," he quickly added. "I've got a guest room you could stay in. And if you're hungry, I could make you something. Or you could just snuggle up with Marley. He's good with"—Zane paused and swallowed—"things like this."

Ann kept her gaze on the black stuffed cat dangling from his rearview mirror, seizing the opportunity to talk about anything other than the fact that she'd just upended her family life.

"Did you name your cat Marley after the singer?"

Zane took a tiny sip of air. "No. That was his shelter name when we adopted him." He let a few beats of silence pass before adding, "A few months after Tessa was diagnosed, we thought it would be good to distract Caroline with a pet. That sounds heartless, but so much was going wrong then. We just wanted something good for her."

Ann nodded, her eyes still trained on the road ahead.

"I'd expected Caroline to pick a kitten. Something as young and frisky as she'd been. But Caroline had walked straight past a veritable basket of them toward Marley, the skinny ten-year-old hiding in the corner, stating 'he needed looking after.' After that, I took care of Tessa, and Caroline took care of Marley. Though things went up and down with Tessa, Marley only got chubby and more sociable. His favorite thing is to sit in your lap and purr."

Ann smiled at Caroline's mature actions. Zane's daughter was usually the first to ask if a fellow student needed a companion, if they were sitting alone on the playground, to make sure everyone was included in recess games. For all of her rigidity and occasional sass, Caroline's tiny ribs housed a compassionate heart.

"I'd like to meet him."

"Yeah?"

Her chest squeezed at the breathless quality of that question.

Normally, she'd use a hard workout session or time alone to work through whatever latest trauma her family had thrown at her, but for the first time in her life, Ann had someone who'd proven to her that she could lean on him.

Ann nodded again, this time looking over and getting swept up in everything Zane: the music reverberating around him, his curls shifting in the slight breeze that blew in from the cracked window, his expressive eyes.

"You won't regret it." Zane's lopsided grin grew. "He's a cuddling pro."

Chapter 22

This spiky unease kept sprinting over his muscles with each item Ann touched. Tessa hadn't cared about decor when they'd moved in. She would have happily left each wall white and forgone decorations, but Zane had lived his whole life with artists. Once he'd had the opportunity and income to customize his home, he'd done so with aplomb.

Now, he wanted to know what Ann thought of his efforts. Her whimsical decor had brought a smile to his lips. It was so perfectly *her*. Did his bring her that same feeling?

His breath unintentionally sucked between his teeth when her fingers trailed over his record collection. Above the custom shelving for his vinyls, a recycled wood countertop held his record player. It was one of three, but the other two were relegated to display only. Caroline's artwork nestled in black frames on the dark-green eucalyptus wallpaper beyond, while brass lamps evened out the space.

Nothing about the interior of his house hinted at its southwestern location. Instead, it held sharp, dark accents, clean lines, and a subdued color pallet more traditionally used in northwestern design. His neighbor, Gwen, had often remarked that she half-expected to step outside into the dewy, Douglas-fir forests of Vancouver instead of his arid, xeriscaped backyard each time she had a plein air lesson with Caroline.

"Do you want to hear something?" Zane asked.

Ann hadn't spoken since she'd entered his home. A pressure had been mounting beneath his collarbones in direct correlation to her silence.

"I wouldn't know what to pick."

He shifted toward her, careful to keep himself a safe distance away as he collected Van Morrison's *Moondance* and set it on the player. It was important Ann understood he'd meant what he'd said earlier. He had no ulterior motives for her being here. The idea of her crumpling into her comfortable couch and crying into the cushions had simply made him want to vomit.

A few seconds of scratchy rasp sounded before "And It Stoned Me" poured from the speakers.

"Most people like this one." Zane allowed himself one slow sweep of her face as she watched the record spin.

"Let's see what Marley is up to. Normally, he trots right over when I get home. Marley? Here, kitty." A few automatic kissing sounds came from his lips as Zane wandered halfway down the hallway. "I brought you a friend."

"Zane?" The unsure nature of his name made him turn.

Ann was hugging her elbows, staring at the hardwood floor. "I think I made a mistake."

The agony hit his chest first, radiating outward in racing streaks until even his toes felt like they were on fire. His knuckles rubbed a pearled button into his sternum.

A part of him had been expecting Ann to say something along these lines. If he didn't need to be her fake date to the wedding, if the bet was off, there was no reason for them to continue . . . this.

Whatever *this* was.

They hadn't even had a chance to discuss it yet, but he'd assumed being intimate with her meant they were real now. It certainly was for him.

"It's okay. I can take you home."

Ann's brow crinkled as her chin lifted, her gaze catching his. "What?"

His fingers tugged at the collar of his shirt, left open when he'd unbuttoned it earlier. "What mistake did you make?"

"With Rene. I should apologize." Ann looked at him for reassurance. "I should apologize and tell her I didn't mean what I said. That, of course, I'll come. It's her *wedding*."

Zane remained silent, feeling Ann had set a healthy boundary earlier.

"Not going to her wedding feels like slicing off my arm at the socket. Like there's no going back."

For a second, Zane wavered. It wasn't his life, his relationship. Every family had their own dynamic. But then he remembered the multiple times he'd seen Ann with her students, with her fellow teachers, relaxed and in her environment, versus how small she seemed to shrink when surrounded by her supposed loved ones.

"You shouldn't text her." He took a small step forward. "You shouldn't apologize. What you did tonight was the kindest, most graceful way to stand up to someone who's been benefiting from your humiliation for decades." Zane intentionally loosened the tension building in his fingers. "There's no good reason for a grown woman to treat her sister that way. Stand your ground because you deserve so much more."

His thoughts were racing quicker than his words, wanting to tell her that he'd give it all to her, whatever she needed. Zane let out a measured breath to keep that last part to himself.

"Don't text her," he said instead.

Ann blinked, her mouth parted, for several beats. "Okay."

His body ached with the desire to touch her, stretching and expanding to the point of pain, but he maintained the distance between them.

"I think—I think I needed to hear that. This last month has been . . ." She slumped against the hallway wall as if she couldn't support her frame any longer. Zane forced his dress shoes to stay rooted to his spot instead of swooping her into his arms like he wanted to. "I'm beginning to think that I'm the problem."

"You're not the problem." His voice was as abrasive as a brick to the jaw.

Ann stared for a moment, eyes wide and locked on his like they'd been earlier . . . when she'd been beneath him. Zane chased that memory away, focusing back on now.

"I just mean that I'm the one that's allowing Rene to use me as a punching bag. We've always bickered. We're sisters." Ann shrugged. "But it's been worse the last few years."

"When Dad was first diagnosed, I wanted to be sure that if he needed anything, I'd be there. It was right after I'd been accepted onto the faculty at Hillcrest. The friends I'd made at my old school fell away as I stopped spending time with them to focus on pouring myself into my new job and spending my free time at home, making sure Dad didn't need help doing all the normal chores that now made him breathless."

Her shoulders rose and fell with a large sigh. "It's surprisingly easy to prioritize yourself last when someone you love is suffering. But since I've been with you, I'm noticing things."

Though Zane tried to keep his attention on Ann's words, it kept tripping and falling over the phrase "been with you."

"Things that my sister and—to a lesser extent—my mom do that other people, like Kennedy and you," Ann paused, "don't."

Zane recalled Ann happily chatting about her co-worker and gym buddy, Kennedy, as they got ready for dinner. His fingers had been massaging his styling cream into his curls, but his heart had been bubbling with joy on Ann's behalf. He couldn't imagine navigating life without his friends at his side.

"I think I'm a bit of a doormat."

"Could you—" Zane halted his giant step forward with a fist to his thigh. Softening his tone, he brushed his suit jacket aside to tuck his hands in his pants pockets. "Could you please have this revelation without calling yourself names? It's not your fault. Even if you now realize that you should've stood up for yourself more, you shouldn't have been walked over in the first place."

Bluesy saxophone resonated from the main room as Ann's shoulders slid back, and she nodded once.

"Okay, good." He ran his hand over his chin. "Are you hungry? Can I make you something?"

Her jaw softened, and she bit the corner of her lip. "Could we make flapjacks?"

Man, she was sweet. He'd been surviving on burnt toast and tannic coffee, and Ann was a dollop of wildflower honey whipped with butter.

Ann's eyebrows knotted at his smile. "What?"

Disbelief that she was here, alone with him, kept flushing over his ribs, but it didn't hamper the broadness of his grin. "I've never met anyone who uses the word flapjacks."

The slightest bashfulness swept her brow, and the urge to kiss it almost undid him.

Zane turned. "I've got some Bisquick. Let's see if we can lure Marley out of hiding with a can of soft food."

He took off his jacket on his way into the kitchen, discarding it on a black-leathered, mid-century chair with wooden arms and legs. It was only after the griddle was warming and all the ingredients and supplies were on his center island that Zane noticed Ann watching his forearms flex as he rolled up his sleeves.

"Why do you have so many suits?" she asked absently. "Most people who work from home don't own this much formal wear."

His fingers paused halfway up his left forearm, his brain fumbling over a suitable lie before everything in him stilled. In that halting moment, another song began, the swinging beat half-timing his racing heartbeat.

Zane wasn't going to layer another interaction with Ann in falsehood. He'd strived to be honest and open with almost everyone in his life, but he'd never felt he could be with her because of the way this had all started. But now, Ann was here without needing to keep up the façade of him being her wedding date. If they were going to move forward, Zane wanted it to be on fresh ground.

"Because this was who you needed me to be." He met her gaze.

A frown twisted her lips, and though Zane steeled himself against its impact, it punched him in the solar plexus. "That must have been expensive."

"It was worth it."

Zane wanted Ann with a ferocity he hadn't known was possible, but more than that, he needed Ann to know—to fully understand in the depths of her soul—that she was worth *everything*.

As expected, Ann struggled with his answer. Years of viewing herself as less than weren't going to be undone overnight.

A soft meow broke the tension as Marley wove between Ann's legs.

"Hi there." She glanced at his black American shorthair. "You must be Marley."

"Why don't you feed him while I get this going?" Zane handed her the cat food and a small dish.

While Ann crouched to feed and pet the very lucky feline, Zane mixed the batter, adding cinnamon last. The sound of the air conditioning clicking on matched that of a squeaky swing, maddening in its irregularity. He made a mental note to find the origin and fix it before he began recording again.

Zane stopped the timer four seconds before it was done and set it back on the island before plating the pancakes. They were three bites into their maple-syrup-covered stacks, standing kitty-corner over the island, when Ann reached for and zeroed out the timer.

The corner of his mouth lifted. "Caroline hates when I do that too."

Ann wrinkled her nose. "I tried to warn you that I do things like this." She set her fork beside her plate. "If we're going to do this, you should know what you're getting into."

Zane's heartbeat kicked up because Ann was talking like they were a couple, but since he always wanted her to feel heard, he asked, "What kinds of things do you do?"

"You know about the weird food combos and my crazy family, but with the way I grew up . . ." She blew out a pursed breath. "I have to keep everything in my home in a specific way, or I can't sleep."

"Okay." He kept his tone even and open.

"I just—" Her expression clouded before it dropped to her wiggling toes. "I don't want my habits to change the way you look at me."

Zane's shoulders rose with an uneven inhale. "How do I look at you?"

The way Ann glanced up made his heart crack open, blood staining his hardwood floor. She struggled over a rough swallow, opening her mouth and then pressing her lips together.

"Like I'm the person you've been waiting for."

His restraint was a single string of spider silk, efficiently snapped. Ann's soft warmth filled his hands as Zane slid his palms up her arms.

How could she be so nervous about him liking her when he'd never seen anything more beautiful in his life? Ann was simultaneously strong and feminine, organized and quirky, earnest and playful. Her deltoids tensed as he leaned forward, but she didn't pull away, so he let his lips brush hers. The featherlight touch was like an EMP explosion, reorienting his nervous system in its wake.

"*Ann,*" he murmured, unable to create any meaningful words with her lips on his.

Her blissful humming noise made letting go impossible. His hands skirted up her neck to frame her face at the same time her fingers clenched the vest at the base of his spine. They came crashing together in that way, the way that felt only possible between *them*. He'd dated, been married, and still, nothing had ever felt the way it did with Ann.

Zane was losing his mind over her, losing his heart. Every part of herself that she viewed as undesirable set a thick, thrumming pulse through him like a plucked bass string. Her frequency and his were perfectly in tune. It was otherworldly.

When her hands pushed up his back and into his hair, Zane set his glasses on the kitchen island.

"I love that," she said between kisses.

"What?"

"When you take your glasses off. The sound of them clanking on the counter sends anticipation spiraling through me."

A growl escaped as Zane gripped her waist. How could she be so articulate while he was reduced to caveman-like noises? Never in his life had he been so verbally incoherent. All he did every day was talk. Vocabulary crowded his brain like a swarm of angry hornets, refusing to organize in a logical manner. Since he couldn't string two words together, he'd have to show her that nothing she could do would make him want to leave.

"I don't want to stay in the guest room." When Ann breathed this against his mouth, that perfectly in-sync feeling flooded his bloodstream again.

"No." He set the hoarse word over her ear before kissing his way down her neck. "You don't belong there." Zane let the implication hover and felt her responsive shudder.

Good. They were on the same page.

Ann belonged with him, beside him, *beneath* him.

Even though he could have easily lifted her onto his kitchen countertop, Zane backed Ann toward his bedroom. When the sun broke through the windows tomorrow, he wanted his sheets to carry the scent of sweet orange blossom.

Chapter 23

Marley's soft fur filtered through Ann's fingers as the chirpy yips of the Gambel's quail sounded from beyond the sliding door in front of them. Pressing one hand against the frame, Ann tilted her head to see the corner of the backyard. A low stucco wall separated Zane's backyard from the strip of desert between his property and his neighbor's. Below a spinning windcatcher grabbing little gulps of air, seven tiny balls of fluff with legs scurried after their mama, her comma-shaped topknot of feathers quivering as they darted in and out of the flowering brittlebush.

Ann dipped her head to mutter to Marley, giving him near-silent instructions like she would to a student struggling with spelling. "You better not think about snacking on those baby quail."

Marley lifted his chin with an *I would never* stare, earning a tender scratch. It was decided. Ann needed a cat. Marley's vibrating body in her lap provided the perfect antidote to the cool hardwood floor beneath her crossed legs.

Despite not having her routine of being at home, the morning had been peaceful. An hour ago, she'd left a sleeping Zane and quietly drew the heavy curtains against the cheerful sunbeams. Marley had greeted her as soon as she'd closed the bedroom door, and Ann had fed him before unpacking the same supplies they'd used last night to make another round of flapjacks. Marley received a banana slice after confirming with a quick internet search that it was safe for him to eat.

Ann wasn't one to snoop, but when Marley had kept meowing at one particular door, Ann opened it to find Zane's recording studio. Trying her hand at being a voice actor, she let one deeply throated, "In a world . . ." escape her lips into the microphone before embarrassment over being caught forced her out of the compact space.

Since then, she and Marley had planted themselves in front of this glass door. Ann was watching the fiery cluster of red flowers atop the ocotillo plant for hummingbirds when Etta James's voice broke through the silence. The Sunday morning lyrics made Ann smile rather than jump at the sudden noise. She liked the idea of Zane's records whispering a soundtrack to his day.

"Good morning," he said, stepping beside her.

The broken-gravel-tumbling-through-a-cement-pipe quality of his voice made her eyes flutter closed. Ann had never spent the morning after with a man, had never heard how his voice sounded first thing. Zane's voice was hypnotizing at noon on a Tuesday. It was almost incapacitating like this.

"What are we looking at?"

"Baby quail." Ann chanced a glance upward. His strong jawline, broad shoulders, and moppy, bed-mussed curls snagged her attention before his lopsided grin turned her way.

"Are we having flapjacks again?"

She shrugged one shoulder even though her breath hitched at his affectionate gaze. "I told you breakfast was my favorite. You didn't have enough eggs for omelets. I couldn't find any bacon, so I cut some fruit to make it different from last night."

Zane's grin broadened. "You won't find any bacon, since I'm a vegetarian, but I'm pretty sure I've got some veggie sausage in the freezer."

After falling apart in each other's arms last night, they'd reheated their cold flapjacks and spent the rest of the evening chatting on his cozy outdoor seating area. It felt like a first date, though they'd been on several already. They'd weaved each of their college experiences together, trying to find a time where they might have intersected.

Then they'd tackled parts of their childhoods. Ann had tiptoed around her family's drama like she often side-stepped her mother's hoarded knick-knacks, highlighting the good moments. She spoke mostly about her father driving her to youth soccer games, playing catch with her in the short gravel driveway in front of their modest home, and being embarrassingly loud when she'd received her Bachelor of Education—the first college degree in her family.

Eventually, they changed for bed and lay side by side as Ann relished in learning the details of Zane growing up in LA. She asked questions about sound studios and movie sets and the intricacies of how many people were involved in making even a small film.

Vegetarianism hadn't come up.

"Oh, no."

He huffed out a breathy laugh. "Oh, no?"

"I love bacon. Behind flapjacks, it's my favorite breakfast food." She bit her lip. "Is that a deal breaker?"

Zane extended his hand to help her off the floor. "You can eat as much bacon as you want. I just won't join you."

Shiny sparks flashed up her arms when her fingers slid into his. "Maybe we should talk about deal breakers, though," she said, standing, much to Marley's disapproval.

"Ann." His hands slipped around her waist, drawing her into him. "Do you know how many years it's been since I slept in?"

Her brows crinkled at the swift topic change. With how late they were up chatting last night, Ann was surprised *she* hadn't slept longer.

"Eight," Zane continued. "I'm pretty sure you could wear a bacon dress and I'd still want to be with you."

Ann's heart was punching her chin as her brain scrambled with a way to deflect. Eight years? What did that mean?

"Didn't someone do that?"

Zane nodded, his face tilting down. "Lady Gaga."

"Right." Her swallow was audible.

"What are your deal breakers?" he murmured, the heat of his loosely wrapped arms searing through her.

This.

But since her mouth was drier than a sun-soaked sidewalk in June, Ann couldn't get out the words. She couldn't state that one of her biggest fears was love itself. Zane wasn't going to take advantage of or hurt her. Ann knew that in her core, so it had to be her that would cause the damage. If this continued, she'd somehow destroy him.

Was she a horrible person that she didn't want to stop being with him even with that knowledge?

Yes.

Decidedly, yes.

"Is that my Marshall Tucker Band shirt?" Impossibly, Zane's voice had dropped another octave.

Ann would like to say that she'd carelessly thrown the shirt on instead of searching through her luggage for the blousy top that went with these shorts, but she'd taken her time in his en suite closet. The door had closed with a whisper, and she'd let her fingers traverse each hung shirt, a ghost of a smile pulling at her cheek when she slipped this beige shirt off its lightly padded hanger. The man took care of his clothes. She hadn't recognized the band name but had liked the horse drawn in the sunset circle and the way it held Zane's subtle sandalwood scent.

"Are you trying to kill me?" This question was accompanied by Zane squeezing her fully to him.

"No," she said weakly.

"You're doing a terrible job of it."

Sweeping strings supported Etta's strong voice as she crescendoed into the next verse, while Zane's lips decimated any lingering thoughts of staying away from him.

Her hands gripped the back of his neck a second before her phone rang on the counter.

"Can you ignore it?" Zane's fingers were gathering the hem of her borrowed shirt.

Ann tilted her head back with a steadying inhale. "Only my dad or my boss call me."

Brief disappointment sprinkled into the pink flush on his perfectly sculpted cheekbones before Zane let go of her. "I'll work on breakfast." He stooped to give Marley a quick scratch before moving into the kitchen.

"Hey," Ann said, answering the unexpected call from Kennedy as she padded into the connected living room.

"Ann, hi. Oh, good. You picked up." Her friend's usually bubbly voice quavered.

"What's wrong?" Her toes clenched the green patterned rug as the distinct sound of medical machinery pinged in the background. Ann's stomach dipped, and nausea swept over her like a storm wind. "Where are you?"

"Tucson General," Kennedy said with a sniff. "In the ER. Matt's out of town for work, and I didn't know who else to call."

"I'll be right there." Ann took one stride toward the bedroom before remembering that she didn't have her car and spun into Zane's firm chest.

"Where are we going?" His blond brows were tense.

"Who's that?" Kennedy asked.

"I'll explain later," she said into the phone. "Call me back if you need me, but I'm on my way."

◊◊◊

Since Zane said there was no earthly way he was dropping her off, Ann left him in the waiting room with his tablet while she followed the admitting assistant back into the bustling emergency room. A weird wash of gratitude over having an empty stomach traipsed through her body. The bile flicking at her tongue would have ruined her favorite breakfast. Ann hated being here, in this place that brought forth her worst memories, but hated the idea of Kennedy being alone more.

Several patients were lying on stretchers in the hallway, including a man muttering about giant spiderwebs on the ceiling, but Kennedy was resting in a glass-doored private room.

"Hey," Ann said, slipping into the maroon chair beside her friend.

Kennedy almost pulled out her IV and disconnected the pulse oximeter attached to her finger when she flung herself over the side to hug Ann.

"Okay, okay." Ann repositioned herself to the edge of the bed, rubbing Kennedy's back in circles.

"I'm so scared." The watery words made Ann's chest seize.

She waited a few beats before asking, "Can you tell me what's going on?"

Kennedy nodded and leaned back to meet Ann's gaze. "I'm pregnant. I haven't told anyone yet because I'm still coming to grips with how my IUD failed. So far, everything's been fine, except for some slight early morning nausea, but at the gym today, I started bleeding a little." Tears streamed down her flushed cheeks. "Just because I didn't expect to be pregnant doesn't mean that I don't want this baby. It's mine and Matt's."

Ann anticipated that familiar gnawing sensation to pinch at her core before crawling through every muscle fiber in her body. With what happened last night, she'd expected tears to rush forward, rendering her unable to give the support Kennedy needed. But instead, a new resonance pulsed through her—hope. A different kind of yearning surged between her ribs because, more than anything, she wanted things to be okay for Kennedy. Ann hoped with everything in her that she got to see her sunny friend hold her healthy child.

And in that moment of hopefulness, the remaining tension that had hovered over her temples abated. As much as Ann knew she couldn't have *one specific* future, that didn't mean that a thousand others weren't possible. If Ann truly wanted a child of her own, she could adopt or foster. She could become the best aunt that Kennedy's baby had ever seen. If things continued with Zane, she could potentially be a stepparent to Caroline. *She* was in control of her future, not one tragic event that happened years ago.

Ann hugged her friend as tightly as she could without hurting her. "I'm right here. I'm going to be right here holding your hand the whole time, no matter what happens, okay?"

Kennedy heaved with a shuddered breath. "Okay."

A quick rap on the glass preceded, "Mrs. Owens? This is Cassidy from ultrasound. Can I come in?"

Kennedy's dark eyes held Ann's as she answered, "Yes."

Cassidy started the ultrasound, immediately confirming that the baby had a viable heartbeat. Relief was almost a visual color change in Kennedy's skin the second that rhythmic *woomp-woomp* echoed off the bland, beige walls. Both of them could have been in a grip strength competition with how they squeezed each other's fingers. The technician confirmed the baby's seventeen-week gestation and made some silent notes before stating that the doctor would be in to review the findings since she wasn't licensed to reveal them herself.

"Baby looks good, though." She gave Kennedy's shoulder a pat before wheeling the ultrasound machine out the door.

Not too much later, a physician with gray in his beard and gentle eyes began asking Kennedy questions. He bristled when Kennedy stated she hadn't been informed of the fact that she had placenta previa at her ten-week ultrasound.

"They should have told you." He shook his head before going through the lifestyle changes she'd need to prevent future bleeding, like not lifting more than twenty pounds, avoiding strenuous exercise, and not standing for more than four hours at a time. "Since you're not having any pain or contractions, the spotting should stop. If it doesn't, come back and see us."

They both thanked the doctor, and he disappeared into the river of activity and noise beyond Kennedy's room.

"I'll teach lying on the floor if that means I get to keep this little bean." Kennedy patted her barely detectable bump, smiling. "I'm sorry we won't be able to be workout buddies for a while."

"You heard the doctor. Walking and lifting low weights are safe. You'll just have to do a hundred five-pound bicep curls instead of your usual heavy ones."

"Oh, joy." Kennedy's laugh filled the sterile room like light obliterating darkness.

Thirty minutes later, the bleeding had stopped. In a moment of calm, while Kennedy was snuggled into a warmed blanket, sipping on an apple juice box, Ann texted Zane.

Ann: *She's okay. We're waiting on discharge paperwork now.*

Ann didn't disclose why Kennedy had been here, not seeing that it was her information to share. When Kennedy decided to announce her pregnancy, Ann would tell Zane then.

Zane: *Good. Anything I can do?*

Ann: *No. Thanks, though.*

Zane: *I'll be out here when you're ready.*

"What's that smile about? Is that the *deep voice* I heard on the phone earlier?" Kennedy winked.

After being given an essential good bill of health, it seemed her friend was back to her jokey antics.

"Maybe." Ann felt the corner of her mouth twitch.

Kennedy squealed like a teenager before swatting at Ann. "You're seeing someone, and you didn't tell me?"

"You're going to send the nurse running in here if you keep jumping around like that," Ann admonished, still a little worried, even though the doctor said Kennedy should be fine.

"What's his name?" Kennedy sing-songed.

"Zane." The word was out before her brain was smart enough to stop it.

Kennedy's dark eyebrows hit her hairline. "Hot single dad? You snagged hot single dad? The one we ran into at the gym? I thought there was some tension there, but I brushed it off since I'm known to imagine things."

Ann's lips twitched, repressing a smile. "You weren't imagining."

Another laugh punched from Kennedy, and Ann's eyes instinctively went to her friend's shaking belly.

"Stop looking so stressed." Her brow wrinkled playfully. "I'm fine. You heard."

"How can you swing from terrified to everything's okay, just like that?" Ann's heartbeat seemed to have taken permanent residence in her left eardrum.

Kennedy tenderly stroked her stomach. "When I went to the bathroom a moment ago, Cassidy stopped me in the hall and asked if I wanted to know if it was a boy or a girl. I know I should've consulted Matt first, but I had to know." Her face was luminescent. "It's a girl. I have no doubt now that this little one is here to stay. Girls are fighters. She's strong like me."

Ann's smile reflected her friend's light back at her. "I'm sure she is."

As the nurse wheeled her to the waiting room, Kennedy jabbered about how much she wanted eegee's ranch fries. Ann smiled. Zane probably wouldn't mind a pit stop at one of his favorite restaurants.

Matt had called to say his flight would be in within the hour, so Ann planned to drive Kennedy's car back to her house and stay with her friend. Zane had texted saying he'd follow behind and wait too.

Except, when they got to the waiting room, Zane wasn't there.

Ann texted, assuming he'd stepped away to get a coffee or something. When several minutes passed without a response, she called, only for it to ring through to his voicemail. Brushing away the disappointment, Ann turned to Kennedy.

"Slight change in plans."

Varied explanations buzzed around Ann's head like springtime gnats. Zane obviously had something important to attend to at a moment's notice. He wasn't getting back to her because his phone must have died.

Throughout their drive, Kennedy added her own explanations—from the practical to the grandiose. Though her friend was trying to make her feel better, suggesting Zane had been abducted by aliens for being the finest male specimen, Ann couldn't help the feeling of abandonment from swelling in her belly.

Chapter 24

His phone was pinging more rapidly than a busy diner kitchen window as Zane accelerated around another slowpoke driver on Speedway. Clips and phrases of Tessa's rushed speech kept pummeling his skull. ". . . can't find her." ". . . looked everywhere." ". . . missing."

After breakfast, Isaac, Tessa, and Caroline had begun painting Caroline's new teal room, when she excused herself to the bathroom. When Caroline didn't return, Tessa went to see if she was okay and found her school backpack and sketching journal gone, the front door unlocked.

His phone rang, and before Zane could pick up Ann's call via his Bluetooth system, Tessa's call rang over it.

"We found my laptop open to an aerial map," Tessa rushed when he answered, neither of them bothering with greetings.

A hushed curse left his lips as Zane swung left through an intersection. "Of what?"

"The house. Isaac's house," she corrected.

Zane knew the neighborhood. His SUV was careening toward it. Once Tessa had announced that she and Isaac were moving in, she'd given Zane the house address and assured that Caroline would have her own bedroom, her own space to decompress. Zane had had Isaac's phone number for months, having met him early on in their relationship. Since then, he'd been effortlessly folded into their co-parenting routine.

When he nearly clipped a Hyundai, Zane tapped the brakes and tried to still the frantic desperation ripping at his chest. He couldn't help if he got into an accident.

"But it's zoomed out enough that your house is on it too." Tessa's voice cracked. "I think she might be trying to walk to you."

Zane blinked to keep his vision from swimming. The distance between their homes was almost four miles. Caroline might be the most self-sufficient child he'd ever met, but she was still only eight. And aside from being his visual doppelgänger, his daughter took after the tiny women in his family.

"Did you—"

"I already called Gwen. She's on her way over to wait for Caroline. My parents are driving through your neighborhood, Isaac's driving this one, and I'm staying put just in case, but . . . there's so much ground to cover."

Both Zane and Tessa were low-tech parents and hadn't bought Caroline a tracking watch or tag for her backpack. She never took a bus to school, so it hadn't seemed necessary. Caroline was always with a parent, grandparent, one of her uncles, or walking on the paver stepstones Zane had placed between his backyard and Gwen's.

Frustration and impotence clawed at the taut tendons in his neck.

"What's the timeline again?"

"I—I don't know. I'm guessing fifteen to thirty minutes. We were busy painting, and you know how Caroline can squirrel away and then get distracted by sketching." A sob echoed over the line. "I honestly thought I'd find her at the kitchen counter, her tongue between her teeth, working on a new drawing."

"I know." Zane let calm he didn't feel imbue his voice. "It's not your fault. I would have thought the same thing."

Caroline had a habit of removing herself from others and spending long periods alone. It'd worried them initially, but then they discovered that, unlike both of them, Caroline was simply an introvert, happy in her own company. Their two-year-old daughter used to say, "Nigh-nigh," grab her baby blanket, and lay herself in her toddler bed for a nap. They'd been the envy of their library storytime group. Later, when Tessa had been diagnosed, Caroline's penchant for independence had been advantageous.

"Did you check the wash?"

A dry, sandy riverbed that only held water briefly during monsoon season—known to locals as a wash—ran between Isaac's property and the houses behind. Caroline had mentioned it was one of her favorite parts of Isaac's house, besides the pool.

"No. That's a good idea." Zane could hear the hesitation in her voice.

"Stay where you are. I'm almost there. I'll park and then check it."

After leaving his car in Isaac's driveway and a quick hug to a shaking Tessa, Zane sprinted down the wash. The deep, beach-like sand sprayed at the back of his legs with each stride. Gratitude that he'd selected sneakers this morning, instead of his standard leather flip-flops, tapped at his temple.

Knowing if Caroline had walked this way was indiscernible, the eight-foot-wide riverbed had been recently traversed by horses, their hoof prints marring the otherwise even terrain. Regardless, he kept moving, needing to rule out each possibility. Sweat dripped down the side of his face as he followed the slight curve, already a mile from the house.

His feet staggered, and Zane almost fell when it became clear that the horses had trotted out of the wash, and Caroline's small footprints continued on. Zane ran faster. Soon this riverbed would intersect the main road, after which there'd be no way to know which way his daughter had gone.

Dread was billowing in his chest, choking him, suffocating his nostrils. Zane struggled for breath until another curve revealed a small colorful ball in the center of the otherwise beige, brown, and green landscape.

"Caroline!" The sound emitting from his throat when she looked up from her crouched, shoe-tying position was inhuman.

His muscles burned, but Zane pushed even harder to close the distance, collapsing into the dirt to wrap his daughter in his arms. A persistent ringing obliterated the sounds of the desert and Caroline's insistent, "Dad."

"Dad." She tapped his chest from her squished position. "Dad. I'm okay."

"What were you thinking?" A hoarse croaking had replaced his normal voice.

"I had it all planned." Zane loosened his arms enough to see her face. "I had four bottles of water, snacks, and a first aid kit. I used sunscreen before I left. I even drew a map."

"Caroline."

She winced at his admonishing tone before her face crumbled. "They made banana pancakes. They made banana pancakes and were dancing in the kitchen like it was completely normal. Like they had a right to do that. That was *our* thing—what we did after Mom had a good day. He doesn't get to do that with us. He wasn't *there*. He didn't have to go through any of it." Gushing tears dampened her thick blonde lashes.

"Oh, honey." Zane pulled his daughter to his chest again, stroking her heaving back.

His phone buzzed in his pocket, but Zane ignored it. Brittlebrush exploded with yellow beneath a trio of thriving creosote plants steps beyond where he sat in the sun-warmed sand, rocking his daughter. A slight breeze tousled his hair into his eyes, and he blew out of the corner of his mouth to relocate the lock.

All these sensations took a backstage position to the feeling of his daughter's ribs expanding against him, her hair tickling his chin. Understanding that Caroline was safe was gradually filtering into his brain, but his arms had yet to relinquish their desperate grip.

"I'm sorry," Caroline squeaked before rubbing her forehead to his chest. "I just wanted to be home. This isn't home."

As much as Zane wanted to comfort her, to say it was okay, it wasn't. No part of putting herself in danger would ever be okay.

"Please don't do anything like this again. Please call me. I would have gotten you."

"But you were camping with your friend Micha." A hiccup punctuated the end of that sentence.

Squeezing pain tightened the muscles of his back as his mind exploded with alternate endings to this day. If she'd made it to the main road . . .

He shook his head, dispelling the terrifying thought. What needed to be done was clear, but first they had to get out of the midday heat. It was already pushing ninety degrees, even though it wasn't even halfway through April.

"Call me anyway. I will drive home. I will stop everything. I will do whatever it takes, Caroline. Please don't put yourself in danger again."

His daughter's tearful gaze met his, and she wiped her nose with her forearm before nodding.

"Okay," Zane said, hugging her tighter.

After calling Tessa, Isaac picked them up. A long family meeting stretched into the late-afternoon hours. Caroline opened up about how she felt about the move, how it added a layer of permanence to Isaac and Tessa's relationship she hadn't expected. It was difficult to watch Caroline struggle to express how hard the change had been, and with each of his daughter's watery words, Zane's mouth felt as dry as the wash he'd just escaped.

He couldn't add another complication to Caroline's already shaky life.

When everyone dispersed, Zane drove blindly. He didn't even realize what he was doing until his knuckles were rapping on Ann's door.

The slight edge in her expression drained when she saw his face. "What happened?"

"Caroline ran away." His voice broke.

Ann's fingers flew to her lips.

"We found her. I found her." Zane shifted to lean on the doorframe, barely cognizant of how his knees were buckling.

Ann secured her arms around him. "I'm so sorry," she whispered.

Though her words cracked with emotion, Ann's frame was steady and strong against him. Zane clutched at her, wrapping himself as tightly as he could. Ann's only response was to grip him back. Though he felt as stable as a glass of water placed on a grain of rice, Ann's steadfastness never wavered.

Maybe he could do this. Maybe he could say goodbye to the best thing that had ever happened to him. She'd be okay. Ann was so strong. His leaving wouldn't break her.

But he didn't *want* to leave. The idea of doing so was like a blowtorch frying his skin.

"Come inside," Ann said after a long while.

It would be so easy to comply.

Caroline was safe with Isaac and Tessa. She'd agreed to staying in her new room for the week as planned. His daughter didn't know about their relationship, didn't know that Zane's life had changed behind the scenes. There was no way anyone could know that the more time Zane spent in Ann's presence, the harder he fell for her. That fact had been resting comfortably in the corner, simply waiting to be acknowledged.

A bloom of emotion stretched up his windpipe, his heart expanding beyond its limits. "I'm sorry I didn't call you back."

Ann's head shook against him. "I understand. It's okay."

How many times had it been him muttering those words, being the one to help, to comfort? Why did it feel more massive than the mountains surrounding them that *she* was the one taking care of him?

"Zane, please. You're trembling. Let's go inside." Ann didn't sound worried, only nurturing.

What he'd almost whispered to her yesterday afternoon surged to the tip of his tongue. The same words that had sung on repeat last night when Ann let him make love to her again. But telling Ann how he felt now would only sully them.

Ann's gaze darted over his face, his shoulders, his hair. "What's your comfort food? I mix green peas with ketchup." She wrinkled her nose, thinking. "Since you're a vegetarian, yours is probably cucumber slices? Jicama? Unpeeled radishes?"

She was trying to lighten the tension with a gentle joke, and it was the sweetest thing.

His chest shuddered with a sigh.

Sweet, sweet Ann.

When she took his hand and tried to lead him into her cozy condo, the rest of him shattered. He'd barely been holding it together since his course of action had become obvious.

"I can't," he rasped, squeezing her fingers and holding his arm taut to halt her movement.

The confusion swathing her gorgeous irises made moisture prick at the edges of his. "I'm sorry, but this can't continue. It's too much change for Caroline. I have to think of her right now."

Zane couldn't believe that the one time in his life he wanted nothing but to stay, *he* was going to be the one leaving.

He let go of Ann's fingers, wishing he'd kissed them one last time.

"Oh." Ann wrapped her hands around her waist. "I understand."

"I'm sorry," he said again.

Ann nodded, and with that action, her gaze dropped. Had Zane known it would have been the last time Ann's breathtaking green would focus on him for more than a second, he would have reveled in it. Instead, he turned, taking unsteady steps away from the woman he loved.

Chapter 25

Tuesday morning, Kennedy swung into Ann's classroom, nearly skidding in her ballet flats before slamming the door closed.

"Hey. Slow down. I don't think you're supposed to be moving like that." Ann took a shaken Kennedy by the elbow toward her desk chair.

She hadn't seen her friend since Sunday afternoon when she'd taken Kennedy home. Yesterday, Ann allowed herself to do something she'd never done—take a personal day. Feigning the stomach flu, she'd stayed home Monday and given herself exactly one day to be devastated by the fact that she'd truly thought her and Zane could have ended differently—because Zane had efficiently decimated her reasons for avoiding relationships like he'd been carelessly popping soap bubbles.

Crazy family?

Not a problem. Zane could keep his sister and mom in check while simultaneously bonding with Denis and her father.

Her strange quirks?

It didn't make sense, but he seemed to relish in them. His acceptance made Ann feel understood in a way she'd never experienced.

That only left one holdout—love's inequality.

The majority of their relationship had been Zane helping her, Zane being there *for her*, but Sunday night, Ann had been given her opportunity. Her throat had been closing off at the idea of something terrible happening to Caroline, but the rest of her had wanted to support Zane through this.

A tiny part of her soul had whispered that this was what real love was about. Give and take. Ups and downs. Love wasn't this wonderful parade of bliss and perfection, or duty and self-sacrifice at a personal cost. It was both. Simultaneously. Teetering one way before plummeting to the other but eventually balancing out.

There'd be days where he would buoy her and times, like Sunday night, when Ann had wanted nothing more than to take care of Zane.

Only, he hadn't let her.

"I know that we're new friends, but you have to believe me. I never want anything bad to happen to you," Kennedy rushed as she sat. "I really thought it was an open thing. I figured everything was in the clear. A-okay. Hunky-dory. Peachy-keen."

Ann's shoulders bunched. "What are you talking about?"

"Benedict," Kennedy squeaked. "I thought he knew."

"Knew about what?"

Her friend bit her lip. "You and Zane."

An icy hand hit her in the chest, and Ann was free-falling thirty stories. There was no *her and Zane* anymore, but Kennedy didn't know that. All Ann had wanted yesterday was to cry and eat wasabi-roasted chickpeas until the sting on her tongue was more intense than the stabbing in her stomach. Ann had planned on telling Kennedy today after school.

What was worse was, a half-hour before dismissal yesterday, Zane had texted her, stating that her luggage—the one she'd left at his house when they'd rushed to the ER—was outside her door, tucked so it wasn't visible to the street. Since her car had been in her small garage, Zane hadn't known she'd been home.

He couldn't have known that she'd missed his texts already. Every morning over the last week, she'd awoken to a new question or a story from him. A grin had lifted her cheeks as she'd removed her teeth-grinding mouth guard and thought of a creative way to answer. In between lessons, Ann had been sneaking messages to him until she'd get home at night, and they'd chat as if they'd been sitting next to each other.

"I just got out of an early meeting with Benedict to inform him of my activity intolerance. To, you know, get ahead of it. I even brought a beanbag from home to rest while teaching the kiddos. I told him about my plans to do more lessons from the rug, things like that." Kennedy winced, like the next part was painful. "Somehow, you being at the hospital with me came up, and then I mentioned Zane had driven you but then gone off somewhere. I'm sorry. It was stupid. So stupid."

Ann hadn't spoken. Her mind was whirring like an overheating computer.

"There's not a lot of people called Zane, and Benedict made the connection." Kennedy made a frantic gesture toward the door. "He's on his way. I only beat him here because Jordan stopped him to ask about the Earth Day fair."

Kennedy was nearly hyperventilating. Something that couldn't be good for the baby.

"It's not your fault." Though every muscle in her body seemed to quiver, Ann set a steady hand on Kennedy's shoulder. "You're right. I should have informed Benedict."

Even though that point became moot the second Zane's bowed head had walked away from her.

"I'm so, so, so, so sorry," she said, her forehead pinching.

Anxiety probably wasn't good for the baby, either.

Ann dropped to eye level with Kennedy like she would with any of her students. "I'll sort it out. Don't worry. Thanks for the warning."

Three sharp knocks reverberated through the room.

Had her future at Hillcrest not been in a precarious position, Kennedy's, *"Eep!"* would have made Ann laugh.

Now she might lose her job over something that was nonexistent. Did it even count if the real part of it lasted less than twenty-four hours? Even though those few hours were the best in her nearly thirty years?

Kennedy could barely keep the despair from her cheekbones as she gave Benedict a weak smile before slipping into the hall.

"Ann." Benedict closed the door behind him. "I assume you know why I'm here."

She took a short inhale before responding, "Yes."

"I know these things can happen." He began striding around her classroom, straightening grammar packets that were already at perfect ninety-degree angles to the edges of the desks. "But it is strongly discouraged for a staff member to date the parent of a student, particularly a student within their instructional realm."

"I understand."

Benedict preferred to hear verbal acknowledgement, something Ann had learned early on at Hillcrest.

"This is a very messy situation." He tapped a desk a few times, the slight gray at his temples more pronounced today. "Who besides me knows about . . . *this?*" Disdain dropped into the room and swirled noxiously with the ever-present scent of pencil shavings.

Though her mouth was lined with cactus spines, she managed, "You, Kennedy, and Ms. Liske."

It wasn't necessary to say Zane's name. She probably couldn't have done it without her voice breaking.

His eyebrow arched, though Benedict's gaze remained on the desks. "His daughter isn't aware?"

"No, but I should—"

"Hm." He tapped the desk again. Each reverberation sounded like a nail in the coffin that was her career at Hillcrest.

Ann knew she would be picked up by another school. So many were short-staffed. But Ann loved it here. She loved working with the rest of the third-grade team to implement new lessons at a moment's notice. She loved knowing she had the flexibility to do what was best for her class without pushback. She loved the eccentric after-school fairs, clubs, and projects that dominated her schedule. She loved that moment when the class ran itself like a well-oiled machine, when the kids knew what they should be working on, were engaged in their individualized curriculum, and everything hummed.

Benedict's voice broke through the dread seeping into her stomach. "I suppose as long as you can assure me that your relationship will in no way affect your ability to teach and grade with fairness, and that no other personnel or parents will discover this like I did, there won't be a need for further action."

She'd been unconsciously hugging herself, her eyes on her crossed arms. When Ann blinked up, Benedict's face held a magnanimous expression, like he was the purveyor of pardons—pardons that needn't be given since said relationship was over.

"Next year will not be an issue as she'll no longer be your student, but you'll need to keep this under wraps until summer break."

Ann's mouth opened, closed, opened again. Three seconds passed before her brain could remember how words worked. "Thank you, Benedict."

It was easier to say that than to explain the problem was no longer an issue. Boisterous noises and the stampeding feet of children echoed outside the closed door.

"I'll leave you to it, then." He smiled again and allowed her students to flood her classroom.

◊◊◊

Ann was grateful that she'd been too busy playing catch-up all day to allow her emotions too much wiggle room. It looked like she was going to be able to get out of this day alive, until Caroline stopped at her desk with a somber expression right before dismissal. Outside of the hug she'd given Caroline at the door this morning—holding a little longer than usual because Ann was relieved that she was safe—Ann had been attempting to keep her focus off of Zane's daughter.

"Ms. Powell?"

"What is it?" Ann struggled to keep her voice even.

"I'm sorry, but I decided to change my essay again. Do you think you could edit this before the contest's due date on Thursday?" Caroline chewed her lip.

"Of course." Ann chided herself for how mechanical she was being. Eventually, she'd be able to look at Zane's daughter and not see his freckles on her face, but today wasn't that day. She forced her lips to lift. "Let's see it."

After dismissal, finishing her classroom cleanup, and preparing for tomorrow, Ann slumped into her desk chair with a red pen and a heavy sigh.

The importence of telling the truth by Caroline West

A searing scorched down her neck and over her shoulder, but Ann forced her eyes back to the lined sheet of paper.

It's important to tell the truth because it can be dangrous if you don't. Sometimes when you tell others a lie it can hurt them, and you to. It's hard for kids to say things to adults, but its important so you don't get hurt. A good reazon to tell the truth are that you'll feel better after. Most adults want to listen! If you say something is okay, and it's not, it can make you fell upset. Then you might make a bad choice. I did this once, and could have got hurt. I'm glad I didn't and I don't want you to either!

Ann's heart ached. The idea of Caroline sitting in her newly painted room, penning this after being found by Zane, flashed in her mind. As much as Ann wished things were different between her and Zane, she understood his decision to put Caroline first.

Her red pen was changing spelling, adding commas, and reminding Caroline to give additional examples to strengthen her case when Ann's phone began ringing.

Tension tightened her ribs, forcing her to take a deep breath before answering.

"Hi, Dad. I'm sorry I didn't come over Sunday. Would it be okay if I helped out tomorrow? I've got tutoring tonight."

Dad stuttered like he hadn't expected Ann to answer that way. "Oh, uh . . . Sure. Yeah, that'd be fine, but . . ."

Her grip on the phone intensified.

"Rene says you're not coming to the wedding." His tone was calm but held a hint of dubiousness.

"That's right." Ann allowed herself two seizing heartbeats before continuing. "I'm sorry, Dad. We've had a falling out that I don't think can be repaired in time."

As she was finishing that sentence, her father began coughing. Ann waited for him to be able to continue.

"Sorry about that."

All her limbs suddenly felt too heavy. "You don't have to apologize every time you cough. You're sick. It's not your fault."

Just like it wasn't her fault that Rene had chosen to pick on her for most of her life. It simply was.

Her father made a non-verbal noise, not quite agreeing or disagreeing. "I'm sorry to hear that the two of you are fighting. I know you wouldn't not come unless there was a really good reason, so I guess I wanted to say I'm sorry."

Her inhale was sharp. "You're sorry?"

"I'm sorry this is happening to you. I only want the best for you. You and Rene and your mom." He sighed. "I just love you girls so much."

There it was, folks. Love bleeding a good man dry. One who'd worked his fingers to the bone to provide for his two daughters and to keep his stay-at-home wife in whatever possessions she'd wanted—which, in her mom's case, were excessive.

"I know, Dad," she whispered, struggling to keep her voice even. "I love you too."

Tomorrow, she'd make sure the yard was immaculate, the garage spotless, the small pool devoid of miniscule mesquite leaves. Ann would make sure her father received some of the love he dispensed so freely. She'd right the imbalance.

"Okay. I'll see you tomorrow, then?" A dry chuckle skipped over the line. "I'll try to keep your mother from harpin' on you about the wedding."

"Maybe I'll get the silent treatment," she said, placing fake hopefulness into her words.

"Yeah, maybe." The skeptical tone of her father's voice made Ann laugh.

They both knew she'd have no such luck.

A seizing thought tightened the knot at the base of Ann's neck as she fought afternoon traffic on the way to the public library where she tutored. Though she shouldn't have, Ann had mentally distributed that four thousand dollars. She'd planned on using most of it to supplement classrooms but had wanted to use a couple hundred to buy new books for her tutoring students and their siblings. Now that money—and the numerous supplies it could have purchased—was gone.

As expected, Jalen was waiting outside alone, balancing atop the wave-style bike rack. A single wheel was still attached to a black U-Lock beneath Jalen's swinging legs. Beyond him, two young teens stood with heads bowed to their phones, any remnants of childhood joy missing from their curving spines.

Ann's mouth twitched up seeing one of her favorite tutoring students. Unlike the few she had who only sat with her because their teachers or parents had forced them, Jalen loved learning. When he'd started with her at the beginning of the year, he'd been at a third-grade reading level but had swiftly progressed. He was *so close* to catching up to the rest of his fifth-grade class.

"Hey, Miss P."

"Hi, Jalen. You ready?"

"Yep." He jumped onto the gravel beneath the bike rack, ran to her side, and snuck his small fingers between hers.

Ann smiled at him as a car ambled past, Tejano music spilling into the street. The joyous upbeat of the accordion radiated through her bloodstream. As long as she could teach and there were students who wanted to learn, it would be okay. She'd just have to be more creative with the money she used from her salary. Ann made a mental note to stop by Bookman's used bookstore on the way home and scour the middle-grade section.

"What do you want to start with today? Fiction or nonfiction?" she asked softly, steering them along the stacks to her tutoring table.

"Fiction." Jalen's hushed voice held a smile. "I like that better than the real world."

A somberness slithered through her belly as the heartbreak of the last few days took up permanent residence.

"Yeah." Fortunately, being at whisper level meant the wobble in Ann's response wasn't as detectable. "Me too."

Chapter 26

Though he'd been getting thrice-daily updates from Tessa about Caroline and had eaten dinner at Isaac's Monday through Thursday to show a united front about this new living situation, Zane was grateful that he hadn't been the primary parent this past week.

Nothing had been accomplished in the six days since he'd shot himself in the heart. At first, Zane had thought that being locked in his darkened, four-by-six room, living in an alternate world, would have helped. But every recording he attempted was full of distracting mouth sounds and him stumbling over words. Then his eyes couldn't focus long enough to effectively book prep. He'd even texted Micha to let him know he'd be missing this week's football practice.

Zane had never experienced the soul-satiating connection he'd felt with Ann. It was reality shifting, as if the sun had tilted into a novel orientation. Now, however, the relentless sunshine felt like it was there just to burn his retinas. The unchanging weather was unfair, really. Arizonans couldn't curl into a ball and cry their way through a melodramatic rainstorm. They had to be miserable in cheery, blatant sunshine.

Marley looked up from his position in Zane's lap. Somehow, his friendly feline companion seemed to defy science and cross species to give him puppy-dog eyes.

"I know. I'll get up in a minute."

He'd been spending a disproportionate amount of time on his couch, but Zane hadn't wanted to sleep in his bed.

That was where Ann had slept.

The memory of Ann's sleepy, angelic smile sliced through his ribs. She had shifted in his arms that night, waking him. Then she'd nuzzled closer as this perfect arch graced her lips. Zane had never felt his heart race like that, never felt split apart and rearranged. It'd been as if Ann had become part of his cellular structure. But now Zane had to extricate her from his life, pull apart his soul and forcefully remove her even though he didn't want to.

When Marley hopped to the floor, Zane stood and stretched his aching chest.

Tessa would be here with Caroline within the hour, and Zane needed to get the house in order. Usually, he kept things tidy—a habit he'd learned from his mother. Dad would have papers, sticky notes, and his multitude of pens sprawled over his compact desk, but Mom would insist that the rest of their small space hold some organization. The Foley studio was always overwrought with props and chaos, so she insisted on some order at home.

The garage door opened a second after Zane finished loading the dishwasher.

"Dad." Caroline shared a long, pointed look with him while striding straight to her room, sketchbook secure in her arms.

That look meant she was either mid-design and wanted to finish, or she needed space. Either way, she wasn't coming into the kitchen.

Tessa dropped Caroline's backpack on the island. "So that's how my week went," she said, like they hadn't been in constant contact.

He, Tessa, and Isaac had been on high alert all week after Caroline's field trip into the desert. Twice he'd texted her in the middle of the night, and Tessa had crept into Caroline's room to send Zane a picture of their daughter sleeping. Monday, they'd decided that Caroline's houndstooth watch should be exchanged with a kid's smartwatch. By Tuesday afternoon, Caroline was back to her usual self and was annoyed that everyone was hovering.

"I guess teen years start really early nowadays." Tessa widened her eyes dramatically before her expression shifted to one of concern. "Are you okay? You look like you lost ten pounds in two days."

He probably had. Food hadn't seemed appealing with his intestines chaotically rearranging themselves every six minutes. He'd only managed to swallow whatever Tessa and Isaac had made throughout the week because he'd had to. Eating on his own felt as unnecessary as sleeping.

"I ate some bad sushi yesterday," he lied.

If Zane told Tessa about him and Ann, she'd interfere. That was Tessa's way. She meddled. Right now, he didn't have the strength to fight her. Zane was already using every iota of his willpower to do the best thing for their family.

Tessa tilted her head, sympathy tugging her lips down. "Do you want me to make minestrone?"

Though it was his second favorite recipe of hers, Zane shook his head. "I'll be fine. Water and time are all I need."

Time.

Maybe with time, it wouldn't feel like a mountain lion was pulling his flesh from his bones.

"Okay, then. I'll see you next Saturday. I might text for proof of life like you did."

A sad smile shifted his lips. "You know I'll be up."

Forty-five minutes later, Zane was attempting to work through an initial read of a new book for work when his daughter finally ventured out of her room.

"Isaac is a lot." Caroline's voice was over his head, behind the couch.

Zane placed a virtual bookmark and closed the cover to his tablet, setting it beside his blanketed, jean-covered legs. The outdoor digital thermometer stated it was eighty-five degrees in the shade, but a shiver had run through him since Sunday.

"It's not like you just met the man."

Tessa had begun dating Isaac almost exactly a year ago.

"Yeah, but seeing him for a few hours is not the same as living with him." She plopped next to Zane, folding her legs so the soles of her bare feet touched. Two unspoken rules in this house were: never use the overhead lights and be barefoot as much as humanly possible. "He sings in the shower."

Zane sucked in a sharp inhale. "The audacity."

"Dad." Caroline narrowed her gaze. "I'm serious. You can hear it from the main room. And he sings old-timey lollypop songs."

He couldn't help laughing. "What kind of songs now?"

"Nothing good." She fluttered her hands around, startling Marley, who'd moved from his outstretched legs to hers. "No Clapton. No Stevie Ray Vaughan."

His grin only grew. "Oh, my sweet child. I've spoiled you."

Caroline ignored him, running her fingers through Marley's fur. "And his favorite eegee is Red Licorice." She stuck out her tongue, the expression at visual odds with today's chosen outfit.

Her fully buttoned Arizona-red polo was snugly tucked into her khaki bermuda shorts. If he had to guess, Caroline had probably asked Tessa to iron them this morning since they held creases down the centers of her thighs.

"We don't yuck other people's yums. Everyone's taste buds are different," he told her, even though *his* taste buds agreed with her. "Remember the poor cilantro souls."

Sadly, four to fourteen percent of the population tastes soap instead of incredibleness when eating cilantro.

"I always feel so bad for them," Caroline said into the distance before focusing back on her rant. "But he was just so *nice* the whole time."

"How dare he," Zane deadpanned.

He decided against reminding her why they'd all been more attentive than usual this week. Zane knew she understood the gravity of the situation. After Monday's dinner, Caroline had pulled him aside and apologized for frightening him. Messy tears had run down both of their faces as they'd held each other. In that moment, while holding his daughter as they both cried over the idea of losing each other, the decision he'd made about Ann made sense. Zane tried to hold on to that memory in all the other moments when it didn't.

Caroline huffed before silence decided to join them on the couch.

"Why don't you have music playing?" Caroline's question sling-shotted him back to the room.

Though he was used to subsisting on barely any sleep, the extra deprivation of this week was starting to sneak up on him. Zane wasn't sure he hadn't just nodded off with his eyes open.

"Hm?"

"Is the record player broken?"

"No." His exhausted brain finally clicked into her line of questioning. "I just wanted some quiet."

Zane should have been listening to the blues greats, telling stories much sadder than his, but even perfectly strummed chords and soulful voices had lost their appeal over the week.

"Weird." Caroline plopped Marley on his lap and stood. "Can I see if Gwen is free?"

When Zane hesitated to grant permission to a request that had never garnered it before, Caroline waved her wrist at him, flashing her neon-orange smart watch.

"Sure. Okay." He nodded, ignoring the stampede of horses trampling his chest.

Not that he'd been doing a great job of focusing before, but Zane decided to put work away for the moment and bite the bullet on the other task he'd been putting off.

Like usual, Ethan picked up on the second ring, "Hey. What's up?"

A turn signal clicked in the background. Ethan must have been alone, because had Haley been in the passenger seat of his sleek sports car, she would have announced her presence.

Zane scratched the back of his head, stalling for a second. "I have a big favor to ask."

"Anything. What is it?"

"I know you were trying to find charities to donate to, and . . . Caroline's teacher"—using that descriptor sounded like brakes squealing—"donates to underserved classrooms at other schools. I was wondering if I set up some way to distribute to those teachers in need, would you mind helping with funding?"

His back muscles seized. Zane had never asked anyone for money, even though one of his closest friends was an actual billionaire. Besides his car, Ethan was still the down-to-earth guy who preferred apartment living to mansions. He'd recently decided to use the money he'd earned from creating the most successful social media app of all time to do some good.

"Absolutely. What are you thinking? A hundred thousand? Quarter million?" Ethan made it sound like they were going in on a pizza, not distributing massive amounts of money.

"I—I don't know. I need to do some research to find out how it would all work."

Zane didn't want to take Ann's charity work away from her, only to help supplement it. He needed a way to support her, since he couldn't stand by her side. It was already going to eviscerate him to see Ann at the Earth Day Fair next weekend.

When he'd signed up for the event, the first week of their fake dating, he'd never expected to be here. Zane had anticipated having to restrict the urge to slide his palms up her arms, to whisper a joke over her ear, to keep himself from kissing her after hearing her raspy chuckle. Not wrestle with the hollowing knowledge that he'd pushed away his chance at real love.

"Whatever you need, Zane. It's yours."

"Thanks." He swallowed. At least this was something good to come from his time with Ann. "It means a lot."

Chapter 27

"Happy Birthday, Ms. Powell!" shouted Abigail, one of her students, as she bounded through the door the following Friday.

Normally, her students wouldn't have been aware of her birthday, but a well-intentioned Kennedy had decided to leak that information during her free period on Monday. Then she'd done the same thing Tuesday through Thursday, claiming that eight-year-olds have short memories.

Though Ann would have preferred to continue living in a denial bubble, her closest friend had brought up Zane with gushing enthusiasm at their Wednesday after-school workout last week. Since she'd been at the gym, Ann had been able to almost remove herself from her body. Being side by side had made it easier for her to flay her veins open and tell Kennedy everything.

The bet. Her real relationship with her sister. How it had been awkward with her mom when she'd visited her parents' house but that her father had supported her decision to create space away from Rene. Caroline going missing. Zane's mature decision to put his daughter first.

There was no way she could have opened up like that if she hadn't been lifting at the same time. Kennedy's ultra-light, seated reps slowed to a staggering pace, but her friend seemed to understand that face-to-face was too direct for Ann, staying quiet and listening.

Since then, Kennedy had been working overtime to lift Ann up—dropping off a bag of her favorite dried mangoes, asking if she needed any copies made for class, showing up early and claiming their favorite weight bench at the gym before the teenage boys got to it.

Giving Abigail a big squeeze, a familiar scent filled Ann's nostrils a moment before Sal, the school security officer, walked through her door. His white mustache tugged up to reveal uneven teeth.

"You didn't tell me it was your birthday," he said, holding an obscenely large floral arrangement in a pale-pink vase.

Two dozen stargazer lilies were accompanied by white snapdragons, pink baby carnations, peach chrysanthemums, and edged with eucalyptus and lemon leaves. The edges of the flowers blurred before Ann blinked away the tears sheening her eyes.

Zane.

"I wanted to get you bubblegum gelato, but Dad said it wasn't very practical to bring to school," Caroline pouted from her position beside Sal before she fiddled with the strap of her backpack. "Are these okay? I *know* you would have loved bubblegum gelato."

Ann's flowy-skirted dress draped on the ground as she dropped to her knees to be eye level with Caroline. "They are the most beautiful flowers I have ever received." Ann took her small, soft hand and squeezed it. "Thank you."

Caroline's smile was aimed at the floor as Sal placed the vase on her desk.

"I heard there was a special birthday girl in here." Kennedy's voice wove around the ten mylar balloons crowding her face, two of which were a gigantic three and zero. "Are we going to be the best students for Ms. Powell tod—whoa." Her eyes landed on the flowers before darting to Ann's and then resuming their normal cheerful appearance.

"Mrs. Owens!" her students cheered.

They began talking over each other, explaining their various gifts, cards, and tokens they'd brought for Ann, pleased with their ability to follow Kennedy's instructions to 'show their favorite third-grade teacher some love.' The four-toned bell rang overhead, indicating that the day was to begin. Kennedy gave Ann a quick hug, whispering, "We'll chat later," before disappearing.

The day got off to a disjointed start, the kids too excited to focus, but they'd calmed down by the time Ann took them to their wellness class with Mr. Kalder, the school's guidance counselor.

Her phone vibrated in her cardigan pocket, and Ann opened it to find separate messages from her parents—a simple text from Mom and a voice text from Dad. She clicked on the voice message when a female scream in the hallway had Ann tossing her phone on the desk and racing to the door.

The second the lockdown alarm sounded, Ann's heart bottomed out. Her kids. They weren't with her. She couldn't protect them. Her fingers gripped the door frame, wanting to sprint through it, though knowing she should follow protocol. *They're safe with Mr. Kalder,* she reasoned. Ann was about to close and lock her door when Zane came sprinting down the hall.

Her breath hitched in her throat.

No. He can't be here too. He can't—

But before that thought could finish, the coordinated sound of four little hooves slapping the vinyl flooring echoed off the student-art-filled walls. Ann blinked, not believing that a large male javelina had just rounded the corner, chasing Zane's sneakered feet. The first scenario that had flooded her mind had been unimaginably terrifying, but this was still a version of Ann's childhood nightmares come to life.

"Zane!"

His concentrated gaze was already on her, closing the distance. Zane slid through the door a second before Ann slammed it shut. The javelina didn't change direction. It kept pounding down the hallway, disappearing behind another curve.

"What in the—"

"The door—HVAC guy—" He paused, waving his hand over his heaving chest before doubling over and taking a moment to collect his breath. "He had a half-dozen donuts on an overturned bucket."

The AC to the school gym had been out all week, making P.E. impossible. Each teacher had to contend with extra bouncy kids until the repair was scheduled.

"I was using that door to bring in a few pop-up tents for tomorrow's fair. When I came through the propped-open door the second time, the repairman was gone, and the javelina was halfway through a Boston creme." An expletive rushed from his mouth as his hands came to his sides. "We spooked each other, and he took off after me."

Ann could only stare. Too many emotions had flooded her at the idea of Zane being harmed. Though she logically realized that the threat had been less fatal, adrenaline was kickboxing her common sense. And winning. She wanted to run her trembling fingers over his strong chest, to feel his heartbeat even though she could see his pulse thrumming in his neck.

The PA system crackled, and both of their gazes snapped to the speaker in the corner.

"Please stay in your classrooms," Benedict's voice came through. "We have a startled javelina running the halls. Maintenance and security have opened the exterior doors to help it find its way out. Do not leave your rooms. Do not engage with the animal. They can be very dangerous when scared. Listen for the all-clear signal."

"Only in Tucson," Zane muttered, moving to pace in the narrow space between her desk and her students'.

It was good that he'd stepped away, because she'd been seconds away from throwing herself into his sweat-glistened arms.

His gaze fell to the bouquet overtaking her desk, his feet slowing to a stop. Without fear coursing through her system, Ann noticed that Zane's eyes were underlined with shadow, that his beautiful cheekbones were more prominent than usual.

"Thank you for the flowers." It was impossible to keep the rasp out of her voice.

The sound of her speaking made him flinch like he'd been punched, but he kept his gaze on her desk. Zane adjusted his glasses before rotating and sliding her apple an inch inward. "Caroline wanted to get you something."

Her bones felt like they'd liquified. Only the door at her back was supporting her at this point. It hadn't been Caroline's idea to get her favorite flowers. This type of bouquet couldn't have been purchased at the last minute. Zane had probably called and overseen the order, making sure every detail was correct. Each bloom matched her favorite colors, the ones she dressed in almost daily.

The last two weeks of her avoiding this feeling, of relegating it to the corners of her mind, trying to remove it from her brain with activity and working herself to exhaustion, was all for naught.

Since she couldn't say the words that pummeled her intestines, Ann asked the question that popped into her mind whenever Zane was in her classroom.

"Why do you always do that? Move my apple?"

"It's a way to touch you when I can't." His head snapped up like he shouldn't have said that, like he couldn't believe he'd answered honestly. "Um." Zane rubbed his sternum, grimacing. "I mean—"

His words evaporated with her determined steps. The logical part of Ann's brain was shouting at her to stop, to think for a minute, but this might be the last time . . .

Her lips came crashing over his parted mouth as her fingers wove over his jaw. Zane hesitated only a second, groaning into the deep kiss as his arms squeezed her body to his. Of all the things—Zane's goofy eyebrows bouncing, Zane's tender, lopsided smile, Zane's toes against her shin and his fingers combing her hair as she drifted to sleep—Ann missed his lips the most.

Here, she could tell him what her heart was attempting to climb out of her body and show him. With his curls firmly against her fingertips, Ann knew Zane wanted this as much as she did. Life was the only thing getting in the way.

His palms smoothed down her spine as a pained sound escaped him, almost as if he couldn't believe she was here, that she was molding into his hands again. The sentiment echoed through her nervous system. Ann wanted to live here, pause time and make the real world vanish. Zane seemed to understand, giving back to her with each ounce she poured into him.

Only when the all-clear bell sounded did he lift his face. A hard exhale washed over her lips as he brought their foreheads together.

"I don't want to say no to you." The tortured sound of his voice sent squeezing pain along her arms.

"I know," she whispered, her stinging fingertips sliding down his neck.

He rocked his forehead against hers, struggling for breath.

"Zane, I—" She swallowed. "I—"

Zane's devastated eyes lifted to meet hers as he shook his head. "Please don't. Don't tell me. That way I can pretend I don't know."

A short, painful breath puffed from her open mouth as tears welled.

Zane's hands left her waist to frame her face, kissing her like he was never going to see her again, like he was heading off to another country, to war, to space.

"Me too," he murmured over her mouth before taking her lips in his again, splintering what was left of her heart. "I do too."

The sounds of people milling through the halls entered into Ann's consciousness in the background, but her entire world was placing one last, soft kiss on her lips. Zane took several deep breaths before the warmth of his fingers left her jaw. When her eyelids finally fluttered open, the look on Zane's face made Ann feel like someone took a sledgehammer to her sternum.

"I need to—" He stopped, rubbing his knuckles over his lips.

Inane excuses were useless. They both knew that.

Ann focused on the courtyard straight ahead, trying her best not to tremble as Zane took a step toward the door. He paused at her shoulder for a fraction of a second before walking out of her life again.

Chapter 28

"**D**ad? You okay?"

Zane was staring out into the desert, his fingers running over the grooves of the wicker armrest of his patio furniture just to see if his sensory system was still working. He couldn't feel anything besides numbness. The last time he'd had any sensation was when Ann's warmth had been beneath his palms, hours ago.

"Did you know that if you really pay attention, it makes a noise when you blink?" His brain had apparently joined the rest of his body because now he was answering simple questions with gibberish.

But it wasn't a simple question. It was a question that contained a catastrophic answer.

Caroline sat beside him, using the back of her wrist to feel his forehead.

That action snapped him back to reality.

"Hey, I'm okay." He gave her his goofiest grin. "I'm just messing with you because you got me with the spider in my coffee tumbler this morning."

It should have sent joy sprinting to the tips of his toes, finding the black, plastic tarantula look-alike at the bottom of his steel cup this morning. The game of placing the spider had begun when Caroline had been in pre-K. She'd received the arachnid monstrosity in a Halloween goodie bag and then had thought it would be funny to leave it as a surprise on his microphone. Zane had retaliated by placing it in her vanity cabinet, right next to her toothbrush. Most of the time, they'd see the spider, mutter, "That stinker," and try to outdo the other. Occasionally, they'd genuinely startle each other. The game had continued off and on over the years, stalling during the hardest months.

"Are you sure? You didn't give me a horrendous nickname when you picked me up this afternoon." Her gaze bounced worriedly over his face.

"Horrendous. That's a good word." He sat up and stretched, trying to encourage his blood not to stagnate in his broken heart.

"We're working on synonyms and antonyms. Horrendous means awful or bad," Caroline explained.

The side of his mouth quirked. "Good to know."

"You never forget a nickname." For as much as Caroline was his duplicate, she possessed Tessa's tenacity. "And Mom's right, you're getting too skinny." She poked at his bicep with one finger.

"Hey now." He opened his palms facing out. "Every body is different. And you know you two are only allowed to talk about me behind my back if you're planning on surprising me with a new record." Zane shrugged. "I don't make the rules."

"You do make—" She cut off the sentence with a huff, briefly glancing at the patio's ceiling.

When Caroline rotated her body to face him, placing her hands calmly in her lap, Zane had to press his lips together to keep them from quirking. His daughter was trying to be calm and collected, though he'd clearly razzed her.

"Dad. I'm going to be nine soon. In six weeks, two days, and"—Caroline consulted her smartwatch—"twelveish hours to be exact."

"Ish," he quipped.

Caroline wrinkled her nose with a *let-me-finish* stare.

Adjusting his glasses, Zane suppressed another smile.

His daughter took a steadying breath. "If you're sick like Mom was, please tell me. I'm old enough to help. I can make us peanut butter sandwiches for dinner tonight if you're not feeling good enough."

"Oh, honey." Zane pulled Caroline into a hug. "I'm okay. I'm not sick like Mom was."

"You haven't been the same since that day." Her small arms squeezed him as she burrowed into his Sister Hazel T-shirt. "Was it me? Did I break you?"

The fear and uncertainty in her voice *was* breaking him. Whatever had been left after he'd walked away from Ann a second time now lay splintered on the cement patio floor.

"No." He leaned back to level his eyes with Caroline's. "You have done nothing wrong. I'm just dealing with some adult things. None of which has to do with you."

Even though that sentence wasn't technically true, there was no reality in which Zane would blame his daughter for life's circumstances.

Caroline bit the corner of her lip. "Will you tell me what's wrong?"

"No."

She nodded, unhappy but accepting his answer. "Mr. Kalder says that if you're having trouble, you should talk it out with someone. Like how I had to tell you I was upset about things changing. Do you want me to call Uncle Kevin?" She lifted her wrist. "He always makes me feel better when I'm grumpy."

"I thought you were only supposed to have me, Isaac, and Mom on there."

Caroline shrugged. "Mom said only family. My uncles are family." She dropped her hand. "You're not going to meet with them tomorrow because of the fair. Do you want me to see if they can come over? I can have Mom get me a day early."

The fact that his almost-nine-year-old daughter was trying to stage an intervention on his behalf and offering to spend an additional night at Isaac's house meant that Zane had done a terrible job not letting the damage from this morning show. Shame flooded his system, efficiently replacing the numbness.

"No. I'm okay." He sat up straighter. "Really."

Caroline leveled her gaze with a skeptical raise of her blonde eyebrows.

"I'm going to see if Gwen is free." She hopped up. "At least call Grandma."

As Zane rose from his position, a low-toned gonging sound from his neighbor's wind chimes echoed over the buzz of the bees. They'd been blissfully collecting pollen from the palo verde blooms in the corner of his yard. Zane hoped the vibrant tree would be spared when they broke ground on pool construction next week.

Caroline's concern was the kick in the pants Zane needed to get his sorry behind moving. This whole situation stunk like rancid meat, but his dwelling in what couldn't be was poisoning those around him. He needed to get it together. Life wasn't always fair. He knew that firsthand.

Relegating the call with his mother to later, Zane went inside but left the screen door to the backyard open and powered his laptop from its nook in the kitchen. Ethan had texted him an hour ago that he'd given Zane permission to access his charity account.

"Dang, Ethan." He blew a low whistle, opening the account named Alpine Investments.

Ethan had given him access to the entire account, but the sum they'd spoken about last week was set aside in a digital folder for Zane to use.

Ethan's former business manager had created the entity for Ethan to anonymously donate. The sleek website for the account even had a custom emblem—a crisp-lined, snow-capped mountain. Zane snickered at the iconography. It likely had something to do with the nickname Ethan's girlfriend had bestowed on him.

Zane hadn't needed to establish some way to get the money to teachers in need. Turned out, there were already dedicated donation websites. Teachers just had to fill out an account and request a sum for their class. Most of the profiles explained what the money would be used for, be it books, art supplies, etc. A few other corporations and individuals had donated to several of the classrooms in the Tucson area, but many of the teacher's profiles were still in the red.

Completely meeting each teacher's couple-hundred-dollar monetary request was a soothing endeavor. After he'd finished with the schools within a hundred-mile radius, ample funds remained. Zane supposed he could wait for each teacher to set up a new request page for the following year and fill those over the summer.

The doorbell rang, and Zane ignored it. He'd get the package later. When the door opened, Zane rose from his position.

"You're in trouble now, dishhead." Tessa kicked off her sandals while walking, a small bottle of whiskey in her hand.

"Dishhead? That's a new one." He put his hands in the pockets of his shorts.

"It's supposed to be double dishhead. Like, you're being a double dishhead by making our daughter call me to find your mother's phone number because apparently 'you're in crisis and not accepting help.'" Tessa set the bottle on the island with a clunk. "Caroline's words, not mine."

Zane ran his hand over his five o'clock scruff.

"She also said to call her when it was safe to come home." Tessa rolled her eyes in an expression that very much matched their daughter's. "Maybe the smartwatch was a bad idea."

"Too late now." Maybe if they went back and forth about Caroline, Zane could avoid detailing his devastating morning.

"Okay. I'm spilling the whiskey. You spill the tea." She broke the seal on the bottle of Bulleit, looking out the open screen door. "I'm guessing this is about *Micha*. What happened?"

Zane exhaled, leaning his elbows on the countertop while Tessa pushed a highball glass under his nose. "I had to end things. . . with Micha."

"'Had to?' Why?" Tessa took a gulp from her glass and hissed with a grimace. "I don't know why you like this stuff."

His ex-wife preferred sweet cocktails—the more sugar, the better. Tessa only ever drank bourbon when he needed her to.

Zane let his own sip scorch down his throat. "It was best for Caroline. You saw how she reacted to you moving in with Isaac. I don't need to add another complication to her life right now. She deserves consistency."

"So you're going to deny yourself love?" Tessa looked as decimated as he felt. "Z. That's the exact reason why we finally got divorced, so we could *both* be with who we wanted. To have that all-encompassing, firecracker love. You deserve to have what I have with Isaac. I know I'm not in your relationship, but I think"—Tessa looked around even though they were alone— "Micha's that person for you. The few seconds of seeing you two together . . ." Tessa paused, pressing her lips tight. "She's crazy about you."

Zane thought back to the words they'd shared in Ann's classroom. If he hadn't interrupted her, Ann would have told him she loved him. Since he couldn't bear hearing that and walking away, he'd done the only thing he could think of and let his body tell her how much he did too, how badly he wanted to be with her.

It took a minute to realize that his head was shaking. "I can't do that to Caroline."

"Can't do what to me?" Her hand was raised to open the screen door. Zane had never been more thankful for code names in his life.

Tessa shared a wordless conversation with him as Caroline padded over, picking up Marley and holding him to her chest like a shield.

"What's happening?" his daughter asked.

"Nothing." Zane ran his hand over his hair.

"I thought you were going to stay at Gwen's until I called." Tessa's voice was unnaturally high.

Caroline leaned against the refrigerator. "I was, but she's started dating someone—a guy with a motorcycle—and he showed up to pick her up."

That would explain the errant engine noises over the last three weeks.

Tessa's pointed, raised brow grated on his already exhausted brain. Caroline's art mentor dating was not the same as her father.

In usual Tessa fashion, she said what she wanted, anyway. "What do you think about your dad dating, like me and Gwen?"

It was slight, but Caroline's lower lip flickered down before she pulled it between her teeth.

All the proof he needed.

"That's not going to happen," Zane reassured her.

"Is that why you've been so off? Why you've stopped playing

music?" Her quiet question was aimed at Marley's silky fur.

Tessa spun toward him, and Zane begged her not to ask any follow-up questions with wide eyes.

"Would she live here?"

"No, of course not," Tessa answered. "Dad might spend his free time with her, and maybe you'd see her a few hours here and there, like you did with Isaac in the beginning."

Caroline still hadn't brought her head up. Her fingers rotated the identification tag on Marley's green collar. "I guess." One shoulder lifted. "If that makes Dad stop acting weird."

"Oh, honey. There's nothing that can keep your dad from being weird." Tessa's loaded wink was met by his narrowing eyes, but Caroline's snort melted the tension.

"That ship has sunk." Caroline's gaze rose and caught his.

"That ship has sailed," Tessa corrected.

The second that hovered between them before his daughter's lip curled, almost imperceptibly, hit his chest like a strobe light. That kinship feeling hummed in his veins as she bounced her eyebrows. As much as mispronunciation irked him, Tessa was a stickler for grammar and getting phrases correct. Whenever Caroline wanted to annoy her mother, she dropped a few double negatives or an *ain't*.

Caroline broke eye contact first, blinking down for a moment before raising her gaze with a determined inhale. "I want you to be happy."

Zane hadn't fully processed the implication of Caroline's words when Tessa's dramatic inhale stole everyone's attention.

"You know what this means?" She nearly squealed in the impending pause caused by his and Caroline's confusion.

"Grand gesture!"

"What's a grand gesture?" Caroline set Marley on the ground before leaning her arms over the island.

"Could be anything," Tessa began. "Singing her favorite song over the loudspeaker. Showing up on horseback. Commissioning a painting of her favorite animal."

Their daughter nodded. "Writing their name in chalk on every sidewalk."

"You're getting it." Tessa tapped her cheek. "Messy, public declarations of love and how stupid you've been for pushing her away."

"Buy all her favorite treats and stash them everywhere so she'll find them later," Caroline suggested.

"Get a giant bouquet of their favorite flowers." Tessa hummed. "What else?"

Though Zane could feel Caroline's gaze on him after that last suggestion, he didn't flinch.

"Dad."

Caroline's tone held the same no-nonsense, tell-me-the-truth inflection it'd had when he'd first explained to her how special effects work.

Tessa was about to tick another suggestion out when she froze, mouth open.

"*Dad.*"

Zane pressed his eyes closed with a defeated exhale.

"Ms. Powell?" Caroline's voice rose in volume.

"It's over. Okay?" Zane said, leveling his gaze with his daughter's so she knew he was telling the truth. "I couldn't tell you because I didn't want it to be complicated for you. Your mom and I moving on with our lives is already really hard without involving your teacher."

Caroline leaned back, her palms flat on the countertop as she silently processed this piece of information. When she lifted her head, she asked Tessa, "Why would Dad being with Ms. Powell make things harder?"

Tessa flicked her gaze to his before answering. "There are rules about parents and teachers dating."

Caroline nodded, picking at her cuticle. "What about when the school year ends? We only have a month left." Her matching brown eyes found Zane's. "Ms. Powell is my favorite non-family member. I guess if you're going to start dating again, she'd be the best person."

The kitchen was entirely too quiet before Tessa popped her lips in Caroline's direction. "Well, this just proves the point I made yesterday. Sometimes, men are idiots."

"Seriously, Tess?" He adjusted his frames. "You're teaching her that?"

"I'm not wrong." She crossed her arms. "You could have simply had this conversation with your daughter, but instead, you made a unilateral decision with little to no input from the others involved and potentially screwed up something great."

A string of expletives ran through his mind as fingers pressed over his forehead. In one simplistic sentence, Tessa had efficiently outlined how stupid he'd been.

"Okay. You're not wrong. I'm an idiot."

Several seconds of cricket song bled into the silent kitchen before Tessa asked, "Is that a yes to the grand gesture?"

Chapter 29

Ann would have never pinned Kennedy, who embodied the word bubbly, to have a penchant for slasher films. She would have never put *Kennedy* and *killing* in the same sentence. But her friend was practically salivating, watching a campy scene of the deranged female lead using a chef's knife to mutilate the guests at a house party. Sepia styling complemented the film's seventies vibe as Ann tried to place the soulful voice singing "Into the Mystic" over the action.

A painful cough left Ann's mouth when recognition finally landed. The song had been playing when Zane had kissed her in his kitchen. Right before he'd worshiped her and made her feel more beautiful and loved than she'd ever experienced.

The bottle-blonde with feathered hair wiped blood splatter off her forehead with the back of her wrist as hot tears silently streamed down Ann's face. Since she'd already cried for the better part of an hour when Kennedy had first arrived, Ann tried to keep this tear session from her friend's attention.

Kennedy interlaced her fingers in hers but kept her gaze on the screen. "It's okay. Let it out."

"I'm sorry," she whispered.

Her friend only shook her head, squeezing her hand.

"I need some air." Ann wiggled free and escaped to her compact patio.

The neighborhood had quieted down for the evening, only the occasional car driving with the windows down spilled song into the warm evening. Pretty soon, it would be uncomfortable to sit out here, even with the sun gone from the sky. Tucsonans anticipated the harsh realities of summer like the rest of the world forebode winter. A heavy exhale left her lungs as Ann slumped onto her outdoor daybed and hugged a pillow to her chest.

The unfairness of this situation dug at her like a bra strap that had been flipped all day, yet Ann couldn't fault Zane. There was nothing to do but process this heartache and try to move on. On paper. Internally, Ann knew she'd never find something like this again. Zane had loved the parts of her that she'd thought she needed to hide. Nothing could have made her feel more cherished.

She'd just have to give herself time. Each morning, she'd have to give herself extra moments to deal with the disappointment. Ann would have to lie in bed while the onslaught of emotions writhed through her before organizing her grading folders and making herself scrambled eggs and coffee.

Heartbreak would become one of her routines. Perhaps she should even give it a color-coded folder. Red for math. Green for science. Blue for English. Yellow for social studies. Purple for heartbreak.

Several long minutes passed before the sliding door opened and shut. Ann kept her gaze on the trio of potted cacti along the stucco wall with a petulant sigh. Kennedy undoubtedly wanted to hash this out again. Her friend kept trying to find angles in which things could work, but it was simple. Zane had made his decision.

The end.

Her elbow plopped onto the teak armrest, sending shooting pain up her arm. "Ow." Ann rubbed her stinging elbow. "It's not really funny when you hit your funny bone."

"No, it isn't." Zane's deep, grumbly voice ripped her focus away from the wall.

Ann gripped the armrest like it was the only thing keeping her from falling off a steep, craggy cliff. "What are you—" She looked behind him to see Kennedy wave from inside, hold up her purse and keys, and make a *call me later* gesture.

Zane cautiously sat on the other end of the daybed, leaving space between them. Space that Ann wanted to annihilate like the murderous knife-wielding lead in the film she'd just abandoned.

"I wanted to give you something." Zane held out a purple file folder.

Oh, the irony.

Swallowing was near impossible with the way her throat was closing up, but Ann took the folder, opening it to see . . . herself. A colored-pencil portrait of herself. A collection of vibrant stargazer lilies crowned her head while other flowers flowed down her brunette waves. It was simplistic yet breathtaking.

"Caroline wouldn't let me leave without this." He gestured to the thick paper in her trembling fingers before gripping the back of his neck. "Actually, the second she finished, she made me take a picture so she could recreate it in full detail like she wanted to. She said to apologize for the quality, since my antsy hovering made her rush."

"It's the most beautiful thing I've ever seen." Ann wanted to press the image to her chest. Caroline had made her appear ethereal, whimsical, and powerful all at once. "Please thank her for me."

When he shifted to kneel in front of her, Ann leaned back slightly. "Could you tell her yourself? She'd like you to join us for gelato tonight."

Ann could barely hear him over the blood rushing in her ears. "What?"

Zane rubbed his temple. "It's been brought to my attention that I've been an idiot. That if I had simply had a conversation with my daughter instead of making a decision for her, you and I could have avoided the last two weeks."

"What are you talking about?" Ann looked around, questioning for a second if Zane was actually here or if her exhausted brain was dreaming all of this after she'd passed out on the couch.

"I want to be with you. I'm so sorry for being a complete dishhead, but if you'll let me, I'll make it up to you."

"Dishhead?" This was definitely a dream. Zane wasn't even using real words.

His lopsided smile hit his mouth. "One of the creative descriptors Tessa deemed should apply to me and my behavior."

"You were trying to do what was best for your daughter. I never blamed you."

Zane rose like he wanted to touch her but halted. "Will you?"

"Will I what?" Her teeth bit her cheek so hard metallic flavor soured her taste buds.

Not a dream, then.

A staggered exhale left his parted lips. "Will you let me love you?"

Her eyes widened, but her brain couldn't formulate an answer. Words jumbled together, the simplest, three-letter one stuck somewhere between her temporal lobe and her brainstem. For as brazen as she'd been in her classroom earlier, Ann was wading through thick, green Jell-O now.

Zane seemed to understand her anyway, leaning forward and brushing her hair over her shoulder. He laid a soft kiss on her cheek, gently whisked away the tears that remained, and then paused.

"Ann?"

She blinked, bringing her gaze from the crook of his collarbones to his face. Just like every time before, Zane was waiting for permission.

Eyes locked on his, her chin dipped in a slight nod.

Zane's fingers shook as they made their way into her hair. Her entire body lit up, and pinpricks raced to every exterior surface. She'd expected them to crash together like two atoms combining, forever changing their structure, but Zane took his time. His nose brushed hers, his breath over her hypersensitive lips.

"I love you."

Her heart was vibrating in her chest. "I love you too."

A heavy inhale raised his shoulders as if he was letting those words sink in. He rocked his forehead against hers so subtly Ann wasn't sure she'd imagined the contact. The tendons in her neck tensed, her tight calves threatened to charley horse, and her abs compressed to her spine.

Then Zane's rushed exhale washed over her mouth a second before his lips crushed hers. The blissful relief coating every nerve ending was incapacitating. They were both insatiable, like the last two weeks had been two years. Everything was frantic and simultaneously familiar.

There was a softness to his sandalwood skin, like he'd shaved right before driving over. The taut muscles of his back filled her greedy palms. His swirling tongue held the unmistakable remnants of bubblegum toothpaste. Ann smiled against his lips before they deviated down her neck, his hands brushing her hair out of the way. When Zane kissed the sensitive skin beneath her ear, a throaty rasp escaped her.

Zane's masculine moan resonated as he shifted her forward, picked her up, and effortlessly carried her inside. A stack of papers slid to the floor as he bumped the dining table on the way through the door.

Growling, Zane set her down to collect the papers. It was clear that he'd rather have bull-in-a-china-shopped his way to her bedroom, but the fact that he'd stop doing what he wanted to make sure something that was important to her happened first made Ann's skin shimmer.

"Leave it." She grabbed the stack from his hands, flung it on the table, and pushed his chest.

His eyebrows rose, but Zane didn't argue.

They were halfway across the room, taking stumbly steps while still kissing, when her front door opened.

There was only one person . . .

"Gah." Rene covered her eyes. "I'm sorry. I should have—" Her sister turned around, closed the front door, and then knocked—*loudly*—as if she hadn't just trespassed.

Zane's hands were still gripping her waist, and Ann's fingers were still clenching the collar of his T-shirt as they stared at the dried-flower wreath hanging on the back of her door.

"Um, Ann?" Rene called out from behind the wooden barrier. "Could I please talk to you?"

Ann blinked. She hadn't been aware that *please* had been in Rene's vocabulary.

"It's your decision." Zane placed a soft kiss at her temple.

A deep inhale filled her lungs before she opened the door.

"May I come in?" Rene asked. The manners were really throwing Ann for a loop.

"No. This is good." Ann leaned against the jamb, crossing her arms to protect the wounded organ in her chest.

Her sister nodded. "That's fair." She tugged at her ponytail. "I wanted to apologize for my behavior at the resort, and during the bet, and—" Rene took a pained inhale. "Basically, my whole life."

Ann's forehead wrinkled.

"Denis is a really good guy." The corner of Rene's mouth lifted. "Like, he treats me better than I deserve, but he makes me want to do the same thing for him—which is new." Her sister shifted her shoulders. "You get it, right? Our whole lives have been Mom picking at Dad. Dad doting on Mom, giving her whatever she wanted, loving her despite her weird eccentricities. That's not healthy. I'd always mimicked their relationship, and it's always failed."

Rene sank with a sigh. "As cliche as it sounds, Denis makes me want to be a better person. We've got this playful power-struggle thing going on, but it's not that way at home. He holds me accountable. Won't put up with my nonsense." She laughed dryly. "Our first week of dating, I tried to pull some trick, and he literally said, 'That's not how people behave.'" Rene bit her lip. "I'm slowly learning that our family has some really maladaptive ways of dealing with things."

Statement of the century.

"Denis was pissed about that dinner, about my behavior. And then he was *really* pissed when I told him I'd faked my ankle injury. At the time, I did the only thing I could think of when I felt threatened or boxed into a corner—I took it out on you." Rene's shrug was shockingly abashed.

"I shouldn't have done that. I shouldn't have done *a lot* of things, but—" She dropped her hands to her sides. "I understand you don't want anything to do with me, but I wanted you to know that I'm sorry."

Rene leaned to the side, catching sight of Zane, who'd been hovering just beyond the entryway. "I'm sorry to you too. I kept throwing myself at you when Denis wasn't looking because I was hoping I could get you to choose me and admit that your relationship wasn't real." She paused, biting her lip again. "I shouldn't have denied your relationship. I'm glad you have each other."

"Okay." Her sister exhaled again, stepping back.

"Thank you," Ann said. It was something she'd taught her students. You don't have to say, "It's okay," after someone apologizes, especially if it isn't, but you can acknowledge their effort.

"Yep." Rene shifted her keys to the other hand, and Ann caught the tremble in her fingertips.

That apology had been hard for her sister, not just another manipulation.

In the movie version of Ann's life, she would have caught Rene in a rib-squeezing hug, and their relationship would've immediately transferred to one of mutual respect and love, but this was real life. Real relationships were messy and complex. Her and Rene's couldn't be fixed overnight with one heartfelt apology. It would probably take years, but her sister had just stepped them on a new path.

Zane's hands framed her upper arms the second Ann shut her door. "What can I do?"

Not, "Are you okay?" because she clearly wasn't. How could he be there for her?

"You're doing it." She leaned into his broad chest, releasing the tension gripping her muscles when he wrapped his arms around her.

After a few seconds, an unfamiliar ringtone pierced the room. It was a standard beeping one. Not a song. Exactly the opposite she'd have expected for the man who loved music.

"How is that your ringtone?" she mumbled against him.

"It's too hard to pick one song."

Ann lifted her head and laughed. When Zane brushed a strand of hair out of her face, his affectionate gaze following his hand, a part of her melted. As stupid and rom-commy as that sounded, that was how Ann felt. Puddlely. Gooey. Cloyingly happy.

"Should you get it?"

"No." The word was husked over her lips. "I have everything I need right here."

Ann arched into him but then remembered. "Aren't we supposed to be meeting Caroline?"

A curse left his mouth before he leaned back to pull his phone from his pocket. Zane had a brief conversation with Caroline, in which Ann could hear Tessa cheering in the background. Ann tried to keep her chuckle to herself, covering her mouth with her hand. Zane gave her that bone-melting smile with a wink, lifting his index finger to his lips.

Ann wasn't sure what part of that gesture was inexplicably attractive—the smile, the wink, or being shushed—but she wanted to thoroughly explore each option.

Zane placed his phone over his chest. "Are you still up for gelato?"

Was she ready for their relationship to fully be real? Was she ready to spend time with Caroline, not just as her teacher, but as the woman in love with her father?

A slow smile lifted her lips as she nodded.

"We'll be there in fifteen minutes," Zane said before hanging up.

His thumb traced her collarbone, sending sensation corkscrewing through her. "Ready?"

Her chest quivered with a shaky exhale as she nodded again.

Zane's hand clenched as it pulled away from her, his teeth biting his lower lip. The tension between them escalated as he watched her wash her makeup-streaked face, find her shoes, and collect her purse. Though she wasn't sure how dessert with Caroline would go, Ann knew with absolute certainty what Zane had planned for the rest of their evening.

Chapter 30

Do you remember when . . .

Ann blinked at the subject line of the email that had arrived in her inbox earlier that day. She had seven other identical ones from Rene—all unread. When the first email had shown up the day after her sister's apology, Ann had ignored it—just like the others she'd received throughout the week. Now the uneven stack was staring back at her, demanding attention.

Setting her phone down on her couch with a sigh, Ann nestled further into Zane's strong shoulder.

"What is it?" His lips brushed her forehead.

"Rene."

Zane's muscles stiffened beneath her. "What did she do?"

Before she could answer, her phone pinged again. Another email from Rene, this one titled, *I'm sorry for bothering you. I won't reach out again.*

Ann's chest squeezed.

"You don't have to read those." Zane's deep voice felt like it was reverberating through her. The sensation was enticing and soothing all at once.

"I know." She took her gaze from the phone to his eyes, drinking him in.

This last week had been something Ann had never imagined possible. Following Benedict's instructions not to be seen together in public until after the school year ended, Zane had met Ann at her condo every evening. They'd fallen into a comfortable routine of dinners in, followed by a little grading/book prep, before ending the night with mind-blowing intimacy.

Today, however, Zane had been at the gym when she'd shown up for her solo Friday workout. The muggy room seemed even steamier with stolen glances through the mirrors as they pretended they didn't know each other. They'd barely made it through her front door before sweat-sodden clothes were stripped to the tile floor.

Zane's hand framed her face, brushing away a few shower-damp strands, before bringing his lips to hers. The kiss was tender and tasted slightly of the Mongolian-style tofu-and-veggie stir-fry he'd prepared for dinner.

"It's going to bother me not to read them," she admitted after he'd leaned back.

The corner of his mouth quirked knowingly.

Bucking the impulse to follow the emails in order, Ann settled back into her new favorite spot and opened the last one first. Zane picked up his tablet, returning to his reading and giving her the privacy she needed while still having his arm snug around her waist.

I realize now that I probably should have asked for permission before spamming your inbox like this. I thought it was a good idea to apologize for specific things I'd done wrong, but then today, when I brought it up to my therapist, she said that I was essentially forcing myself into your life when you might not want me there. Sorry for that. I won't email again.

Ann's heart stumbled, recovered, and then tripped again.

Rene was going to therapy?

Quickly, Ann went back to the first email.

Do you remember when Dad was first diagnosed, and it felt like the world veered to the left? I couldn't get my footing. I'd just married Travis, and all I could think about was how pointless that was because my dad was going to die.

I was paralyzed by the idea that the one person who genuinely loved me was leaving me. Travis wanted me as a trophy he could flaunt in front of his business partners. Mom had only really cared for me when I was in sync with her, doing her bidding. Dad was the only one who looked at me and actually saw me, you know?

And I couldn't help him.

You could, though. You were right there, cleaning things, fixing things, cooking meals. You knew what he needed. I became obsolete overnight, and I resented you for it more than I resented how Dad had always liked you best. Mom knew that too. That's why she's always picking at you.

You'd always been the perfect daughter. Smart. Kind. Athletic. And here again, you knew just what to do. You had everything under control. You weren't scared like I was.

I was so jealous and angry.

What I should have done was channel that fear into something positive like you did, but I couldn't see that kind of outcome because it'd never been presented to me. Does that make sense? You don't know what's right if you've never seen it. I should have paid more attention to how you'd grown and changed with going to college and getting experiences outside of our toxic little world. Instead, I dug in deeper and made you the enemy. For that, I'm sorry.

A train had just rolled over Ann's bones, splintering them into infinitesimal pieces. Zane's arm tightened around her, sensing the tension raking through her muscles. As much as she wanted to stop, Ann opened the second email and then the third. The rest of them hadn't been as reality-tilting as the first one. They were mostly Rene bringing up a time when she'd been intentionally cruel to Ann and apologizing for it. The last one was simply a memory.

Do you remember when we were in middle school and Mom had been gone when we'd gotten off the bus? Neither of us had remembered our key, and I had bet you that you couldn't climb the side wall and use it to get onto the roof. Once you did, you helped me climb up, and we sat there all afternoon. I was posting my clever mischief on social media while you studied, but then the sun began to set.

I'd remembered I'd bought a KitKat from the vending machine before getting on the bus. It was goo since we'd been in the sun for hours, but I split it with you. Sitting shoulder to shoulder with you as the sun set, licking melted chocolate from our fingertips, is one of my better memories of growing up. I wish I had more of those. I wish I could make more of those with you now.

The salt of her tears hit her lips before Ann realized they'd fallen. She'd never heard—or rather, read—Rene be so honest before. Vulnerable. Her sister had always hidden behind an impassive or snarky façade.

"What did she do?" The protective growl in Zane's voice zipped down her spine.

"She's—She's apologizing." Ann couldn't take her gaze off Rene's last sentence.

I wish I could make more of those with you now.

Ann glanced up. "I think she genuinely wants to make this right."

Skepticism skirted across Zane's freckled cheeks before he evened his expression. "What do you want to do?"

Though these seven emails threw a clarifying lens over her sister's behavior, Ann wasn't sure if it was too little too late.

"I don't know yet."

◊◊◊

The next week didn't fly by as quickly, since Zane had spent the week at his home with Caroline. Though they texted every night like they'd done before, Ann already missed falling asleep beside him.

Nervous spiders raced up and down Ann's spine as she pulled into the busy parking lot of Ground Street Coffee Saturday morning. She'd been prepared to follow Benedict's rule to the letter, but it'd been Caroline who'd wanted Ann to meet her uncles. Zane had called last night with the idea for Ann to "run into" him and his friends at their bi-monthly get-together, assuring her that no one would be the wiser.

"Ms. Powell!" Caroline ran over and gave her legs a hug. "What a complete surprise to see you outside of school," she said loudly, looking around.

Zane left a table of men, a goofy smile lifting his lips. "Yes, how strange to see you here. Tucson can be such a small place sometimes."

The wink he sent Ann singed her collarbones. Zane stood behind Caroline, almost using her as a shield against the incomprehensible magnetism that flowed between them. Had Zane not also been meeting Tessa to drop off Caroline, the tension of being near him without being able to run her hands up his back and into his hair would have been too great.

A man with tortoise-shell glasses who had colorful tattoos covering his arms intercepted her first. "I'm Kyle. I hear you're Caroline's teacher." When he let go of her hand, his grin broadened. "She talks about you a lot."

"Oh?" Ann looked at Caroline, who ducked her head in response.

"Kevin." A short man wearing an olive fedora stepped in front of her. "Thrilled to meet you." Though Kevin shook her hand with both of his, the gesture was more energetic than smarmy.

Ann met Rowan last. He was the broadest of the men, but his warm smile and gentle demeanor instantly put her at ease.

As they made idle small talk, Ann stood slightly outside the group, keeping a safe distance between her and Zane, just in case anyone else from Hillcrest should happen by. Before long, Tessa arrived, and her shocked declarations were almost as transparent as Caroline's. Clearly, the women in Zane's life didn't possess any acting prowess.

The conversation eased as ribbing jokes were tossed before counter-arguments and fond memories were lobbed in defense. Ann found herself laughing along with the group, feeling submerged like one would in a soothing bath after a hard workout. She could see why Zane loved each of these people so much, why he spoke about them so often.

They were his family.

That thought brought her back to last night, when she'd gone home to help Dad move some things around in the garage. Her mother had ventured outside while Ann was mid-task, critiquing her form.

"Mom, if you don't have anything helpful to add, would you mind stepping inside?" she asked, wiping sweat from her brow.

Ann didn't cower under her mother's disapproving gaze. She held the same even expression she'd used hundreds of times with the unreasonable parents at Hillcrest.

Though nothing outwardly had changed between her and her mom, Ann felt different because she'd realized something while driving here. She didn't want retribution. Even if she'd laid out all the past injustices against her in a cinematic reveal, the only person who would've felt shame or guilt over them would've been her father. And he didn't deserve that pain. Not when it hadn't been his fault.

So Ann decided she didn't want to tear open old wounds. She wanted to move forward. It wasn't her responsibility to fix her family. She could only control her own response to any given situation. From now on, that would be standing up for herself.

"Just make sure you leave enough room for both cars," Mom said through pinched lips.

"I will."

Her mother stared Ann down for a few more seconds before retreating into the house.

"Okay." She turned to her father with a smile, shaking off the interaction. "Where did you want these to go?"

Zane's easy laugh brought Ann back to the sun-soaked patio. The way he and Kyle playfully shoved each other while Rowan tried to be annoyed with them was endearing. Happiness radiated from the knowledge that this was the first of many Saturdays with this new group of people.

After a few more minutes—as planned—Ann made her excuses. She'd only driven a mile when Zane called her.

"Hey. We're still good for your place?"

Since there was a pool construction crew working in Zane's backyard, his house wasn't exactly private right now.

"Actually . . ." Ann pressed her lips together. The idea that had been zipping through her mind since last night came to the forefront again. "How do you feel about brunch?"

Chapter 31

"That's four," Ann said to Zane after leaving her parents at a different damask-covered high-top. "You'd think Mom wouldn't criticize Dad's suit since she picked it out for him, but . . ." Ann widened her eyes over the gin martini he'd just handed her, taking a sturdy sip.

"We're not even done with cocktail hour. We'll hit ten for sure." Zane wrapped his arm around her, his thumb playing with the glossy fabric of her strapless maid-of-honor dress.

Two weeks ago, when Ann had asked if he wanted to have brunch with Rene and Denis, a ribbon of protectiveness had pulsed through him. So much of their relationship had been him watching Rene mistreat Ann. But when they'd arrived at Denis's house with an impromptu gas-station gathering of breakfast items, Rene had been nothing but gracious and remorseful.

That casual meal between the foursome had been markedly better than the first. It'd also given Zane an opportunity to come clean about his identity, citing that he hadn't wanted anyone to make the connection that his daughter was in Ann's class. It had turned out that Denis was a huge sci-fi fan and planned on picking up a few of Zane's audiobooks for his commute to his dental practice.

When Zane had told Ann's parents the following weekend, her father had asked a dozen engaging questions about his work life, while her mother simply sat back with crossed arms.

"It's the perfect night for a wedding."

Zane followed Ann's eyeline through the floor-to-ceiling windows toward the happy couple. Rene and Denis were still outside on the expansive outdoor patio overlooking the mountains, having the last of their photos taken.

"It is," he said, watching Ann's lips lift as her gaze remained on the newlyweds.

The ceremony had been beautiful. Soft-pink beams of sunset had highlighted the bride and groom, illuminating every background cactus spine like millions of fairy lights. Ann's evergreen eyes had caught and held his when Denis and Rene ugly-cried with joy as they became each other's forever. It'd been hard to subdue the soul-encompassing knowledge that Zane wanted Ann to be his forever.

But they were still new. They were still discovering the little alcoves of each other, exploring each other's depths. Since the school year finished yesterday, there'd already been a palpable shift in their relationship. Tonight, Zane could hold and kiss Ann as much as he wished.

His hand brushed a ringlet from her updo aside to leave a soft kiss at her temple. Stifling the impulse to shift his lips lower, to that sweet spot beneath the corner of her jaw that made Ann rasp, had taken immense effort.

"Have I told you how stunning you are?"

Ann's smiling lips took another sip of gin. "Only a few dozen times."

"Not nearly enough, then." Zane set down her drink, gripped her hips, and turned her toward him.

The flirty dare in Ann's eyes was going to undo him. Zane had expected that loving her would bolster her confidence in *them*, but he hadn't anticipated that her self-confidence would grow to blinding proportions. The more assured Ann became in every facet of her life, the harder it was for Zane to keep his hands off her.

"Pardon the interruption, but if you'll head through the open ballroom doors, dinner is to be served," a server said from the other side of the table.

His fingers twitched, tightening, before releasing with a resolved sigh. "After you."

Following one of the most decadent dinners Zane had ever eaten, Rene and Denis shared their first dance. Afterward, most of the guests joined them as the exceptionally good band played hit after wedding hit. Their fingers interlaced beneath the table as Ann shimmied in her seat.

"Do you want to dance?" Zane asked over an impressive guitar riff.

The way her forehead wrinkled made his chest ache. "You don't dance."

"I *can't* dance." He emphasized the word, his lips lifting. "Doesn't mean that I won't if you want to. That is, if you won't be too embarrassed by me."

Ann tilted her head thoughtfully. "What if I led?"

"You can try, but remember Kevin and Kyle—who've had extensive dance and fight choreography training—said I was helpless."

"We'll see." Determination brightened her cheeks as she led them to the corner of the dance floor nearest the wall.

Ann didn't get frustrated when even her strong arms couldn't will his body to coordinate with the music. She laughed. Ann collapsed against his chest, mirthful eyes lit from within. Then Zane tried even harder to prove that he was a reanimated sack of potatoes parading as a human man, not stopping his jerky, uncoordinated movement until Ann doubled over in a fit of giggles.

Ann stared at their feet once she'd collected her breath. "Maybe if you thought of it like a football play. Instead of running ten yards, juke left, then sprint right, you step forward, right, then together?"

The upbeat song ended, and a slower one replaced it.

Zane's palms smoothed over the waist of her dress. "How about we high-school sway to this one and keep our feet planted?"

Ann laughed again, a few loose curls from her updo spilling over her bare shoulders, before wrapping her fingers behind his neck and snuggling into his chest. His chin dipped automatically, taking a deep breath of her sweet orange blossom scent.

They'd only made it ten sways when Rene appeared beside them. "Hey." She tucked a lock of her wavy hair behind her ear. "I don't mean to interrupt, but now that things have settled down, I wanted to give you this." A white envelope rested in her outstretched hand.

Ann's brow pinched as she accepted it. "What's this?"

"Four grand." Rene's shoulders slipped back, resolve smoothing out her features. "Like we agreed upon."

"I don't—"

Her sister splayed her hands open wide, her newly acquired wedding ring glistening in the thousands of suspended lights hanging from the ceiling in orderly rows.

"No. A bet is a bet. You brought a date." Rene gestured to Zane with a warm smile. "I brought a check."

"*Rene.*"

"Let me do this." Her French-tipped fingers wrapped around Ann's, crinkling the envelope. "I want this to be the last bet between us. I want to settle *this* score, knowing there's no way I can come close to fixing my errors in the past."

When Rene's lower lip wobbled with her words, Ann wrapped her in a fierce hug.

Shock skirted over Rene's face like a disoriented lizard caught indoors before she closed her eyes and squeezed Ann tight, whispering, "Thank you."

With the envelope tucked into his suit jacket, since Ann's dress didn't have any pockets, they resumed their sophomoric dancing position. Though, originally, Zane hadn't intended on telling Ann about the donations he'd made on her behalf, the paper against his chest made his jaw tense.

"There's something I have to tell you," he murmured against her hair.

"Hmmm."

Zane exhaled slowly. "When we were apart, I'd asked a friend to help me support the underfunded classrooms in the area. He's . . . rather wealthy and has a foundation he uses to donate to charities."

Ann's eyes were guarded as they lifted.

"I didn't want to take anything away from you, but at the time, I knew you'd lost Rene's money. For me, it was another way to be with you while I couldn't be with you. I couldn't hold you, but I could help you with something you were passionate about."

When her expression didn't change, Zane rubbed the back of his neck. "I'm not sure if that makes sense, but that's how I felt."

Ann's fingertips trailed down his chest, stilling over the envelope beneath the fabric of his jacket. "We can add this to the amount you and your friend donated." A small smile tugged at her mouth. "Thank you for doing that for me, for the teachers and the children in need."

Zane was about to mention that there was still a hefty remaining sum to be donated in the allotment Ethan had given him, but Ann's hands flew behind his head as her lips met his. Zane mentally slotted that part of the conversation for later—later, when her fingers in his hair weren't sending sparks cascading down his back to collect at the base of his spine.

"How soon is too soon to leave?" he rasped, subtly pushing her against the nearby wall.

Ann's throaty chuckle did nothing to quell the demanding blood surging in his veins. "We're here till the end."

Zane knew this, but he let a growl resonate in his throat nonetheless, which pulled another laugh from Ann.

The lead singer announced it was time to cut the cake, and Ann wordlessly collected his hand and led him toward the cake table. His fingers smoothed up the back of her dress and drew geometric shapes at the nape of her neck as Ann sighed into his shoulder.

"I'm glad we came," she said as Rene pushed a fistful of cake over Denis's mouth and face, and he gave her a you'll-pay-for-that-later glare.

"Me too," Zane said before pulling her into his arms again.

The thoughts from earlier bombarded him a second time, vibrating like an orchestra warming up. In his mind, Ann's peach bridesmaid dress would be traded for a breathtaking white one. She would walk toward him, those boughs of green unwavering in their intensity before—

Zane startled when a familiar mic'd voice broke into the fantasy.

"Come on, everyone! Line up!"

Zane's gaze shot to the stage as Claire—*Rowan's* Claire—hopped off before positioning herself at the front of the dance floor. The band shouted, "It's electric!" into their microphones, beginning the first few notes of "Electric Boogie."

"There's no way . . ." His brows knotted.

"What?"

"But she's not supposed to be back until July."

His head subtly shook as Claire, in a conservative black dress that might as well have been a yellow sequined one for how brightly she shined, helped Priscilla to follow the steps to the Electric Slide. Denis's prim mother was giggling like a woman two-thirds her age while following along.

The few times Zane had interacted with Claire, it'd been like being drawn to a flame. She had this effortless way of shaking even the most reserved person from their shell. The only person resistant to her charms had been Rowan.

"That's Claire." Zane didn't feel it fair to describe her as Rowan's first love. "Rowan's sister's best friend, but she hasn't been back in Tucson in nine years."

"Oh." Ann followed his eyeline. "You should say hi."

"I will later." And then he'd find a moment to text Rowan and let him know that Claire was back early. "Now it's time for you to decide"—he paused to spin Ann—"if you want to continue watching this train careening into fifteen dumpster fires or if you'd like to get some cake before all the good pieces are gone."

"Would you be mad if I said cake?" The corner of her mouth quirked.

"Who would be mad about choosing cake?" Zane personally loved when Ann devoured food like an excavator demolishing a building. It helped remind him that she was real and not some apparition he'd made up after his long hours of sound-muffled isolation.

"People who don't like sugar." Ann's lips tipped into a full smile. "So, not me."

"Nothing could be as sweet as you." Zane bounced his eyebrows once. "But we should give the cake a fair shot."

Ann shook her head with a slight eye roll before grabbing his hand and pulling him toward what he hoped would be a very long future of moments just like this.

Epilogue

Nearly two years later

Apan flute and its accompanying guitarist soared over the sounds of food vendors shouting out orders, thousands of conversations, and street performers trying to capture a rapt audience. Saturdays were the busiest day of the 4th Avenue Street Fair, but it'd been the perfect place to pick up Caroline from Tessa and Isaac. The biannual event, hosting three hundred artist tents and dozens of performers, was a local favorite. When they'd met up, Tessa had shown off her newly purchased wrought-iron cookbook stand and turquoise earrings.

"Do you want roasted corn?" Zane asked as the three of them entered the intersection of 7th Street, now serving as a food court.

Ann quickly surveyed the nearby food tents, her eyes snagging on the one thirty feet away with glistening pictures of meat.

"Go get your bacon." Zane's teasing voice was beside her temple before he kissed it.

"Meet you by the tables over there?" Ann tipped her head toward the fry bread vendor and the seating area.

"Sounds good."

Ann picked her way through the crowd to stand in the long line for satays and fried rice. While she waited, she couldn't help watching Zane. Zane bending to listen to Caroline over the noise. Zane laughing when his daughter said something funny. Zane looking up to catch Ann's gaze, almost as if he knew it was on him.

He said one more thing to Caroline before stepping in Ann's direction. Passersby of the crowded street fair were mystically choreographed to cross before or behind but not interrupt Zane's determined strides. The myriad of conversations, noises, and music from the nearby performance group dimmed as Ann's heartbeat took precedence in her eardrums. The older woman behind her stepped back slightly as Zane swallowed her into a hug.

"Hey." When the low, quiet word dropped over her ear, Ann's eyes closed with a relieved exhale. The tension he'd built with his purposeful strides receded like the frothy waves being pulled back to sea. "I just had to tell you I love you."

They'd just spent a solid week alone, uttering those words almost carelessly. Like most couples, *I love you* had become their hello and goodbye. But now, Ann felt the difference. Zane's words pulsed in her chest as if she was standing too close to a concert speaker. When Ann opened her suddenly parched mouth to respond, the woman behind them interrupted.

"Why don't you walk up to me like you're parting the Red Sea anymore?" she asked of her husband, who had the misfortune of following Zane, holding two fry bread tacos.

Zane loosened his arms enough for them to watch the husband make a playfully dismissive noise and lift his full hands.

"They're obviously new to the game. Wait until it's been forty-nine years. Then you bring food instead." The white-haired gentleman winked at Zane like he was imparting valuable wisdom.

"Noted." Zane smiled at the man before tilting that lopsided grin down at her.

"So how long has it been?" The man raised a wiry eyebrow.

"Six months, two weeks, and five days." Zane's rapid answer pulled a surprised puff of air from Ann's lungs.

"Told you they were newlyweds." The man gently elbowed his wife.

The din of the boisterous fair was falling away again as Ann whispered, "I didn't think we were keeping track."

One of Zane's curls fell over his glasses as he dipped his head lower. "I'm always keeping track."

"Okay, lovebirds. Scoot forward three steps. The line's moving," the woman said with a slight edge.

Ann mumbled an apology as they shuffled forward. Zane moved beside her, his fingers sliding up her spine and tracing designs above the edge of her pale-pink bandeau-style maxi dress.

"Hon, why don't you get started on these while they're hot. I see an open seat over there. I'll get the satays and sodas." The woman grumbled slightly but headed off with the food. "She gets . . . what's that new word? Oh, right. Hangry," her husband said through a veneer-filled smile.

Ann had to bite the inside of her cheek to keep the chuckle tucked into her mouth while the man continued on. After a moment, Zane excused himself to return to Caroline. Ann received seven more minutes of quality marital advice before reaching the front of the line. Clutching the flimsy paper plate of bacon-wrapped satays, she joined Zane and Caroline on the sun-warmed picnic table.

"Pool when we get home?" Zane asked after swallowing a bite of cotija-covered roasted corn.

"*Yes.*" Caroline elongated her emphatic answer.

Ann took her gaze away from the two of them across the picnic table and glanced at her watch before saying, "That should work."

They had just enough time for a quick dip before she and Caroline had to get ready for Rene's baby shower. Ann smiled at her greasy plate, thinking about becoming an aunt twice over. Kennedy's daughter, Casey, already had two official aunts, but her friend had never made Ann feel like her relationship with Casey was less than. She'd firmly become "Aunt Ann" as soon as Casey could mutter syllables in a coherent manner.

"I can't wait to get into the water," Caroline said after another bite of her honey-and-powdered-sugar fry bread. "It's so hot today."

One particular poolside memory from a year ago came forward almost automatically.

Ann sprayed another coat of sunscreen on herself after finishing touching up Caroline's shoulders, even though her olive skin didn't need it yet. Both Caroline and Zane would turn into lobsters if Ann didn't have a timer on the patio table, reminding her to reapply every forty-five minutes.

The comforting rasp of Zane switching out the record in the house echoed through the outdoor speaker system he'd had set up when the pool was built. Ann smiled when the rhythmic strumming of "Sultans of Swing" sang into the dry desert air.

By now, Ann was familiar with his collection. When they'd begun officially dating, Zane had played a different record each night she stayed over. Though she'd always done her evening grading in silence, certain albums helped her feel less drained after hours of paperwork. And then Zane had been there, reading on the couch, always willing to put his tablet aside for an impromptu makeout session or if she needed to talk through a work dilemma.

"We're out of lemonade, so I'm going to run to the store," Zane said, coming back with ice waters and a tray of goodies.

"No, stay," Ann pouted, pulling her sunglasses down. She made sure not to admire shirtless, swimsuit-clad Zane too obviously, since Caroline was nearby on a pineapple floaty.

"It's your birthday, and you asked for lemonade." He dropped a quick kiss on her frowning lips. "I'll just be a few minutes."

Caroline leisurely paddled herself along for a while before she flung herself to standing in the shallow end. "Good. Now that he's gone, we can get to the business of your present."

Sitting up on her pool chaise, Ann's brow wrinkled. Caroline had already given her a new set of her favorite colored pens and a custom planner. "You gave me a present."

Caroline rolled her eyes while quickly toweling off. "That was the decoy present. Your real present is in here." She quick-stepped over to the patio table and picked up her sketchbook.

Oh. That made sense. Anticipation spiraled through Ann, wondering what piece of art she'd receive. When she'd moved into Zane's house, Ann had received a set of framed drawings to go on her side of the bathroom. They mimicked the woodland-creature art from her condo that now shared space in the living room with Zane's decor. Racoons, deer, and—ironically—possums in pajamas either brushed their teeth or combed their fur.

"Dad really wants to marry you," Caroline said casually, like she was mentioning that it would be sunny tomorrow.

A cold sip of water burned her nose as Ann snorted. "What?"

It wasn't that she and Zane hadn't discussed the topic. They had. Extensively. But Ann had been the one wanting to give Caroline time to adjust after she moved in.

"Yeah." Caroline rotated her opened book, not looking up. "He's been wanting to do it for a long time, but I think he's waiting to talk to me about it, so I'm fixing that."

Though Ann had not stopped staring at Caroline since she'd plopped beside her on the chair, Caroline finally looked up.

"I'm designing your ring." Her expression was even and serious, like when she was focused on a task she wanted to get perfect. Then a small smile flirted with the corner of her mouth. "That way, I can be a part of you marrying Dad." She lifted one still-damp shoulder.

Ann's chest squeezed at the sweetness of Caroline's words.

Caroline was all business again, flipping through what Ann now noticed were ring designs. "I can't exactly decide what would best match your style. Obviously, something feminine because you prefer light colors and soft things like ruffles, but it's hard to do that with metal, you know?" She briefly glanced up but didn't seem to register Ann's shocked expression.

"I was thinking something like this." Caroline pointed to a design with the band to the center diamond split between entwined swirls, one of each lined with tiny accent stones. "But then there's this." She flipped to another page where the center diamond was haloed and what looked like tiny leaves decorated the band. "Because you like woodland things."

Caroline flipped to the last drawing of a stone with a plain, twisted band. "Or something simpler. Either way, I think you should get it in rose gold."

Silence, except for the lapping of the still-shaking pool water and the music from the record player, infiltrated the pool yard while Ann sat stunned.

"Before I go, do you want—" Zane's voice and movement through the patio door halted when he caught sight of Caroline's six-by-eight-inch design. "What's that?"

"The design for Ann's ring." The matter-of-fact tone of Caroline's voice was almost snarky.

Zane strode over. "What kind of ring?"

"Her engagement ring."

He crouched beside the chair, staring at the design. "That's gorgeous, honey, but Ann already has an engagement ring."

"She does?"

"I do?"

Zane pressed his lips together, nodding. "It's been hidden in my studio for the last six months."

Ann blinked as she did the math. He'd gotten her a ring six months after they'd begun officially dating? Before they'd talked about moving in together?

"Well, go get it!" Caroline punched up from the chair, bouncing with juvenile excitement that was endearing coming from her old soul.

Ann spun the ring circling her left finger to face out, admiring it in the blazing Arizona sunlight. It'd slipped inward since it was currently covered in a thick coating of bacon grease. It turned out that Zane had purchased a design that was nearly identical to Caroline's first drawing, set in rose gold. And now, a solid rose-gold wedding band sat beside it.

When she glanced up, Zane was watching her, his affectionate smile lifting his freckled cheeks. Volumes of words passed between them as their eyes linked. Ann was coming to realize how much could be communicated with Zane this way, how they'd been doing it since the minute they'd collided in the Hillcrest hallway years ago. Then his lips twitched as his smile transformed into that bone-melting one that always liquified her insides.

"Why don't you look at me like that anymore?" The older woman was throwing away her trash into the can at the end of their picnic table, glaring at Zane.

Her husband only chuckled and winked in their direction. "I'm not trying to set this whole place on fire. The young one doesn't know better than to unleash that power in the middle of a drought."

Though Zane's skin was already flushed from the midday heat, two cherry spots apexed his breathtaking cheekbones.

The man pulled his wife to his side with an arm around her waist, whispering something that made the gruff woman giggle and playfully swat at his chest.

"Mind that advice I gave you, and this'll be you in a few decades," he said with a parting grin.

Caroline whispered, "Gross," under her breath, tapping away at her smart watch, but Zane's eyes simply found Ann's as he bounced his eyebrows. The mischievous determination in his gaze sent warmth stretching over every muscle.

The corner of her mouth kicked up, accepting his challenge.

Forever it is, then.

Acknowledgements

Eegee's is life. Especially when you live in a place with seasons that are hot, hotter, hot, ooooo this is nice, and then right back to hot. A series about Tucson would not be complete without mentioning the deliciousness of eegee's—specifically the Watermelon and Lucky Lime flavors.

I'm fortunate that each book of mine starts out with a developmental read from Rachel Garber. Thank you for loving this book so much and for your thoughtful proofread. Jenn Lockwood is the best copy editor, and I'm grateful for her and her careful eye. Thank you to my beta readers Lisa Wittrock and Louise Morris who made this book so much stronger. You both are the best!

Thank you to Laura Burrill for letting me pick her teacher's brain for story details. I am in love and awe of Enni Tuomisalo's talent and her ability to create a cover that so articulately captures my characters. Thank you! A huge hug of appreciation to all the members of the book community who read, review, and shout out my books! Thank you for your enthusiasm and loving romance as much as I do.

My two kids were particularly tickled over the possum in a picnic basket idea and encouraged me to go with it. My sweet husband continues to be the best support system and quiet, steady cheerleader. Thank you to my incredible friends, parents, inlaws, and extended family for being there for me. And to the javelinas who terrorized me as a child, you're alright . . . I guess.

To my incredible readers—I'm so excited and grateful you're here. Seriously. I love that you're on this journey with me and I truly hope you enjoyed this story and these characters. Thank you!

About the Author

Laura Langa is an award-winning sweet romance author. She strives to write stories that pull at her readers' heartstrings and create relatable characters you can't help but root for. Laura loves trees and all things green, hates flossing but forces herself to do it every night, drinks tea—not coffee, and believes that salt air can often cure a bad mood.

Visit her website at www.LauraLanga.com

Subscribe to her newsletter for the latest details at www.LauraLanga.com/Newsletter

Follow on Instagram and Facebook @LauraLangaWrites